the library
IN EAST AYRSHIRE

East Ayrshire
COUNCIL

Please return item by last date shown,
or contact library to renew

SUCH WICKED
INTENT

www.**davidficklingbooks**.co.uk

Also by Kenneth Oppel and published by
David Fickling Books:

Half Brother
This Dark Endeavour

SUCH WICKED INTENT

The Apprenticeship of Victor Frankenstein

Book Two

KENNETH OPPEL

SUCH WICKED INTENT

A DAVID FICKLING BOOK 978 0 857 56016 2

Published in Great Britain by David Fickling Books,
a division of Random House Children's Publishers UK
A Random House Group Company

This edition published 2012

1 3 5 7 9 10 8 6 4 2

Set in Deepdene

DAVID FICKLING BOOKS
31 Beaumont Street, Oxford, OX1 2NP

www.kidsatrandomhouse.co.uk
www.totallyrandombooks.co.uk
www.randomhouse.co.uk

Addresses for companies within The Random House Group Limited can be found at:
www.randomhouse.co.uk/offices.htm

THE RANDOM HOUSE GROUP Limited Reg. No. 954009

A CIP catalogue record for this book is available from the British Library.

Printed and bound in Great Britain by Clays Ltd, St Ives plc

For Sophia, Nathaniel, and Julia

CHAPTER ONE

CONSUMED

The books flew open like startled birds trying to escape the flames. One after the other I savagely hurled them into the hottest part of the bonfire, watching them ignite almost before they landed.

We'd hauled everything out of the Dark Library, every alchemical tome, every grimoire, every glass vial and earthenware mortar. Father had ordered that it all be destroyed, and he'd enlisted the help of only our most trusted servants. But even with their assistance it had taken us many hours to carry it all out into the courtyard.

It was well past midnight now. There were no more books left to add to the conflagration, but my body still craved things to tear and throw. I prowled the margins of the fire with a shovel, flinging half-burned debris back into the centre of the inferno. I was hungry for destruction. I looked at my father, the servants, their faces pale and terrible in the dancing light and shadow.

Pain throbbed from the stumps of my two missing fingers. The heat seared my face and brought water to my eyes. There was nothing remarkable about this bonfire, no spectral lights, no demonic whiff of brimstone. It was just cracked glass and burning paper and ink and reeking leather. The smoke lifted into the dark autumn sky, carrying with it all the lies and false promises I'd foolishly believed would save my brother.

The next morning I woke to the sound of the birds' dawn chorus and had my brief blissful moment – always the smallest of moments – before I remembered.

He is gone, truly gone.

There was only a hint of light behind my curtains, but I knew sleep had abandoned me, so I sat up, my body stiff from the previous night. The smell of smoke was still trapped in my hair. I put my bare feet against the cool floor and stared blankly down at my toes. The dull pulses of pain in my right hand were the only reminders that time even continued to pass.

In the three weeks since my twin's death, I'd felt neither fully asleep nor awake. Things happened around me without happening to me. Konrad had shared my experiences for so long that without him as my confidant, nothing seemed properly real. My sorrow had folded itself over and over like a vast sheet of paper, becoming thicker and thicker, harder and harder, until it filled my entire body. I'd avoided everyone and sought out places where I could be alone.

We were a house of ravens, dressed in our mourning black.

I clenched my eyes shut for a moment, then stood and hurriedly dressed. I wanted to be outside. The house was still asleep as I made my way down the grand staircase and opened the door to the courtyard. The sky was just starting to brighten above the mountains, the air crystalline and still. The bonfire had all but burned out, leaving a low, ragged pile of faintly smoking ash and fractured earthenware.

'Can't sleep either?' said a voice, and in surprise I looked over to see Elizabeth.

I shook my head.

'Every morning I wake so early,' she said, 'and there's always just a second when—'

'Me too,' I said.

She gave a quick nod. In the severe lines of her black dress, she appeared thinner and paler, but no less beautiful. As a small child she'd come to live with us, an orphaned and very distant relation. Quickly she'd become part of our family, and a cherished friend to my brother and me – but this past summer my thoughts for her had often been more than friendly. I forced myself to look away. Her heart had always belonged to Konrad.

'So it's done,' she said, staring at the smouldering

remains of the Dark Library. 'I saw you all, last night. Did it make you feel better?'

'Briefly. No, not even that. It was something to do. You didn't feel like burning some books?'

She sighed. 'I couldn't. I felt too heartsick, just thinking of all the hope we'd put into them.'

It seemed an age, but was scarcely three months ago, that Konrad, Elizabeth and I had discovered the secret passage to the Dark Library. It was a hidden storehouse of arcane volumes collected by our ancestor Wilhelm Frankenstein. Father had forbidden us from returning and had said the books were filled with dangerous nonsense, but when Konrad had become desperately ill and no doctor could heal him, I'd taken it upon myself to find a cure. One of the texts in the library held the recipe for the legendary Elixir of Life. With our dearest friend Henry Clerval, and under the guidance of an alchemist called Julius Polidori, we'd sought out the elixir's three ingredients, each more dangerous to obtain than the previous. I glanced at my right hand, my two missing fingers. But even after all we'd risked, it hadn't helped.

Staring over the pathetic remains of the bonfire, for the first time I felt a pang of regret. So many yearning theories and recipes.

'I can't help thinking,' I murmured, 'that perhaps if I'd

been faster, or smarter, or found some other, wiser tome . . .'

'Victor—' she said gently.

'And then other times I wonder . . .' I couldn't finish my sentence.

For a moment she was silent. Then she stepped closer and took my hands. Her skin was soft and cool. 'You didn't kill him. Look at me. We don't know what killed Konrad. Whether it was the elixir we gave him, or just his disease, or something else entirely. You're not responsible.'

'There's no colour or taste to things,' I said, 'no hope of things ever being what they were.'

With determination she inhaled. 'He's dead, and no amount of wishful thinking will bring him back. It's a struggle, but I've resigned myself to that. And you must too.'

'You think his soul is elsewhere, though,' I said, knowing that she often travelled to the church to light her candles and pray. 'I've no such consolation.'

She stepped closer and hugged me. Gratefully, my arms encircled her. I could feel her heart beating against my ribs.

'Nothing will be the same again, you're right,' she said. 'We're in the depths of grief. But we're also built for happiness. That I truly believe. We'll find it again. We must help each other find it.'

She lifted her head to look at me. The sun had just cleared the mountain peaks, and in its pure light I saw the three whisker-thin scratches that Polidori's diabolical lynx had left across her cheek. The urge to kiss her dizzied me – and for the briefest moment I wondered if she might *want* to be kissed.

I looked at the ground. My voice was hoarse when I asked, 'And how will you find it, do you think, this happiness?'

'When things are more settled here,' she said, 'maybe when spring comes, I plan to join a convent.'

In utter disbelief my eyes snapped back to hers. 'A convent?'

'Yes.'

It had been so long since I'd laughed that the noise that burst out of me probably sounded like the cawing of a deranged crow. But I was quite unable to stop.

Elizabeth released me as I staggered back, and crossed her arms, eyebrows compressed.

'And why is this so amusing?' she demanded.

I struggled for speech, swiping tears from my eyes. 'Convent . . . *you*?' And then I could only shake my head.

'Keep your voice down,' she growled. 'I haven't told anyone else my plans yet.'

'I can't . . . imagine . . . why,' I gasped.

'I'll have you know, I've given it a great deal of thought,' she said stormily. 'And I'm determined to accept all that's happened, and place my life in God's hands.'

'I'm sorry . . . I'm sorry,' I said, finally regaining some control of myself. I let out a big breath. It had felt good to laugh. I looked Elizabeth in the eye. 'It's just that . . . I can't quite see you as a nun.'

'You doubt my passion for my faith?'

'No, no. You're *very* passionate. That, I think, might be the problem.'

She began to say something, then cut herself short and narrowed her eyes at me. 'You're such an ass, Victor,' she said. And with that, she stalked off.

I watched her disappear inside the house and, with a sigh, took one last look at the sooty remains of the Dark Library. Amidst the grey debris something bright red suddenly flashed in the sun. I squinted. It was just a bit of glass, surely. But when I stepped closer, I saw that it was the spine of a red book – completely unburned.

With great determination I forced myself to turn back to the house. But halfway there my step faltered.

No paper could have withstood the searing heat of those flames. How could a book not burn?

I swallowed against the heavy thump of my heart. Some birds trilled as they flew overhead. The courtyard was still empty, but it wouldn't be long before the servants came to start removing the debris.

I seized a shovel, stepped into the ash, and carefully slipped the blade under the red object. I lifted it out and deposited it on the cobblestone. Kneeling, I saw its cover wonderfully decorated with scrollwork but bearing no title or name. A book that would not burn.

Walk away.

But I couldn't restrain myself. I reached out, and the moment I touched the cover, pain seared my fingertips. I recoiled with a gasp. What kind of devilish thing was this? Then, feeling ridiculous, I realized that this book was made of metal and was still hot from the blaze.

Sucking my fingertips, I bent my head lower. The illusion was exceedingly clever. Lines had been carefully scored into the metal sides to look like actual page ends. And, squinting, I could now see that there was a single straight seam that ran all the way around the book, with two tiny hinges embedded ingeniously within the spine. It was actually a slim metal container, meant to look, and open, exactly like a book.

Just another strange book from a room of strange books.

I stood, prodded it dismissively with the toe of my shoe. Why would someone bother constructing a book of metal – unless its contents were so important that they needed to withstand an inferno?

Do not do this.

Quickly I took a nearby bucket of water and sluiced some over the metal book. It hissed briefly. Then I took out my handkerchief, wrapped the slim book up, and slipped it inside my pocket.

In the privacy of my bedchamber I opened the metal book. It contained shallow compartments on both the left and right sides.

On the right were packed several bundles of cloth. Hurriedly I unwrapped the first and beheld what looked like some kind of pendant – a narrow loop of slim but sturdy metal with a star-shaped ornament at one end.

In the other bundles were several smaller metal pieces, obviously specially forged, for they were complicated. One was a kind of ball-in-socket pivot, the other like the bits of a miniature horse's harness. They were stiff with rust, but as I moved them they became more supple. Oil was all they needed – to do what, I had no idea.

In the left compartment was a thin sheaf of pages that had clearly been torn from the binding of an ancient book. The first sheet was printed with forceful Gothic type. At the top of the first page was written:

Instructions for the Spirit Board.

What in the world was a spirit board? I flipped through the pages and saw careful blueprints for the construction of some kind of apparatus that required the oddly shaped pieces I'd seen. At the machine's centre was a pendulum, and its weight was the star-shaped ornament. Impatiently I flipped ahead until I found more writing under the heading 'Conversing with the Dead'.

A lump formed in my throat. How many times had I wished it were possible, if only for a few moments? And suddenly, hungrily, I was reading. But I made it through only a few lines before looking away, self-disgust welling within me.

Why had I even taken this book from the bonfire? It was just more medieval nonsense, and unlike the alchemical lore I'd put such faith in, this didn't even pretend to have a veneer of fact or science.

With great determination I folded the crinkled sheaf of pages and stuck them back into their compartment. Then I hurriedly began wrapping up the metal pieces. The star-shaped pendulum was last, and in my angry haste I stabbed myself on one of its sharp points. A drop of blood welled from my finger onto the ornament, and in that instant the thing was as something alive in my hand. It gave only the slightest tremor, but I dropped it in alarm.

It lay in its metal box, an inert object once more.

But an object that contained some strange, compressed power within it.

'Now do that bit up here,' I said to my nine-year-old brother, Ernest, and watched him carefully as he tapped the hammer against the nail. 'That's it. Good!'

I'd had all the materials brought up to the west sitting room and, after Sunday lunch, had set about building a wooden pendulum, in accordance with the instructions in my metal book. Of course, no one needed to know where these instructions had come from, or their true purpose. It was just a fun and educational activity, and one my mother watched over approvingly as she wrote her letters.

'It's good to see you so engaged in something, Victor,' she said, coming over now to place an affectionate hand on my head. Her eyes, I noticed, were moist.

Since Konrad's death, I hated everything. I could not concentrate to read. I could not sit still long enough to listen to music. Neither horseback riding nor sailing offered me any pleasure. The world was going on elsewhere, and I had no part in it. I was locked deep inside myself.

But now . . . after opening that metal book, there was something I wanted.

Down the corridor I could hear the tramp of the

servants whom Father had instructed to seal up the Dark Library for ever. They would fill in the well at the bottom of the shaft to make sure no rats would get inside and bring plague. And then the masons would brick up the entrance to the Dark Library and, after the spiral stairs were destroyed, plaster over the secret entrance from our own library. Even after everything that had happened, I did not like to think of it – something being lost for ever, like the lid closing over Konrad's sarcophagus.

The pendulum tripod was all but finished. It stood some three feet off the ground on its wooden legs. I was quite pleased with myself, for the measurements had had to be precise, and as I looked at it now from every angle, it seemed perfectly level. From the tripod's apex was fixed the strange metal pivot that allowed the pendulum to move in any direction. I still had to attach the final piece of the pivot, a kind of second joint, but I could tell Ernest was getting impatient.

'Let's make it go,' he said eagerly, and with a pang I realized that this was one of the first times since the funeral when I'd seen him look happy. Konrad had always been his favourite. Ashamed, I realized how in my own grief I'd neglected everyone else's. I would have to be a better brother to Ernest.

'All right,' I said. 'But remember it's not quite done yet.

Right now it's just a normal pendulum.'

Quickly I tied a measure of string to the main pivot and at the end attached the star-shaped pendant from the metal book. The star had one point that was longer than all the others, pointing straight down at the floor.

'That's an unusual weight,' Elizabeth said. She'd been reading in an armchair, and now walked over for a closer look at our work. 'Where did you find it?'

'Just something I found lying around,' I replied carelessly.

She frowned. 'I think I've seen it somewhere before.'

'Care to lend a hand?' I asked, hoping to distract her.

'No, thank you,' she replied. 'I'm enjoying my book.'

'Ah, quiet contemplation,' I said. 'Can never have enough of that. Nice and solitary.'

Her eyebrows lifted satirically, and she then returned to her chair.

'Can we make it go now?' Ernest asked impatiently.

Grateful, I pulled back the weight and let it swing in a long arc, back and forth.

'It's not too interesting,' said Ernest after a few moments. 'It just keeps going in the same direction.'

'Yes,' I said.

'But that will change in time,' said Father, and I turned to see him watching over us. I hadn't heard him come in.

He smiled down at Ernest. 'If we leave it long enough, you'll see it change course because of the Earth's revolution.'

Ernest frowned. 'How?'

'The earth is a big ball, remember, making a complete rotation every twenty-four hours.'

'So it would turn the pendulum?' Ernest asked, his small brow furrowed.

'No, the pendulum stays exactly the same. The earth does the moving below it, so it only seems like the pendulum's direction changes.'

I watched Ernest's face, and I wondered how much of this he understood. I wasn't entirely sure I understood it myself.

'How long does that take?' he asked.

'Hours before you'd notice.'

'Oh.' Ernest's eyes strayed to the window, wondering about better entertainments.

My father's gaze settled on me briefly. 'An excellent activity. Well done, Victor.'

And with that he left the room, saying he had some business to attend to in his study. I wondered if he was avoiding me – in the same way that, until today, I had tried to avoid everyone else in the house.

I looked back at Ernest, eager to recapture his attention.

'But watch what happens when we attach the double joint,' I told him. 'Now, I'll need your help here. It's a bit tricky . . .'

It took us some time to fix the double joint to the main pivot, but Ernest proved to be a very focused apprentice, as long as I let him hold a tool or occasionally twist a screw. When we were finished, we tied on the star-shaped pendulum weight once more.

'Now watch this,' I said. 'There are two pivots, each at ninety degrees to each other.'

I pulled back the weight and let go. With each swing the weight careened in a new direction, completely unpredictably, as though it were doing some strange dance.

Ernest laughed, delighted. 'It's like it knows!'

I glanced at him sharply. 'What do you mean?'

'Well, like it knows what it wants to do,' he said.

I smiled. There was indeed something eerily alive about the motion of the thing.

Elizabeth came back over and watched with interest as the pendulum flailed about.

'It goes and goes,' Ernest said.

'It will slow down eventually,' I replied.

I looked at my younger brother, pleased by his delight. 'So, what do you say, Ernest? Is that a good toy?'

'Yes,' he said, stopping the pendulum and then setting

it going in a different direction.

'It's oddly hypnotic,' said Mother, 'like looking at the flames of the fire – never the same from moment to moment.'

I wished Father had not gone off so quickly. I would have liked to feel his hand clap me on the shoulder.

I worried that he blamed me. It was never spoken; it didn't need to be, but I felt it as an invisible barrier between us. During the quest to make the elixir I had deceived him, and kept secrets from him, and he'd ordered us to abandon the search. But I'd ignored him.

I wanted things mended between us. Konrad's death felt like a great fissure through my being, and another blow would crack me apart entirely.

And yet here I was, about to deceive Father again.

As we were finishing dinner, Justine, our nursemaid, came to tell me that William, my littlest brother, had been calling for me.

I quickly finished my torte and left the table. In the dim nursery I saw William in his crib, lying on his stomach, with his arms circled around his favourite two toys, a knitted elephant and a soft flannel horse. He was not quite one yet, and at the sight of me his legs wriggled against the sheets in excitement, and he beamed. A more blissful face I don't think I'd ever seen.

'Tor,' he called me.

'What are you doing, wide awake?' I placed a hand on his back, his warm head. He pushed up, and I leaned down to kiss him. 'I love you, Willy. I'll see you in the morning.'

'Yeah,' he said, and dropped back down, hugging his animals closer to his face.

For a moment my resolve melted. My apparatus was finished and waiting in my bedchamber for my midnight business. I could take it apart. I could put it away. I could sink the metal book in the lake. But I knew I wouldn't. Once an idea had set its course in my head and I'd fixed my destination on the horizon, I'd never been able to tear my gaze away.

I embraced William once more. How I envied him – the world was such a simple, good place. All he needed was a soft bed, two toys, and a kiss on the head.

After midnight, by candlelight, I spread upon the floor the spirit board I'd fashioned. It was a large piece of leather on which I had written the letters of the alphabet, well spaced, around the edges, in the particular manner described in the instructions. Rising from the centre of the board was the wooden tripod that held the pendulum.

I placed more candles around the periphery of the board

so I could see properly. I had a sheaf of paper, two inkwells, and an extra quill nearby for good measure.

I skimmed over the instructions once more. Rain pattered against my window, and when I glanced up, I had the fleeting sensation that someone was looking in at me. I went to close the curtains, then returned to the spirit board. I crouched beside the pendulum and deliberately, in accordance with the instructions, pricked my finger upon one of the weight's points. I felt its purposeful vibration and quickly stood. I picked up a piece of paper, dipped my quill into the well, and cleared my throat.

'I invite you to speak,' I said to the empty room.

No sudden draught chilled my flesh; no candles guttered.

'I invite you to come,' I whispered.

My door opened, and every hair on my neck bristled as a shadow darted into the room. Almost at once the flickering candlelight showed me the face of Elizabeth, and my terror was replaced with indignation.

'What're you doing here?' I demanded.

'What is it *you're* doing?' she countered, staring at the board, and then my pendulum. 'I knew that machine of yours was no mere toy.'

I made no reply.

'What does it do?' she persisted.

'I don't know yet.'

'What is it meant to do?'

'Allow me to talk with Konrad.'

Her face was waxen. 'Is this some invention of yours?'

I shook my head. 'In the bonfire there was a book that wouldn't burn. Well, it wasn't really a book but a metal box, and in it were instructions for conversing with the dead. It claims that their spirits remain a time on the earth, unseen by us, weak and powerless to communicate unless we help them.'

'And who was the author of this book?'

I shrugged. 'Some magician or necromancer. What does it matter?'

'But you don't even believe in such things!'

I chuckled mirthlessly. 'I don't know what I believe any more. My faith in all things is shaken. Modern science failed me. Alchemy failed. I trust nothing but am ready to try anything.'

She looked horrified. 'The occult? I actually believe in a world beyond ours, Victor. I haven't seen them, but there may truly be ghosts – and devils, too – and I think it very unwise to try to summon them.'

'All I know is that I want to talk to Konrad.'

From the corner of my eye I saw the pendulum twitch.

'Look!' I whispered, pointing.

'It's a draught,' she breathed.

'I feel no draught.' The pendulum weight flinched once more and quivered slightly, as though waiting.

'How do you make it move?' she demanded, her voice tinged with both anger and fear.

'I'm doing nothing!' I held out some paper and my extra quill and inkwell. 'Curious? Sit across from me and write down any letters the pendulum points to!'

'I don't like this, Victor!'

'Leave, then! Get thee to a nunnery!'

She looked at me, hesitated for only a split second, and took the paper and quill. I couldn't help smiling. Elizabeth was never one to back down from a challenge.

'I part the veil between our worlds,' I whispered. 'I invite the spirit of my brother Konrad to join us. I invite you to speak, Konrad.'

The pendulum quivered again.

'I beg you, speak.'

Elizabeth gasped as the weight suddenly jerked, and my eyes locked on to its long tip, watching the letters it pointed to as it swung. Hurriedly I began writing.

'Copy them down,' I panted. My entire body felt suddenly sheathed in ice. Back and forth, side to side, the star-shaped weight jerked swiftly.

'They're not forming words!' Elizabeth said.

'Don't worry about that now!' I said, for the

pendulum's movements were becoming faster still. It flailed about the spirit board, and I could scarcely keep up with its wild motions. I was scribbling madly, the ink smearing in my haste.

The pendulum's frenzy thrilled me – and terrified me too, for it was like a bird trapped in a room. I lost track of time and was only aware of filling page after page until, with a final violent spasm, the star-shaped pendulum broke its tether, flew across the room, and hit the wall. I realized I was holding my breath and let it out, feeling as though it had been *my body*, and not the pendulum, lashing about.

I looked at Elizabeth, then down at my pages of desperate letters.

'This isn't some trick, Victor?'

'You saw it moving!'

She moved around the board towards me, and for a moment I thought she was going to embrace me, but her arms caressed only the air in front of me, hands brushing back and forth.

'What're you doing?' I demanded.

'Checking for strings. You might've made it move yourself.'

'Why would I do such a thing?' I retorted, furious.

She was trembling, and I suddenly realized how

frightened she was. I too felt a watery weakness in my joints. Quickly I pulled a blanket from the end of my bed and draped it around her shoulders.

'Some force animated the pendulum,' I said quietly.

'And you truly think it was Konrad?'

'There might be a message.' I was almost afraid to examine the pages I held, but I forced myself.

lksjdflkjlskdjflkjcomelsjdflksjldkfjlksdraiseioureyjnmnsmeoeriy
toiskldfqweqwemlksjdflkjlskdjflkjcomelsjdflksjldkfjlksdrai-
seioureyjnmnsmeoeriytoiskldfmnkjjkhoiulksjdflkjlskdjflkjcomelsj
dflksjldkfjlksdraiseioureyjnmnsmeoeriytoiskldfiucvzxsjkhklksjd-
flkjlskdjflkjcomelsjdflksjldkfjlksdraiseioureyjnmnsmeoeriytoiskld
fioubvwtygflksjdflkjlskdjflkjcomelsjdflksjldkfjlksdraiseioureyjn-
mnsmeoeriytoiskldf . . .

'It's all gibberish,' Elizabeth said, looking up from her own papers. 'Nothing.'

I shook my head in dismay.

'I'm disgusted with myself,' she said vehemently, and then turned on me. 'Isn't there enough misery in this house already, without you inviting more?'

I let the papers slip from my ink-stained hands and sank to the floor.

'You're not the only one who suffers, Victor,' she said.

'Everyone in this family is suffering. I've seen my entire future change.'

'I lost my *twin*,' I growled.

'And I lost my future husband.'

I said nothing, the word 'husband' clattering painfully inside my mind.

'But what if it was Konrad?' I asked. '*Trying* to talk to us?'

Her eyes closed for a moment. 'I should've walked out on this. You'll only torture yourself – and me, too.'

My eyes settled on the pendulum. 'There is a definite power in it,' I persisted. 'I felt it.'

'If there is,' she retorted, 'it's not one we're meant to harness.'

'Where is that written?' I said defiantly. 'By whose law?'

'You didn't need to build this device, Victor,' she said. 'You had a choice. But I can see you're intent on dwelling only on the darkest things.'

I watched as the door closed behind her, and with a sigh I bent to gather my papers from the floor. Blinking to clear my tired eyes, I suddenly saw, among the garble of letters, a word.

I stared, then snatched up my quill and circled it. My eyes roved across the lines, and I circled another word, then another and another. The same three words repeating again and again.

Heat and ice squalled across my flesh. Could it be coincidence? Or my own mind, knowingly forcing my hand to write the words, so desperate was I for a message from my twin?

Outside the window rain pelted the glass. I hurriedly gathered Elizabeth's discarded papers, and my gaze flew over them. There. And there! And there!

Come raise me.

Come raise me.

Come raise me.

CHAPTER TWO

A KEYHOLE IN THE SKY

'It seems beyond dispute,' said our friend Henry Clerval, running a hand through his wispy blond hair as he looked between the two sets of pages. 'You've both recorded the same letters – and words.'

I looked over triumphantly at Elizabeth.

'I never doubted they were the same,' she said. 'But it doesn't mean they came from Konrad.'

On a table in the music room I had spread out our transcripts from the previous night, as well as the red metal book and its contents. We had the chateau to ourselves. After our morning lessons, presided over as usual by Father, both my parents had left for Geneva, Father to attend to his magistrate's duties, and Mother to help ready the city house for our return in October.

Before Konrad's funeral, their pace had been frenetic. They'd received visitors offering condolences from near and far; there had always been preparations and meals to oversee. Our house had always seemed full. And even after, my parents seemed intent on keeping to their usual schedules – if anything, more vigorously than ever. Father resumed our morning lessons with Elizabeth, Henry, and me, and afterwards he carried on with his own work. Mother threw herself into her duties about the house, carving out time to begin another pamphlet on the rights of women.

Henry fluttered his fingers, giving his characteristic impression of an agitated bird. 'And you truly think Konrad spoke to you from beyond the grave?'

'Why would it be anyone else?' I countered.

There was an uncomfortable silence before Elizabeth replied. 'I was taught that the dead who need to atone for their sins are sent to purgatory, and sometimes they wander the earth in the hope of somehow making amends – and that they may try to communicate with the living.'

'Very well, then,' I said. 'By your way of thinking, Konrad is communicating to us from purgatory.'

'But,' Elizabeth continued, 'the Church also believes there are devils whose only aim is to beguile us and lead us into temptation.'

Henry was nodding emphatically. 'Remember that play of Marlowe's, *Doctor Faustus*? The doctor foolishly makes a deal with the devil, and in the end he's dragged down to Hell. I'd never felt such horror – not in the theatre, anyway.' He paused. 'With you two I've felt far greater horror, of course.'

Despite myself I laughed. 'Why, thank you, Henry. I'm flattered.'

'What is it exactly you think you can achieve?' he asked me, removing his spectacles to polish them. I was surprised by the steadiness – the hint of challenge, even – in his blue-eyed gaze.

I took a breath. My own thoughts were far from clear. 'I don't know. To see him again, I suppose. To help him.'

'Admit it, Victor,' said Elizabeth. 'You'd make your own deal with the devil if you could play God.'

'Don't listen to her,' I told Henry dismissively. 'She plans to join a convent.'

Bewildered, Henry looked from me to Elizabeth. 'Is this true?'

Elizabeth glared at me. 'Why did you say that?'

I shrugged. 'Why keep it secret?'

Henry looked truly distressed. 'You really mean to become a . . . a *nun*?'

'Why does everyone seem to find this idea so incredible?' she asked.

'Well, it's just' – Henry cleared his throat – 'you're very, um, *young* to make such a drastic decision – and have you thought about the family? They've just lost a son. If you entered a convent, it would be like losing a daughter, too. They'd be devastated.'

'Of course I've thought of that! Which is why I wasn't planning on doing it right away.'

'Well, that's some comfort,' murmured Henry. 'Still, it would just be such a terrible loss to, well, everyone.'

'She has no intention of becoming a nun,' I said impatiently. 'Anyway, she wouldn't last two days.'

'I resent that very much!' Elizabeth said.

I held up two fingers. '*Two days* before the mother superior throws herself from the bell tower.'

Elizabeth bit at her lips, and by the light in her eyes, I knew she was suppressing a giggle.

But now Henry levelled his gaze at me. 'You, Victor, are just trying to change the subject. What exactly are you planning? You used to joke about being a god. But this is taking things too far, don't you think?'

I rubbed at my temples, impatient. 'I tell you, I want to see my twin again!'

'But how?' Henry demanded.

I sighed. 'I've no idea, not yet. Here's all I know: that the world is uncontrollable. Chaos reigns. That anything and everything might be possible. I won't subscribe to any rational system again. Nothing will bind me.'

'That is the way to madness,' said Elizabeth.

'If it makes me mad, so be it. But leave me to my method, because without it I'll fall into a despair so deep,

I'll never claw my way back out. I'll see him, damn it! As far as I'm concerned, he asked for my help. Come raise me. Over and over he said it. Wherever he is, he's not happy.'

'Stop,' Elizabeth said.

'He's suffering,' I persisted.

'Stop it, Victor!' Her eyes were wet.

'Victor, you're upsetting her,' Henry said, softly but firmly.

'You two don't need to have any part of this. I've bullied you enough – you especially, Henry.'

I was startled to see anger animate his face. 'I'm not quite so easily bullied, Victor. I may not be the bravest of men, but I'm not the weakling you suggest.'

'I wasn't suggesting any such—'

'I was with you when Polidori amputated your fingers and tried to kill us all. I fought then, and I fought that wretched lynx alongside the rest of you.'

'Absolutely you did, Henry, and—'

But he was no longer listening to my reassurances. His eyes had strayed to the red metal book.

'I've seen that before,' he said.

'Possibly in the Dark Library,' I told him. 'We spent enough time looking through the shelves—'

'No. Not there.'

Purposefully he walked past me, opened the door, and

left the music room. Elizabeth and I looked at each other in puzzlement, then followed. We found him in the great hallway, standing before the huge portrait of Wilhelm Frankenstein, our notorious ancestor who'd built this chateau some three hundred years before.

His face was handsome and pale, unblemished except for a mole on his left cheek. His full mouth was well-moulded, almost feminine. His eyes were a piercing blue, with a curious speck of brown in the lower part of each iris. Eerily he stared out at me, meeting my gaze directly, his right eyebrow lifted slightly, conveying a hint of mockery.

'There,' Henry said, pointing.

I looked and shook my head in amazement. 'How is it possible I've lived here my entire life and—'

'Precisely for that reason,' Henry said. 'We stop seeing what's before our eyes every day.'

'Incredible,' I murmured. One of Wilhelm's hands held a slim book. There could be no mistaking its colour, nor the elaborate decoration on the cover. 'The metal book.'

I heard Elizabeth give a small gasp. 'And that's not all. Around his neck, look.'

Wilhelm wore a black doublet with a ruffled collar in the Spanish style fashionable for the time. Half hidden in the lace flourishes was a chain with an unusual pendant.

Without a doubt it was the star-shaped pendulum weight.

'This is the fellow who built the chateau, isn't it?' asked Henry.

'And the Dark Library within it,' I replied. 'Remember, he's the one who got on his horse one day and was never seen again.'

'Your father mentioned that he attempted to converse with spirits and raise ghosts,' Elizabeth said quietly.

'Perhaps his attempts were successful,' I said. I stared up at his face. His smug smile seemed to be congratulating us for our discovery. 'The fellow knows something.'

'You can learn a lot from a painting,' said Henry, peering more closely at the canvas. 'And there's a great deal of detail in this one. Remarkable. It could have been painted with a magnifying glass.'

'There's fruit on the windowsill,' said Elizabeth. 'Limes and oranges and apples.'

'What of them?' I said impatiently.

'Fruit was terribly expensive three hundred years ago,' said Henry. 'They're a display of his wealth. He's bragging. *Look at my limes and oranges! The elaborate brass chandelier! The tapestries on my wall!*'

I couldn't help laughing at Henry's pompous voice.

'His money's new to him,' my clever friend continued. 'He wants to show it off.'

Elizabeth looked at him with real admiration, and I felt an unexpected pang of jealousy. 'That was well observed, Henry!'

'I'm a merchant's son,' he replied, flushing. 'I know the cost of things, that's all.'

'But there's symbolism to it as well,' Elizabeth said. 'The apple's always a sign of the forbidden fruit of the tree of knowledge, and' – she pointed – 'that one there has a bite out of it.'

I leaned closer. 'So it does. You think that refers to his endeavours in alchemy?'

'The occult, more likely.'

'Look at the chandelier,' Henry said. 'There are eight holders but only one candle.'

'Does that have significance?' I asked, starting to feel more than a little irritated by my ignorance amidst all this scholarly brilliance.

'On the altar at church,' Elizabeth said, 'a lit candle is the sign of God's presence, that He is among us. But' – and she shivered – 'that one is unlit.'

'Perhaps he's saying he doesn't believe in God,' I said.

Elizabeth sniffed. 'More like His presence is not invited, but if he thinks he can hide from God, he is sadly mistaken.'

'But he *wants* to be seen,' Henry said. 'That's the point

of the whole painting. He *wants* to show us something.'

'What does he want to show you?' asked a voice behind us, and with a start I turned to see Maria, our housekeeper, staring at us in surprise. Of all our servants Maria had been with us the longest. She had been nurse to both Konrad and me (Konrad being her favourite, naturally) and was practically a member of the family. Indeed, when we were seeking the Elixir of Life, she helped us find the disgraced alchemist Polidori, and kept our secret for us. And when we finally gave the elixir to Konrad, she was in his bedroom, watching. But I never told my parents that – and never would.

'Hello, Maria,' I said breezily. 'We've just been amusing ourselves with our ancestors' portraits. It turns out Henry here has a connoisseur's eye when it comes to evaluating a painting. He was just pointing out all the signs of wealth in the portrait. The clothing, the fruit, and so forth.'

'Is that right?' Maria said, looking from me to Henry with some suspicion, then up at Wilhelm Frankenstein. 'That fellow, I always look away when I pass him.'

'Why's that, Maria?' Elizabeth inquired.

'The way his eyes follow you. Makes my skin crawl.'

'Yes, it's quite a feat to paint the eyes for that effect,' said Henry, playing the part of the eager expert.

Once more Maria turned her gaze on me, and I knew she suspected something. She'd known me since I was a babe and of late knew what secrecy I was capable of. We would have to be very careful. Then her face softened and she smiled. 'I like seeing you all together, enjoying yourselves.'

'Thank you, Maria,' I said.

We made bland comments about the painting until she walked off to resume her work. We waited for her tread to fade away.

'Do you think she heard anything beforehand?' Henry asked.

'No,' I said. 'But let's be quick.' I stared at the portrait hard, willing it to open up its secret meaning. 'What of that mirror?' I said, squinting.

Near the top of the painting, in the background, hung an oval mirror in an ornate gilt frame. I could see that there was something reflected in it, but the images were too small, and too high up for me to see.

Elizabeth nodded. 'There may be something interesting up there.'

I ran to a cupboard that I knew contained a stepladder, and when I returned, I saw that Henry had taken a magnifying glass from Father's study.

'It's really quite amazing,' he said, examining the

painting. 'Did you know that there's virtually no craquelure on this canvas?'

'Craquelure?' I said.

'Those little wrinkly cracks you get on old paintings as the oils dry over time. This piece was done three hundred years ago and has hardly a blemish.'

An unexpected shiver went through me then. 'You really do know a great deal about paintings,' I said.

'My father deals in antiquities sometimes.' Henry climbed the rungs of the stepladder so that his face was almost perfectly level with the mirror. 'Did you know this was a self-portrait?' he asked.

'No one ever mentioned it.'

'He was a talented man,' Elizabeth said. 'Your father said as much.'

Henry leaned closer. 'He shows himself painting, with a brush in his . . .' His voice trailed off.

'What?' I demanded, stepping up the ladder and jostling with Henry.

He passed me the magnifying glass, looking a bit pale.

Truly the painted details were amazing, for even through the lens my view was as crystalline as something seen beyond a window. Within the mirror Wilhelm Frankenstein stood behind an easel, his right hand raised. But his fingers held no brush, only pointed to the canvas, as though giving directions, while the actual brush hovered just above, in midair.

'What do you see?' Elizabeth asked impatiently.

'The brush is floating,' I said. 'It must be some joke. He's just congratulating himself, saying it's like magic.'

'Look more closely,' said Henry.

I squinted at the brush 'Is that not shadow?'

Henry shook his head. 'The light comes from the other direction.'

What I'd mistaken for shadow was in fact a pair of black butterflies who together held the paintbrush, wings aflutter.

'Let me have a look,' said Elizabeth, and Henry stepped down to allow her room. Her warm body pressed against mine as I passed her the glass. She studied the painting.

'It gives me gooseflesh to see it,' she said.

Henry cleared his throat. 'Victor's right, of course. It could all be a joke.'

'Or he could truly be commanding some spectral force to do his work,' I said.

Elizabeth was slowly moving the magnifying glass across the painted image within the mirror. 'Behind him, did you see the large window? And is that . . .'

'What?' I demanded. 'What do you see in the window?'

'The sky. There are clouds, some of them in the shape of angels, I think. But in the middle of the sky . . .' She swallowed. 'You'd better look at this.'

Almost reluctantly she passed me the magnifying glass. I found the window, marvelling once again at the painting's clarity. I saw the blue of the sky, the feathered clouds – and there, in the centre of this blue sky, was a keyhole.

A star-shaped keyhole.

I lowered the glass and looked back at the pendant hanging from Wilhelm Frankenstein's neck.

'The pendulum weight is a key,' I said.

Elizabeth nodded.

'We must find this lock,' I said.

'A keyhole in the sky?' Henry said sceptically.

'It must be somewhere in the house, surely,' I replied.

'You've lived here your entire life,' Henry said. 'Have you ever seen a keyhole like this?'

'No, but it may be covered up. Wilhelm built the chateau three hundred years ago. It's been added on to considerably over the years, but it would have to be in the oldest part, the original part. A window,' I said, thinking aloud, 'or perhaps somewhere on the ramparts, where the chateau is closest to the sky—'

'I know where it is,' said Elizabeth quietly.

Henry and I turned to her together. 'You do?' I said.

'In the painting – that's not the sky. It's the ceiling of our chapel.'

We never used the chapel in Chateau Frankenstein. My parents did not believe in God, and my siblings and I had been brought up to believe that only mankind could make a heaven or hell of earth. So no candle burned on the chapel's altar to signal Christ's presence. No priest ever came to say Mass here. Yet in Wilhelm's time it had surely been a place of Roman Catholic worship.

It was on the chateau's main floor, in the very oldest part. A narrow room, the chapel had only a few windows covered with stained glass, and a stone altar at one end. A large chandelier hung from the high ceiling.

My entire life I don't think I'd ever spent more than a few seconds at a time in this room. It offered no hiding places for games. It was cold and draughty and un-welcoming. And I'd certainly never taken the time to gaze up at the ceiling, as the three of us did now, with great attention. We'd made sure to close the door securely behind us, and turn the lock so Maria or any of the other servants couldn't wander in and see us.

The ceiling had once been painted but had been left to fade and flake, though you could still see the traces of what once must have been a brilliant and colourful fresco.

Through the painter's skill the ceiling had been transformed into a vast vault of heavenly blue sky, and all around the base peered smiling cherubs and angels.

Head tilted back, I said, 'The chandelier.'

'Same as in the portrait,' Elizabeth concurred. 'Only larger.'

'The ceiling's too high to see if there's any keyhole,' I muttered.

The chandelier was suspended by a stout rope that ran along the ceiling, through a complicated pulley, and then down the wall, where it was tied off at a cleat. Like all the other chandeliers in the house, it needed to be lowered so the candles could be lit.

I walked over to the cleat, un-looped the rope, and braced myself for the chandelier's weight. Given its size, it was surprisingly light. Hand over hand I lowered it, and tied it off a few feet above the floor.

'It seems solid enough,' I said, gripping and testing the strength of its brawny wooden arms. 'One could easily sit on one of these braces.'

Henry looked at me in surprise. 'You don't mean—'

'Yes,' I said. 'I'll have a much better view. Hoist me up, will you?'

I sat near the middle and gripped the tall central column with one hand, and a wooden brace with my other.

Henry grasped the rope and hoisted me towards the painted sky.

'Is it difficult?' I asked.

'No,' said Henry, 'and I don't quite understand why.'

'It must be the pulley system,' I said, peering up at the mechanism on the ceiling. 'And the chandelier itself is made of some light wood.'

For a giddy moment I felt like a child again, and pumped my legs.

'Stop rocking it, Victor!' Elizabeth cautioned.

But I wasn't ready to surrender the moment just yet, and kicked out my legs, straining for the sky.

I was nearly at the ceiling when I heard the crack and felt the brace beneath me fracture. I was spilled off my perch so quickly that I scarcely had time to get both hands around the central column. Legs kicking, I dangled from the chandelier, which was still swinging crazily, some fourteen feet above the merciless stone floor.

'Hold on!' I heard Henry gasp. 'I'll bring you down!'

In his haste Henry lowered the chandelier so violently that my left hand – the one with all its fingers – was jerked off the column.

'Stop, stop!' I grunted, struggling to hold on as the chandelier lurched and spun. 'Do nothing!' I flailed about for another brace to grip, but felt my three-fingered hand begin to slip, and knew my time was running out. I swung my legs with all my might and managed to hook one over a solid brace. Grasping it with my right hand, I swiftly hauled my belly up over the top of the brace, and prayed it would hold.

'Thank God,' I heard Elizabeth murmur below. 'Victor, you idiot!'

With both hands I seized the central column and pulled myself into a sitting position, making sure to move very slowly. The chandelier was swinging only a little now. My pulse slowed.

'I'll lower you,' Henry called out. 'Hold on.'

'No! Raise me. All the way.'

'Are you mad?' said Elizabeth. 'The thing's clearly unsafe!'

I looked at the splintered brace, angling down slightly like a broken branch. I wondered if it would be noticed. No one really ever came into the chapel, after all, but I was grateful it hadn't snapped off completely.

'I just put too much strain on it,' I said. 'It's fine. Haul away, Henry!'

'You're sure you—' Henry began, and then laughed abruptly. 'Of course you're sure. Very well. Up! You! Go!'

I turned my attention to the ceiling and the fresco painted there. Closer, I could appreciate how clever its illusion was, for even though the paint was faded and cracked, for a moment I thought there was no ceiling at all, only sky.

'This is as high as it goes,' said Henry.

Directly above me, not two feet away, was the great loop that supported the chandelier, and next to it was another cleat for tying off a rope, which confused me for a moment before I realized what it was for.

'*He* did this!' I called down to the others.

'What?' Elizabeth said.

'Wilhelm Frankenstein. He sat on the chandelier and hauled himself up to the ceiling. He could tie off the rope right up here.'

I knew what this meant. I looked at the ceiling, among the shadows of clouds, the flaking paint. It would have to be nearby . . . and there it was. From the ground I would have missed it altogether, or mistaken it for a blemish on the fresco.

A key-shaped hole in the sky.

'Found it!' I called down to Elizabeth and Henry.

'You're certain?' Henry asked.

'Well, let's find out.' From my jacket pocket I took the key.

'Wait, Victor,' said Elizabeth. 'Are you sure this is a door you want opened?'

42

'What else does one do with a door?' I said.

'How do you know it's not a portal to—' Henry began.

'Hell?' I said, smiling down at him. 'In a sky filled with angels?'

I reached up and pushed the star-shaped key into the hole. I turned it. I heard a click, and at once a trapdoor sprang down, a little ladder attached to one side.

Ruined angels watched as I climbed up inside the vault of heaven.

CHAPTER THREE

THE DEATH ELIXIR

I crouched at the threshold, waiting for my eyes to adjust. It was a tiny room, low-ceilinged and airless. Near my hand I saw a candle in a holder, and I took a match from my pocket and lit it.

A reclining sofa. A small table, and on it a book, a pocket watch, a glass flask, a dropper and a star-shaped key. I picked it up and saw that it was identical to my own. Wilhelm Frankenstein must have had a second copy made, for safekeeping. Dust carpeted everything.

'Victor?' Elizabeth called from below.

I peered down through the trapdoor. 'Come up. You should see this. Henry, you hoist Elizabeth, and then take the rope and haul yourself up.'

'I hardly think that's safe,' Henry objected.

'It held me; it can hold you,' I replied. 'Just keep your head, Henry, and no swinging.'

'Ah, hilarious,' he said, swiftly lowering the chandelier and casting a wary eye over it. 'The thing's clearly rotted through.'

But I smiled when I saw Elizabeth immediately perch upon the braces and hold tight.

'I'm ready,' she said to Henry.

It did not take long before both of them had joined me in the chamber, the chandelier tied off at the ceiling cleat. We closed the trapdoor, just in case a servant should enter the chapel, and dust swirled up into a dense mist.

'Do you think your father knows about this room?' Elizabeth asked when her sneezing abated.

It was possible, of course. Father was full of surprises, as I knew better than anyone else. Over the summer I'd discovered that he'd tried his hand at alchemy as a young man. He'd failed to transmute lead to gold. But it hadn't stopped him from selling the fake substance in faraway lands to ensure his family fortune.

'I don't know,' I said, handing my handkerchief to her.

'Strange man, your Wilhelm Frankenstein,' said Henry, dabbing his nose. 'Most men are satisfied with one secret room, but he apparently needed two.'

We'd all gathered around the small table and the book atop it. I quickly picked it up and opened it.

'Some kind of workbook,' Henry said at my shoulder, for the early pages were dense with scribbling and crossing-outs, and numerical charts, written any which way across the page. Page after page of ink so dense and dark it appeared like thunderclouds – and then, on a calm page, some orderly lines of handwriting.

'This must be Wilhelm Frankenstein's hand,' I said. 'Written in Latin – of course,' I added with a sigh. 'What is everyone's obsession with Latin? It's absurd. Henry, will you do the honours?'

My long-suffering friend took the notebook and exhaled. 'This feels too similar to our last adventures in the Dark Library.'

'If you don't read it, I'll only puzzle it out myself,' I told him with a smile.

'I don't doubt it,' he said. 'The first line says here *One drop and one drop only, taken on the tongue.*'

Elizabeth took up the flask. The glass was a dark green, but through it I could see the darker shadow of some liquid near the bottom.

'I'm amazed it hasn't all dried up,' she murmured. 'Could it have been here for three hundred years?' With some difficulty she uncorked the flask.

She took a sniff at the neck and recoiled. 'It smells like something that should not be drunk under any circumstances.'

'Who said I'm going to drink it?' I asked.

Elizabeth raised a doubtful eyebrow. 'Do you think Wilhelm Frankenstein actually drank this?'

'We don't know yet,' I said. 'Go on, Henry.'

'*In your right hand take firm hold of the spirit clock . . .*'

'Spirit clock,' I repeated, and from the table grabbed hold of the pocket watch. I stared for some time before understanding what I was looking at. I swallowed.

Beyond the scratched, smoky glass was what looked like the skeletal remains of a fetal bird, perhaps a sparrow. Its collapsed ribs, bent neck, and crushed skull occupied the centre of the clock face. A spindly leg protruded straight up from this bundle of bones, its tiny clawed foot pointing at what in a normal timepiece would have been twelve o'clock. Yet there were no numerals anywhere on the face.

'How delightful,' said Henry with a hoarse chuckle. 'I'm sure they'll be all the rage in Paris before long.'

I turned the clock in my hands. There was no keyhole for winding it. I put it to my ear.

'It doesn't tick.' I looked at Henry and asked, 'Does it say how it works?'

Henry looked back down and continued translating, but almost instantly broke off. 'Look here,' he said to me firmly, 'before I read any more I want a promise from you that you're not going to do anything rash. A promise, Victor, or not another word.'

'Henry, I promise.'

He held my eye a little longer and then read on. '*In your*

left hand hold the talisman that will bring you back to your body. The item itself is of no significance, so long as it is clenched tightly in the left hand when you make your entry – and your exit.' Henry looked up, his eyes wide behind his spectacles. 'Entry and exit where?'

'It's obvious enough, isn't it?' I said, a quickening excitement beating in my ears. 'Here's what I think. Wilhelm discovered those instructions for the spirit board and used them to communicate with the dead. And maybe the dead told him how to enter their realm. Or, who knows, he might have figured out how to get there himself!'

'It's not possible,' said Elizabeth. 'Beyond our world there's heaven, hell, and purgatory – and the living can't go there.'

'Keep reading, Henry!' I urged.

He swallowed. *'The talisman allows your body to recognize your spirit as its rightful owner. You must return to your body when the hand of the spirit clock has made one full revolution.'* Henry paused briefly. *'Tarry too long and your body will die.'*

'So, it seems,' I said, 'that your spirit leaves your body when you enter this other world. And you have a limited time to be parted from it.'

Henry continued reading. *'Beware, because time is unreliable in the spirit world. Your allotted time might seem an age, or the blink of an eye – though, with practise the spirit clock can be manipulated.'*

I snatched up the dropper and poked it deep into the flask.

'Are you mad?' Elizabeth said, grabbing my arm.

I tried to grin. 'You know I am.'

'Victor, you promised!' Henry exclaimed.

'I lied.'

Elizabeth tried to snatch at the dropper. 'It could be poison!' But before she could stop me, I squeezed a drop of the fluid onto my tongue.

No one said anything for a moment.

'You fool,' she breathed.

'It's done,' I said through gritted teeth. 'It cannot be undone! If it's nonsense, we'll all be the wiser.'

And if it kills me, I will go where Konrad has gone. I'll be a twin again.

'How do you feel?' Henry asked.

'Completely unchanged,' I said, reaching out for the bottle. 'Are you sure I took enough?'

Henry stopped me with his free hand, glancing down at the book. *'Never take more than a single drop. Its effect is potent, and the elixir cannot be taken more than once a day, lest your body fall into a dangerous torpor.'*

'There's something now . . .' I grimaced. A bitter metallic taste suddenly blossomed in my mouth, and an unsettling warmth swept through my veins.

'Make yourself vomit it up!' Henry urged me. 'We've no idea what it really does!'

The anxiety in his face sent the first jolts of panic through me. What if it truly were poison? I forced myself to focus. Heavily I sat down on the reclining sofa and took up the spirit clock.

'Right hand?' I said, looking at Henry, feeling light-headed.

'Yes, yes, right hand!'

I closed the three fingers of my right hand around the clock's smooth contours.

'And you must have something in your left!' Elizabeth said. 'Your talisman!'

'My ring!' I said, and tried to pull the Frankenstein family ring from my finger, but a strange numbness was overpowering me. I lay down.

'Here, let me,' she said, and tugged it from my finger. She put it in my left hand and folded my fingers tightly around it.

'Henry, is there anything else written?' I asked urgently.

My friend frantically flipped ahead in the notebook. 'No, that's all. That's everything.'

'Your eyes are drooping,' I heard Henry say as though from a great distance.

'Victor, get up!' cried Elizabeth. 'Don't fall asleep! Henry, help me get him up!'

I blinked again—

—and Henry and Elizabeth are both gone.

I'm still lying on the sofa, in Wilhelm Frankenstein's secret room in the chapel ceiling. I must've dozed off and been deserted, which seems more than a bit inconsiderate. The trapdoor is closed. I frown. Why would they leave me here alone?

I'm suddenly aware of my clenched hands. I open my left and see my ring. And in my right hand is the smooth round shape of the spirit clock, its silver cool against my warm skin, and what I thought was just my body's pulse echoed in my fingers is actually the ticking of the clock.

I hold it to my ear. The ticking is unmistakable, and the skeletal leg of the bird, which once pointed straight up, has twisted a bit to the right.

And then my gaze shifts from the clock to the hand that holds it. My three-fingered hand now has five fingers. I drop the clock onto my lap and stare in amazement, wiggling the fingers before my eyes.

'They're healed!' I cry, wanting Elizabeth and Henry to be here so I can show them.

The dull drumming pain is gone, completely gone. I make a fist.

How can this be real? I thump my body. I'm solid and awake. This is no dream.

But I am . . . elsewhere.

I slip my ring back onto my finger and look once more at the clock. When it has made one full revolution, I must return to my body. Does that mean this sofa here, where I now sit?

I look about myself. Are Elizabeth and Henry still here somewhere, in the real world, unseen and unseeing?

Slowly I stand, expecting to feel light-headed, but I feel absolutely fine. Better than fine. I feel as though I've shed the gloom that hung upon me like a leaden cloak. Instead an eager vigour courses through me. I'm a spirit, yet I have substance and strength. I'm no bit of ghostly vapour – and most curious of all, I've never felt more alive. Every beat of my heart cries, *Now*.

I reach for the trapdoor and have no idea what awaits me on the other side. A barren plain? A fiery swamp filled with torment? Or a blissful meadow faintly vibrating with harp music? Heaven, hell, or purgatory – those were the possibilities Elizabeth had mentioned. So which will it be?

I look once more at my miraculously healed hand and

realize that I am not remotely afraid. All I feel is exhilaration. I open the trapdoor.

There is the chandelier, still tied off at its cleat. Below, the chapel looks completely unchanged. I swing my legs out over the edge of the hatch, and step carefully down onto one of the braces. I untie the rope from its cleat and sit down, lowering myself slowly. It's easy work, especially with two able hands. Within moments I am at the floor.

I let my eyes linger on the ceiling, and the dull fresco suddenly pulses, showing me its former glory in a blaze of vibrant blues and golds. It's as though, by mere will, I am making the house remember its past! I turn my gaze to the walls, where I know nothing hangs any more, but, concentrating, I now see heavy tapestries depicting Jesus and the stations of the cross. At the altar a candle burns. Rows of simple wooden pews swim into view.

I step towards one of them, and as I rap it with my knuckles, it becomes truly solid. I stroke my fingertips across the grain – the feeling is intense, strangely pleasurable. And when I sit down upon the pew, it's no surprise that it's as solid as can be. It doesn't evaporate and spill me out, though when I stand, it starts to fade, as though it takes my gaze, my touch, to properly remind it of its existence. I smile at the wonder of it, my power to make this happen.

A feeling of being watched crawls over me, and I turn towards the doorway. I am alone but suddenly conscious of what else I might see here.

I leave the chapel and walk towards the chateau's great entrance hall. The place is so still and quiet, yet seems to pulse with energy and expectation. At first everything around me seems utterly familiar, but I need only to let my gaze rest awhile somewhere and suddenly I see spectral tapestries and paintings, bits of unknown furniture, different doorways, flagstones, wall sconces and mouldings – everything that was once in the house, or was once part of it, is still here, waiting to be seen and touched again.

I reach the entrance hall. Flanking the great wooden door are two leaded glass windows, beyond which is a fog so thick, I cannot see the courtyard.

Once more I'm aware of being watched. I whirl back to the stairs to find no one upon them. But fluttering lazily down towards me is a black butterfly. I remember the two dark creatures in Wilhelm Frankenstein's self portrait, holding the paintbrush. But this butterfly here is surprisingly large, with a dark blue eyespot on each of its wings, and with every wing-beat I can actually hear a strangely musical thrum.

As I watch, the creature circles above my head, tentative, as though asking permission. Instinctively I stretch out my hand, and cautiously the butterfly lands upon my finger. At its touch a thrill of pleasure passes through me – and something else too, which reminds me of both hunger and being fed – and as I watch in amazement, the butterfly is illuminated with colour more intense than any stained glass.

When it flutters away, gloriously ablaze, I feel a twinge of sadness. I check the spirit clock. The fetal bird leg points straight down. Half my time already gone!

I hurry upstairs, and as I near Konrad's bedchamber, my step falters. If I find him inside, what will he look like? What will I say? I force myself onward. The door is ajar—

Sitting at his table before a chessboard, he's turned away from me, dressed in the suit he was buried in. I can only stare in wonder. My voice abandons me. My brother is not gone. He has been here all along, just waiting. He moves a rook, then turns the board around, considering his next move, and I realize this is the same game we were playing at his bedside before he died.

I push the door open, enter the room. 'Konrad,' I whisper.

Immediately he turns, throwing an arm across his face, as though shielding himself from a blinding glare. He stands, upsetting his chair. In shock I see him snatch up a rapier and back away from me in terror.

'Are you an angel?' he cries out. 'Or a demon come to punish me?'

I walk deeper into his room, arms spread wide. 'Konrad, it's just me: Victor!'

He cowers, squinting, still shielding his face. I look over my shoulder and can't see the source of any glare. Can it be me?

'No!' he shouts. 'You lie! My brother's alive! What are you?'

'Victor!' I insist. 'And I *am* alive! But I found a way inside! I came to find you!'

He tightens his grip on the hilt, but I can see the blade shaking. 'Prove it.'

'Ask me anything – something only we would know.'

'When we were four years old,' he begins, 'there was a cat we both loved, and—'

'One day in the stables we had a contest to see who could lure it to him first. It preferred you, of course, and you gloated, so when your back was turned, I picked up a large stone and dropped it onto your head. I promised you my dessert if you wouldn't tell anyone.'

'Victor?' Konrad says quietly. 'Is it really you?'

I draw closer to embrace him, but he staggers back wincing, hand outstretched to ward me off. 'No, don't touch me! Your heat!'

'My heat?'

'It burns!'

I stop, confused and hurt – and then another thought blossoms, unbidden, in my mind:

I am light and heat. I have total control over him.

'Why do you have a rapier with you?' I ask him. 'What are you afraid of?'

'The house is different now.'

'What do you mean? Are there others here?'

'Yes,' he says, 'but—'

In my pocket I feel a strange vibration, and I hurriedly pull out the spirit clock. Its skeletal leg points straight up, and the tiny clenched claw is ghoulishly tapping at the glass.

'What's that you're holding?' Konrad says, squinting.

'I must go,' I say to my twin, remembering the notebook's strict instructions. 'Are you safe here?'

'I don't know! Don't go yet!'

'I'll come back! I promise!'

I run, the ring on my hand guiding me like some supernatural magnet, in the direction of my body in the real world. It knows. It impels me.

'Victor!' I hear Konrad call from the hallway. 'Don't go!'

The despair in his voice is like a chisel to my heart. 'I have to,' I call back over my shoulder, and see he's following me from a distance. But I move like a current of wind, outstripping him. I hurtle down the grand staircase, and on the final steps a low moan of wind from outside draws my eyes to the windows. The fog is even thicker now, and eerily bright, swirling in strangely hypnotic patterns.

A dangerous curiosity stirs in me, and I want to go closer, to look deeper, but the ring on my hand sends an insistent jolt through me. I must leave. But my mind feels addled now, and as I begin to run back towards the chapel, before me suddenly stands a wall where there should be none. Without thinking I rush through a doorway I've never known.

'Victor, where are you going?' my twin cries out, as though from a great distance.

Panting, I find myself in a part of the chateau that must have only existed centuries ago, a totally unfamiliar ante-room. Feeling woozy and confused, I look back to the doorway, only to find it gone. There is no other entrance.

It's as if the house is remembering its former selves so quickly that I can't navigate it.

Concentrate!

But I'm trapped, fighting panic. With a faint musical thrum a black butterfly suddenly lands upon my shoulder, and becomes colourful. And in the moment before it flutters away, I take a great breath into my lungs and remember my light and heat, the power of my gaze.

I fix my eyes upon the walls of the room, and reluctantly the stone softens and melts away into a new doorway. I run through it before it can close, and find myself in another unfamiliar passage. I've spent my life in this place, and I'm truly lost. For the first time I start to feel a weakness in my limbs. I burst into a kitchen so ancient, it must be the original one built for the chateau, nothing more than a hearth and a drain in the floor. I turn around wildly, looking for an exit, my pulse beating in my ears. Stairs leading down. No. A small, low doorway. I duck through it into a long doorless corridor lined with the mounted heads of boar and deer – another place I do not recognize.

Where is the chapel? It's one of the oldest parts of the chateau; it must be close by!

I stagger on, the floor seeming to tilt, the end of the hallway receding faster than I can reach it.

A great anger stirs within me. I am being defied.

'All doors will be revealed to me!' I shout. I glare at the walls until a familiar arched doorway etches itself in the stone. Relief surges through my limbs. I burst into the chapel. The room is alive in a way it wasn't earlier, bounding through all its ages one after another, the ceilings and walls throbbing with colour. I can barely focus on the chandelier waiting for me near the floor.

I collapse upon it, swallow, pray that I have strength enough to pull the rope. I haul, hand after hand, lifting myself with increasing effort. Halfway to the ceiling I have to pause, gasping for air.

Tap-ta-tap. Tap, tap, tap, vibrates the spirit clock in my pocket.

I reach the ceiling and heave myself through the trap-door, my fingers numb. I lurch to the sofa and lie down. Clumsily I pull the ring from my finger and grasp it in my left hand, clenching the vibrating spirit clock in my right. A great breath is pulled from my lungs and—

—Elizabeth and Henry peered down at me, their foreheads creased with anxiety.

'Victor! Oh, thank God!' Elizabeth gasped. 'Are you all right?'

I nodded.

'You were so still and pale,' she said, 'and your breath so faint.'

Henry put his hand to my wrist. 'Your pulse is stronger now. In the last few moments it was very weak . . .'

'How long?' I croaked, my body still heavy with fatigue.

'A full minute exactly,' said Henry, looking at his pocket watch.

'It felt much longer,' I said, opening my right hand to reveal the silent spirit clock.

'You're such an idiot, Victor,' said Elizabeth. 'You could've died!'

'And yet here I am,' I said. I dragged in a deep breath and sat up, steadied by Henry. The world slewed, and I clung tightly to my friend.

They were both looking at me, expectant, but wary, too.

I smiled, feeling suddenly exultant. 'It's real! I was there!'

'*Where* exactly?' Henry asked.

'Here! It was our chateau, the same but different. It remembers itself somehow. Or at least my gaze made it remember.'

'What do you mean?' Henry asked.

'When I stared hard at a place – a wall, a corridor – I could see how it used to look in every age! Towards the end it got a bit confusing. There is a trickiness to the place, and I lost my way for a moment trying to get back to the chapel. And the butterflies! There are butterflies, just like the ones in the painting, and they helped me remember the power I had, and—'

'Did you *see* him?' Elizabeth asked emphatically.

I licked my dry lips. 'I saw him.'

'How did he look?'

'Not like a ghost. Like himself, healthy. He was in his room, playing chess.'

'And what did he say?'

'He was afraid of me. He held his arm across his eyes as though I were a torrent of light. He said I blinded him, and gave off a powerful heat. He didn't know who I was, not at first – he asked if I was angel or demon – and it took him a while to believe it was me.'

'What else?' she demanded.

'He said there was something different about the house, that he wasn't alone.'

'You saw others?' Henry asked.

'No. He seemed ill at ease, though.' I thought it best not to mention the rapier, not yet.

Elizabeth chewed at her lower lip. 'Anything more?'

'The spirit clock told me my time was up.' I looked down at the device with wonder. 'Its little claw actually taps against the glass.'

Elizabeth looked at me hard, shaking her head. 'It makes no sense. The dead go to heaven, or hell, or purgatory. Our chateau can't be these places.'

Henry cleared his throat. 'I'm no expert, but there's very little description in the Bible of the afterlife. Purgatory especially might look like anywhere.'

'What matters,' I insisted, 'is that I went to the world

of the dead and came back! It can be done! So what does that say about all your rules?'

Elizabeth was silent.

'It means,' I said, 'that religion doesn't know all the answers. The things it tells us aren't true – or at least they're incomplete.'

Elizabeth's eyes flashed. 'You're astonishingly arrogant. Why this still surprises me, I've no idea. But has it occurred to you that you only *dreamed*, and what you saw was a hallucination caused by that elixir?'

'No, it was real . . .' But I trailed off, for I hadn't considered this possibility. Already my memories had a dreamlike aura.

'That's the most likely explanation,' she went on. 'What do you say, Henry?'

My best friend regarded me carefully, then blew air out of his cheeks and gave a rueful smile. 'I'd have to agree that Elizabeth's is the most likely explanation.'

'Well,' I said, 'there's only one way to find out for certain.'

Elizabeth frowned. 'Which is?'

'Two of us must go in at the same time.'

She shrugged. 'Two people might both hallucinate.'

'Or have *exactly* the same real experience.'

For a moment no one spoke. I looked at Henry.

'It does make sense,' he conceded. 'It's the only way to be sure.'

'Will you come, then, Henry?' I asked.

'Well, I'd leap at it normally, if it weren't for a certain rare phobia of mine.'

'Which is?'

'Fear of death,' he replied.

'I'll go,' Elizabeth said.

I turned to her in surprise. 'But what of your beliefs? Isn't it a grave sin to dabble with the occult?'

'As you say, it's the only way. Next time we'll both go in, Victor, and that will tell us the truth.'

'Which is why you'll need me to watch over you,' said Henry, nodding as if this had been his design all along. 'And when you return, you'll each write your account in silence, and I will compare them with utter impartiality.'

'Excellent,' I said. 'Tonight, then, when the house is asleep.'

'Too soon,' Elizabeth said, looking distrustfully at the green bottle of elixir. 'Remember Wilhelm's notes. Not more than once a day.'

'It's just as well,' said Henry. 'I need to go home this afternoon. My father's returning from a business trip, and I should be there to greet him. And,' he added with a grimace, 'there will soon be preparations for a trip of my own.'

Startled, I looked at him. 'What trip?'

'You're going away?' Elizabeth said in genuine distress. 'Why didn't you tell us sooner!'

He laughed. 'Difficult to fit in, what with all the excitement at Chateau Frankenstein. Well, yes, Father has decided it's time for me to accompany him on one of his merchant voyages.'

'When?' I asked.

'Two weeks.'

'For how long?' Elizabeth wanted to know.

'Two months.'

'So long?' Elizabeth said, and I saw Henry blush at this show of attention. 'Well, then, we must see as much of you as we can. Tell your father you've been invited to be our houseguest for the next two weeks.'

'Absolutely,' I said. 'Mother and Father will insist on it.'

'Well, I'm very touched,' said Henry.

I smiled at him and raised my eyebrows devilishly. 'It will be excellent to have you so close at hand, Henry, at such an exciting time.'

'Yes, how lucky I am always to be included.'

With great care we made our separate descents on the chandelier, making sure to take all the apparatus from the secret chamber: the elixir, the spirit clock, the notebook. It would be too tricky – and possibly dangerous

– to return here to make our next trip to the spirit world.

Before opening the door to the chapel, I put my ear to the door to listen for servants.

'Tomorrow night, then,' I said to the others, 'and not a word of this to anyone.'

That night I dreamed I was in my room, undressing for bed, and the door drifted open just a bit. I knew it was only a draught, for my window was open as well, the evening was so warm and fine. I walked over to close the door properly, but when I pushed it, I met with resistance, and I knew there was someone, waiting, on the other side.

CHAPTER FOUR

MOMENTOUS DISCOVERIES

'And so you can see,' Father told us at our lessons the next morning, 'that throughout Ovid's *Metamorphoses* there is a constant theme of transformation. Daphne is turned into a tree, Narcissus into a flower, Actaeon into a stag – all of these the work of the gods, of course. But perhaps we can take away from this an appreciation of the endless and fascinating mutability of our own world and—'

There was a knock at the door, and Klaus, one of our servants, poked his head apologetically into the room.

'I'm very sorry to disturb you, sir,' he said, 'but there's been a bit of a problem at the bottom of the shaft.'

'No one's injured, I hope,' Father said.

'No, sir. It's just that we started filling in the well down there, like you wanted, and, um, it's not a well.'

'What do you mean, Klaus?'

'There's a false bottom in it, sir, and it gave out under the weight of the gravel.'

'What's below, then?' I couldn't help asking.

'Looks to be a cave of some sort. We didn't want to do anything until we told you about it first, sir.'

I was watching Father's face carefully, trying to guess if this was news to him. He was, I knew, an able keeper of secrets. But his face looked genuinely surprised.

'Have you a ladder long enough to reach down?' Father asked.

'We have, sir.'

'Let's have a look, then,' Father said.

'Can we come too?' I asked.

He looked at me, and must have sensed my honest excitement, for he smiled and nodded. 'Very well. You'll be sensible and do as you're told. Klaus, if you'd make sure we have enough lanterns, please.'

I leaped to my feet, and grinned at Elizabeth and Henry. Chateau Frankenstein was not just a home but had also been the most exciting playground a child could imagine, with its dungeons and ramparts and concealed passages, most of which had been discovered long ago by Elizabeth and Konrad and me.

'What an endlessly fascinating home you have, Victor,' said Henry with a wry smile. 'Imagine having your own cave!'

Apart from the night of the book burning, this was the

first time I'd been inside our grand library since it had become a construction site. It was now kept under lock and key, to make sure my younger brothers didn't wander in and fall down the perilous secret stairwell, now permanently open while the workers went about their labours.

The carpets had been rolled up, and boards laid down to protect the floors from wheelbarrows loaded with gravel and brick; the shelves of books were hung with thick curtains to guard them from dust. The hinged shelf that had concealed the secret doorway had been dismantled, leaving the portal wide open.

It felt most strange to once more be making my way down these narrow steps. Even though they'd been properly reinforced by the workers, and the shaft was well lit with lanterns, I acutely remembered my first dark and secret descent with Elizabeth and Konrad. Halfway down, as we passed the entrance to the now vacant Dark Library, my heart gave a quick, sad squeeze, for my twin was not with me now.

At the bottom of the shaft, two workers were peering down the well, into which they'd lowered a lantern on a rope. I saw they had a long ladder at the ready.

'Let's get that down and have a look,' Father said, turning to me with a wink. His look of true pleasure cheered me. There were few men in the republic who loved learning as much as my father, and for the first time I realized that, though I was a sloppy student, raw and abundant curiosity was something we both shared.

The workers lowered the ladder, made sure it was secure, and then stepped back. 'There you go, Klaus,' one of them said.

Klaus looked at his fellow workers. 'Not keen to come, then?' he said mockingly, though I noticed he himself looked less than thrilled as he swung himself over the short wall. Father went next, and then it was my turn.

Rung by rung I descended, feeling the subterranean chill climb my body. I passed the splintered plank remnants of the well's false bottom, and then the cave opened out around me. Lantern light lapped at pale stone.

I stepped down into the pile of gravel and earth that had collapsed earlier, looked around the large cavern – and sucked in my breath as I beheld the giant image of a horse drawn in black.

It was not alone. Other horses galloped and leaped across the walls and ceiling, the simplicity of their lines only enhancing their grace and sense of speed.

'I've never seen anything like this,' said Father, holding his lantern close to one painting. 'They must be very old indeed.'

Elizabeth and Henry were soon among us, gazing about

with wide eyes.

'Incredible,' Henry breathed.

'So beautiful,' said Elizabeth, smiling at me with such simple joy and wonder that I could not help but smile back. For a few blissful moments the pain that drummed in my missing fingers almost evaporated.

'It keeps going, this way,' said Klaus, holding his lantern high and showing us a passageway with corrugated walls that made me think of some great leviathan's gullet. Though the passage was narrow, its ceiling was vaulted high, and on the stone were yet more animals – giant bulls with bristling crests of hair, and great horns, powerfully painted in a rich terracotta so you could practically feel the sheer bulk of their flanks, the bundled muscle of their haunches.

'Look!' said Elizabeth, pointing. 'That one has a spear in its side.'

'Well spotted,' said my father. 'And this one's been felled.'

In the wash of his lantern light, I saw one of the mammoth creatures on its side, head drooped lifelessly.

'It's like some kind of primitive art gallery,' Henry said.

'Museum, too,' Father said. 'Look at these markings here, beneath the fallen bull.'

I saw the series of simple black marks with strokes through them. 'It's like a tally,' I remarked. 'They wanted to keep track of their kills.'

Father nodded. 'Whoever made these pictures was recording their history.'

The passageway turned to the right and opened up into another cavern. Elizabeth called out excitedly, 'An ibex, look! When did ibexes last live in Geneva?'

'Is that a bear?' Henry said.

'Must be,' I remarked, 'though I've never seen one so big. Look at it there, compared to the bull! What a monster!'

A short tunnel led out from this cavern into a series of narrow vaulted galleries. We walked through them, sometimes awed into silence, other times excitedly calling out the new animals we saw in this underground bestiary. One gallery was filled with brown stags. In another knelt a strange horse with a horn growing from its forehead. Crouching beneath it was some kind of tiger, ready to pounce and kill, with two great teeth curving from its upper jaw. And beside the tiger was something I'd not seen before now.

'A handprint,' I said. It was red, made with paint – or perhaps blood.

'Is it like a signature, do you think?' Elizabeth said. 'An artist taking credit for his work?'

Instinctively I went and placed my spread fingers

against it. The print dwarfed my own hand.

'They were bigger than us,' I said.

Klaus was looking ill at ease, his eyes straying into the darkness, as though half expecting someone or something to emerge.

'There are more here,' said Henry, swinging his lantern to a stretch of wall where there were numerous hand-prints, of all different sizes.

'*This is us*,' Elizabeth murmured.

I looked at her strangely. 'What do you mean?'

'The handprints – it's like a way of saying *Here we are. This is us*. Maybe it showed how many people lived in their family, or clan, or whatever it was. A family portrait.'

'Why didn't they just draw pictures of themselves?' Henry asked. 'They were obviously excellent artists. Doesn't it seem strange they wouldn't have done any people?'

'It does indeed,' said Father, 'especially when they had language, too.'

'Language?' I looked at him, startled. 'How do you know that?'

Eagerly he beckoned me closer and showed me, in the flicker of his lantern, a long string of curious geometric markings.

'Surely these are words of some kind,' he said, 'though

in an alphabet I've never seen.'

I had seen some strange scribblings in alchemical tomes, but these were altogether more primitive.

'They're nothing like Egyptian hieroglyphs,' I murmured.

'No,' said Father, 'and yet the longer I look at them, the more variety I see.'

'You're right,' I said. 'There seems an infinite number of ways they've arranged the lines and dots.'

He placed a hand upon my shoulder, gave me a squeeze and a smile. It felt good to be together like this, talking and sleuthing. I hadn't felt this close to him for a long time, and in the coldness of the cave, I felt the warmth of his large hand all the more.

'Passage branches up ahead,' Klaus said.

'Then we must stop here,' Father said. 'We're not equipped for a proper exploration, and I won't risk getting lost.'

'Do you think Wilhelm Frankenstein knew about the caves?' I asked.

'Most probably. He would've discovered them when he laid the chateau's foundations. And no doubt it was he who built the false well to conceal them.'

'But why would he keep them hidden?' Elizabeth wondered. 'They're so wonderful.'

'He was a mysterious and secretive man,' my father said.

'I don't think we'll ever know the extent of it, or what happened to him.' He regarded us more sternly now. 'You're not to go exploring alone. Do you understand?'

'Yes,' I said, and I truly meant it. Despite the caves' appeal, my thoughts were fixed on different matters.

'Good,' Father said. 'The last time you went caving, you nearly perished. Your mother could not endure any more trauma at the moment.'

'You won't seal all this up, will you?' I asked.

He looked at me carefully for a moment, as if trying to gauge my trustworthiness. 'I mean to send word to a historian acquaintance of mine at the university. He'll be most interested to see all this, and I'm sure he'll have a better idea of its origins than we do.'

'Where's Mother?' I asked at lunch, for I was eager to tell her about the caves.

'She won't be joining us,' my father said.

'Is she unwell?' Elizabeth asked with concern.

I watched Father, waiting for his answer.

'No, she's not ill, just tired.' But his leonine head seemed to sag upon his broad shoulders. How had I not noticed until now? 'During the past weeks, since the funeral, she's been very strong for all of us, but now she needs her rest.' He tried to smile reassuringly. 'You're not to worry. It's not uncommon after a great sadness. All she needs is time, and she'll be up and about again.'

The food set out before us suddenly lost its appeal. I felt ashamed of myself. Elizabeth had been right when she'd said I was blind to any but my own suffering. I wondered if my mother's frantic pace had been her way of escaping grief – but grief was the swifter, and had overtaken her in the end. And I wondered if there were some way I could vanquish her grief. What if it were in my power?

'Perhaps, sir,' Henry began awkwardly, 'this is not the best time for me to stay.'

Father shook his head. 'No, no, Henry. You're like family to us, and we'll miss you sorely when you go on your trip. Until then, stay. Your presence brings light into our house.'

'That's very generous,' said Henry, looking uneasy, and I wondered if he, like me, was thinking of what we planned to do tonight, in darkness.

After the church bells in Bellerive struck one, first Henry and then Elizabeth joined me in my bedchamber, fully clothed like myself.

By the light of a single candle, I took from the locked drawer in my desk the spirit clock and the green flask of elixir.

'Are you ready?' I said.

Elizabeth was staring at the green flask, chewing on her lower lip. I thought she might be shivering.

'Have you chosen a talisman?' I asked her.

From her wrist she carefully pulled a bracelet made of tightly coiled hair. 'It's from my mother. After she died, my father cut some and had this fashioned for me. It's one of the only things of hers I have.'

I knew this was a common enough practice, making keepsakes out of the departed's hair, but I still found something rather ghoulish about it.

Henry cleared his throat. 'I would just, at this point, like to make one final – probably doomed – plea for reason. I urge you not to do this.'

'Thank you for that, Henry,' I said. I looked at Elizabeth. 'You don't have to do this.'

'I'm not afraid,' she said, 'if that's what you think.'

'I never think you're afraid,' I told her. 'You're the bravest person I know. But I also know you think this is a—'

'What I *think* is that we'll both hallucinate and prove this is all nonsense. And that will put a stop to it. But if you're right, well . . . then I'll be proved right as well.'

'How's that?' I asked, confused.

'If there's a world beyond our own, a life after death, that means there's also a God.'

'Does one have to follow upon the other?' I asked.

'You two, please,' said Henry, 'not another riveting theological debate right now.'

'So that's the only reason you're coming?' I said mockingly. 'To make a believer of me?'

She couldn't help smiling. 'To save your miserable little soul, that's right.'

'Nothing to do with Konrad whatsoever?' I inquired.

'Just pass me the elixir.'

She took a deep breath, hesitated for only a second, and then placed a drop upon her tongue and handed the flask to me so I might do the same.

'You can recline on my bed if you like,' I told her.

'I'll be perfectly comfortable in this armchair, thank you,' she replied, settling herself and gripping her hair bracelet in her left hand. 'You have the spirit clock ready?'

'Yes,' I said, lying back against my pillow. 'Do you taste it, metallic in your mouth, and feel the strange heat washing through your body?'

She nodded. 'Henry, you'll watch over us carefully?'

'I will indeed,' he promised.

'It comes quickly,' I told her. 'The blink of an eye.'

I yawned and—

* * *

—look over. There she is, sitting on my chair: Elizabeth.

She's the most beautiful thing I've ever seen. Her amber hair spills like silk around her radiant face, over her shoulders. Her eyes are open, and she smiles at me. I smile back. There is absolutely nothing between my gaze and her face. It's like I'm stroking her skin. It feels almost wicked, deliciously so.

There is no need of candlelight, for beyond the windows of my bedchamber comes a surprisingly strong white light from the thick, impenetrable fog.

I push myself up off the bed and stand, feeling that same vital energy coursing through me. And with every step I take, with each hot squeeze of blood through my veins, with each flex and pull of my muscles, I am thrillingly aware of myself as never before. It's as though every hair on my head, every pore, every surface of my body is twice as sensitive.

There is nothing I could not do here.

I put the spirit clock in my pocket, slip the ring back onto my finger. I step towards Elizabeth. My nostrils flare to take in her scent – her hair, her skin, her breath. Her hazel eyes draw me closer. I have a distant memory of two wolves in the night forest.

'Are we here?' she asks.

It takes me a moment to understand, for here is so immediate and real, how could there be anywhere else *but* here and now?

In answer to her question I stretch out my right hand and show her how my two missing fingers have been returned to me. In amazement she frowns and reaches out – and I know, beyond any doubt, that once we touch, we will be unable to resist each other.

But this current of desire is severed suddenly by a few simple notes of music wafting through the air.

Elizabeth lets her hand drop as she stands. 'Piano,' she says.

Eagerly she walks past me and opens the door to my bedchamber.

'Konrad played that piece all the time.'

Played it for you, I think, for I remember how they used to steal away to the music room to be alone.

I follow her as she strides purposefully down the hallway.

'Konrad?' she calls out, and the music abruptly stops. We reach the doors of the music room, and Elizabeth throws them wide and walks in ahead of me.

Half turned on the bench, arm shielding his eyes, is my twin. I see his rapier, tipped up against the piano.

'Elizabeth?' he breathes.

She weeps with total abandon, tears spilling down her cheeks. Despite what I've told her, she steps towards Konrad to embrace him.

'I'd give anything to hold you,' my brother says, standing and retreating, 'but I can't.'

'It's too unfair,' she says, her words jerking out.

'Your heat's so intense, it nearly sears me, even from this distance.'

I see his eyes move to me briefly, squinting, and he smiles.

'Victor. You came back.'

'I promised I would. This light of ours, we can't see it.'

'It radiates from you like an aura. You're like something drawn with the sun's fire, and I can take only little glimpses of you.'

He stands now before us, his head bowed, like a man awaiting sentence from the magistrate. I feel like both angel and devil, radiating glorious light but also demonic heat, and once again I feel a surge of excitement to think myself so powerful.

'How long have I been dead?' he asks. 'Time seems to have no meaning here.'

'Nearly a month,' Elizabeth tells him. 'I never even had the chance to say goodbye to you. It was so sudden.'

'Tell us,' I ask him impetuously. 'What was it like?'

'To die? I can't really say. When I first woke in bed, I was alone. No one answered my calls. So I got up – and was surprised by my strength. I felt completely well, like my old self. I wanted to tell you all, but when I left my room, I couldn't find anyone. The house was completely deserted, and seemed somehow unfamiliar, even though everything seemed to be in the right place. That was when I first began to wonder if I'd died in my sleep, though I hoped it was just a nightmare. But I didn't wake.'

'You don't . . . *look* dead,' I tell him.

He gives a small laugh. 'Well, I'm glad to hear it.'

I am suddenly ravenous with curiosity. 'Do you float above things, or do you feel the floor beneath your feet?'

'I feel the floor.'

'And you can open doors, exert force on objects?'

'You heard me playing the piano.'

'If you punch the wall, is there pain?'

'Yes. I've tried.'

'Do you sleep?'

'Victor, enough,' Elizabeth says.

'I don't seem to, no,' Konrad replies.

'And are you hungry?'

'Not thirsty, either. Victor, am I to be another scientific experiment of yours?' He gives a wry smile, and I chuckle apologetically.

'I'm sorry. It's just that there are so many things to discover here.'

'For me too,' my brother says. 'How is it possible you're here?'

'We got your message and came to find you,' I say.

His confusion is obvious. 'My message?'

'Come raise me. That's what you said, over and over again.'

'Victor built a spirit board to speak with the dead,' Elizabeth explains. 'You didn't hear him calling out to you?'

Konrad looks shaken. 'There was a moment – I don't know how long ago – when I felt you so strongly, as though you were somewhere in the house. And I looked for you, and called out, but heard no reply. I thought I must just be hallucinating. But I don't remember saying *Come raise me.*'

'Well, maybe it doesn't need speaking aloud,' I reply. 'Maybe your wishes alone conveyed themselves to our world.'

But Elizabeth looks uneasy. 'Who else is here?'

'There's a girl our age called Analiese. She was a servant in the household and died of fever long before we were born. When I was wandering the house, I met her in the kitchen. She was very kind to me, as kind as anyone can be when they're telling you you're actually dead.'

'Where is she?' Elizabeth wants to know.

'She often seems to prefer the servants' quarters.' He gives a small smile. 'I think she feels she's being too familiar, coming upstairs to speak with me, though God knows I welcome her company.'

'Yes,' Elizabeth says a bit stiffly, 'I can imagine it must be terribly lonely for you. So you two are the only ones here?'

Konrad hesitates a moment. 'I don't know. Sometimes I hear sounds, deep in the house. Like someone slumbering fitfully.'

'Well, I'd like to meet this Analiese,' Elizabeth says. 'Maybe she can explain why you're here.'

'She already has. She says everyone who dies in the house comes here for a time.'

'I simply don't understand it,' says Elizabeth. 'Your soul ought to have gone straight to heaven – or at least purgatory.'

'Unless this house is purgatory,' Konrad replies.

'Isn't it obvious,' I say with an impatient laugh, 'that everything is different from what you've been taught by the Church?'

'No, it isn't,' says Elizabeth.

Konrad sighs. 'Things are very strange here.' He turns

to the windows and the impenetrable fog beyond. 'I feel so trapped.'

My eyes remain fixed on the fog, watching its slow, mesmerizing swirl.

I begin walking towards it. 'You should open a window,' I say.

'No, don't!' he shouts, and his urgency stops me in my tracks.

I laugh. 'How can it hurt to open a window?'

'One of the first things Analiese told me was never to open the windows or doors.'

'Why ever not?' Elizabeth wants to know.

'Because, miss, there's an evil spirit outside who wants to enter.'

I whirl round to see a young woman, no older than me, standing in the doorway, one hand shielding her face from our glare.

'Are you Analiese?' I ask.

'I am, sir. And you must be Mr Konrad's brother. He told me you'd been, and I could scarce believe it – the living visiting the world of the dead.'

She is beautiful, I see immediately, with long plaited hair so blonde it is almost white, and eyes of a most arresting blue. Her porcelain skin bears a bewitching beauty spot on one cheek. She wears a simple black dress

– her best, no doubt – that, though modest, cannot conceal her very pleasing figure.

'What do you mean, "an evil spirit"?' Elizabeth asks.

As if in answer the fog outside the windows intensifies and thumps menacingly against the glass, so hard that the panes actually rattle.

I hear Analiese gasp, and see her take a step back.

Once more the fog pounds at the glass like an angry fist, and I realize I am not frightened but strangely expectant, wondering: *What will happen if the glass breaks?*

But the glass does not break, and I feel a curious disappointment when the windows stop their shaking and the fog disperses slightly, though nowhere near enough to allow any view.

'It has intent, no question,' says Elizabeth, not fearfully but with the same fascination I myself feel.

'It's only what I was told, miss,' Analiese says, eyes averted humbly. 'When I died and came here, there was only one other person in the house. She was one of the ladies of the house, and she was the one who told me about the devilish spirit and how we mustn't let it in, lest we be tempted.'

'It's like some great coiled serpent,' Konrad says uneasily, 'hungry and waiting.'

Analiese continues, 'And the lady said we must bide

our time here, until we are gathered.'

'Gathered?' I say.

'Yes, sir. I saw it happen to her, not long after. A beautiful winged light, even brighter than yours, and musical, entered the house and wrapped itself around her, and she was gone.'

'Angels!' says Elizabeth, looking at me triumphantly.

Analiese smiles happily. 'I think so too, miss! And I can only hope that my turn will come before long.'

At that moment two large black butterflies flutter into view, circling high over Elizabeth and me.

'What are they?' I ask Analiese.

'Oh, they've always been here I think, sir.'

'You don't have to call me sir. We're a very liberal household, and besides, you're much older than me.'

Her eyes are still averted, showing her lovely long eyelashes to great advantage. 'It's habit, I'm afraid, sir, but I'll try.' She looks up at the butterflies. 'I've always thought of them as a kind of angelic presence, to keep us company and give us hope for the life to come.'

'I think you must be right,' Elizabeth remarks as one bobs down towards her. 'They certainly don't fear our light and heat.'

When it alights upon her shoulder, she gives a little gasp of delight, and her cheeks flush.

'So beautiful,' she breathes as the butterfly's black wings radiate with colour, and then it flutters away.

Elizabeth's eyes meet mine briefly, then look away almost secretively. I hold out my hand, and the second butterfly lands upon me, and I feel the same surge of pleasure as the first time.

It lingers upon my finger, brilliantly glowing, and I feel a powerful calm settle over my mind – all its jumbled drawers and cluttered surfaces organized – and with it a great sense of strength and readiness, like a sprinter upon the start line.

'How much time is left us, Victor?' I hear Elizabeth ask.

With my free hand I take the spirit clock from my pocket. The skeletal leg has almost made its full revolution. Elizabeth draws closer to look and gives a sigh of disappointment.

'How does it work?' Konrad asks. 'You still haven't told me how you even *got* here!'

As Elizabeth explains, I suddenly remember Wilhelm's handwritten instructions: *With practise the spirit clock can be manipulated.*

I put it to my ear and listen. *Tick, tick, tick* . . .

The butterfly is still perched upon my finger as I touch the clock face, above the skeletal bird leg.

Slow.

'What're you doing with it, Victor?' Elizabeth asks.

And slower still.

I put it to my ear once more and listen intently. *Tick . . . tick . . . tick . . .*

'I think I've done it!' I exclaim.

'Done what?' Elizabeth asks.

'Slowed it down! Remember, the notebook said it could be done. It ticks slower now! I've bought us a little more time!'

I see Elizabeth gaze at Konrad with a look of such undisguised love and desire that I feel both awkward and jealous. I cannot watch.

'These butterflies,' I say to Analiese as mine flutters away, 'they have a power to them.'

'I wouldn't know, sir. They show no interest in me.'

'Nor me,' Konrad says.

'What about these noises you've heard in the house?' I ask my brother.

'I still hear them from time to time,' he says uneasily.

I turn to Analiese. She has a pretty habit, I notice, of absentmindedly stroking her earlobe, which draws attention to both her lovely throat and hair. 'You've been here much longer. Do you know anything about this?'

'I've never seen anyone else in this house, sir, but I think

I've heard the same sounds as your brother. Like someone who wants to wake up but can't.'

'Are you frightened?' Elizabeth asks Konrad.

'No,' he says, and I know he's lying.

'Then why's there a rapier by the piano?' Elizabeth demands.

For a moment my twin says nothing. 'It gives me peace of mind, foolish as it may be. Moment by moment I don't know what to expect. Whether I'm to be gathered to heaven – or to hell.'

'No—' Elizabeth says, shaking her head fervently.

Konrad cuts her off, a look of wildness in his eyes. 'There's a spirit outside the windows that wants to come in, and something inside that wants to wake. I doubt my rapier will make a difference, but if need be, I'll wield it for all it's worth.'

'I can't bear it if you're in any danger here,' Elizabeth says, aggrieved.

'I've not come to any harm here,' Analiese tells Konrad soothingly. 'All will be well, sir, you'll see.'

Konrad looks at her gratefully, and exhales with a nod. 'Thank you, Analiese.'

I watch Elizabeth, her eyes moving between them. 'It's too unfair,' she says to my twin, 'to have come so far and not be able to touch you.'

'Right now just seeing you and hearing your voice is great comfort,' he replies.

I feel a faint vibration in my pocket and remove the spirit clock to see the little clawed fist *tap-tap-tapping* against the glass.

'Our time is done now,' I say.

In dismay Elizabeth looks at me. 'Get us more time!'

'It's too late for that now,' I say.

'But I'm not ready to say goodbye!'

'Will you return?' Konrad asks, sounding bereft.

'I promise you,' I tell him. 'But now we must go.'

'Where do you go, and how?' Konrad asks in frustration.

'To the place where we left our bodies in the real world. Come,' I say to Elizabeth, and she seems finally to understand my urgency, for her eyes move to the door. 'Our bodies need us back.'

'Goodbye,' she says miserably, stretching out her hand towards Konrad. 'I shouldn't have come. It's torture to leave you again.'

I head for the door, into the hallway, and look back to make sure Elizabeth is following. Down the hall we hurry with our unnatural speed, no doubt blazing trails of light for Konrad and Analiese, who stand watching us from the doorway.

Entering my bedchamber, I falter, for it looks entirely different. The furniture is all in different places, and the pieces themselves are much grander and older. The walls pulse with different colours and paintings and tapestries.

'Victor,' I hear Elizabeth say, and when I glance at her, she touches the wall as if to steady herself. 'What's going on?'

'It's the house, remembering itself,' I say in wonder. 'Our living presence seems to agitate it.'

I look at the ornate carving of the grand canopied bed and see on the pillowcases the monogram WF.

'This used to be his room,' I whisper. 'Wilhelm Frankenstein's!'

'Make it go back to normal,' she says, sounding scared for the first time.

'If you concentrate, it'll return to its present age. You have the power to do it too.'

I take a breath, focusing my gaze on the place where my bed should be. From the corner of my eye I see the entire room shimmer and begin to reshape itself. And for just a moment I see, set within the wall, a strange cupboard containing a book – and then it's gone and is nothing but brick and plaster. Suddenly my bed is where it ought to be, and when I look about the room, it is altogether mine again.

Elizabeth seems confused, and moves towards my bed.

'You're on the chair, remember,' I tell her, and take her hand to guide her.

The effect is instant. It's the first time I've touched her in this world, and the simple contact of her skin against mine sends an urgent heat coursing through my entire body. I stare down at my hand, her hand, breathing hard. My spirit world heart thrashes within my chest like a firefly trapped in a jar. I feel weak, slightly sick – and completely, hypnotically helpless to the desire that grips me. I swallow and look up at Elizabeth and know from her gaze that she is possessed by the same sensation.

'This is a dream,' she says.

I shake my head. 'No dream.'

'I am dreaming.'

In one step I am against her, my hand in her hair. Her arms lift and encircle me, her fingers pulling hard against my neck, urging me to her. Our mouths meet hungrily, and it's as though some spectral current has been completed, and there is nothing more than this moment, all sensation, every nerve in my body attentive to her.

But our frenzy is interrupted by the ever more insistent pattering of the spirit clock in my pocket, and a real weakness seeps through me. Not a pleasurable, giddy one this time but true exhaustion and breathlessness.

'We must get back,' I pant, forcing myself away from her, and I see the look of disappointment and anger in her face. Once more she draws closer to me.

'Our bodies need us,' I say, pushing her into the chair. 'Take hold of your bracelet. Hurry!'

Breathless, I tug my ring free, clench it tight in one hand, the spirit clock in the other, and throw myself onto the bed, my limbs weirdly moving of their own volition to shape this spectral body to my real one and—

CHAPTER FIVE

THE SECOND DEATH

We woke gasping at the same moment. Henry paced between us anxiously, looking at his stopwatch.

'Slightly over a minute this time!' he said. 'What kept you?'

'I stretched time a little.' I swung my legs over the side of the bed and faced Elizabeth. 'Tell me what you saw!'

'No!' commanded Henry. 'Say nothing, either of you!' From my desk he took quills and paper and handed them to us. 'Remember our plan. Write down what happened, in as much detail as you can. Events, dialogue. Then I'll read them.'

I exhaled. 'Yes, of course. I was forgetting.'

As I scribbled out my account, I kept glancing over at Elizabeth, wondering if she'd truly had the same experiences as me – right up to the moment before we'd left the spirit world. I wrote and wrote and heard the church bells toll the half hour. As I neared the end of my account, I hesitated and decided to leave out the passionate embrace Elizabeth and I had shared. If it had all merely been a dream, I'd only embarrass myself, and if it were true, I would mortify Elizabeth. Surely she'd omit it. I looked up and saw her watching me. We'd finished at the same time, and we silently handed our sheets to Henry.

Waiting as he read both our accounts was excruciating. Elizabeth's fingertips traced the lace embroidery of her hem. I covered my maimed hand with my whole one, wishing I could hide it away forever, wishing I could obliterate the throbbing pain that dogged me. We avoided each other's gaze, and then, when we'd run out of nooks and crannies to focus on, our eyes finally met.

Your tongue touched mine, I thought, staring at her. And then I had to look away, for my cheeks burned, and the memory of our intimacy was like a blaring presence in the room.

Henry was now making low sounds in his throat as he looked between our accounts.

'For heaven's sake!' exclaimed Elizabeth. 'You must be done reading our dreams by now.'

Henry looked over, pale in the candlelight. 'It seems,' he said, 'you've had virtually the same dream.'

I leaped to my feet, exultant. 'No dream! The exact same *experience*!'

'Only the very endings differ slightly,' said Henry, scratching at his hair. 'Elizabeth, you say that just before you exited, Victor seemed . . . confused?'

I looked at her in surprise, then amusement.

'Just before we returned, yes,' she murmured. 'Rambling a bit, possibly delusional.'

Henry turned to me. 'Victor, you have no recollection of this?'

I looked at Elizabeth, a smile dormant on my lips. 'It's possible. Things can get a bit hazy after the spirit clock rings. The house tends to shift. But what we experienced was real, every bit of it. Do you believe now?'

'Of course. And you must believe that there's a world beyond ours.'

'Certainly.'

'And that it's filled with spirits and angels and devils, and could only be governed by an all-powerful God.'

'Ah. Let's just say I believe it's a world filled with wonders, and one I plan to visit many more times.'

'Is that wise?' Henry asked.

Elizabeth said nothing for a moment, then, 'I won't go again.'

Aghast, I stared at her. 'What do you mean? You saw him.'

She put her face in her hands. 'But I don't know if it was more solace or torment. He could barely look at us. I couldn't even touch him. He's *gone* from us, Victor. In time he'll be gathered and taken to his final home.'

'I mean to bring him back,' I said quietly.

Silence boiled through the room like a thundercloud.

Elizabeth was shaking her head. 'We can't bring him back, Victor.'

'I don't accept that. And you shouldn't either. Two days ago you didn't believe a door could be opened to the spirit world. We've opened it. We've passed through. Why can't Konrad pass out?'

She was trembling. To my surprise Henry lifted a blanket from my bed and draped it over her shoulders, kneeling beside her. 'You're exhausted by all this.'

'Don't play nursemaid, Henry,' I said impatiently. 'She's as strong as me, and you don't see me traumatized.'

At this Elizabeth stood, threw off her blanket, and glared at me. 'I should've known this was your intent all along. Just when I think your egotism has found its limit, you amaze me afresh. Yes, we've passed into the realm of the dead – a place we likely shouldn't have – and yes, we saw Konrad's spirit. But do you actually think you have any authority in that place?'

'We'll see.'

'No. We will *not* see. Only God resurrects people, Victor, and, as startling as this might be to you, *you are not God!*'

'I never said I was,' I retorted. 'You see, this is exactly

my point. You think only your God has the power to govern these worlds. All I'm doing is raising a question: Might we as well?'

She swallowed. 'I feel sickened by all this. It was a mistake.'

'What about Konrad? I thought you loved—'

'Yes, and that's precisely why I can't bear it again. It's torture, Victor, for him and me. I vowed to let him go.' More quietly she said, 'Nothing good can come of it. I won't go again.'

I took a moment to marshal my thoughts. I nodded. 'I understand. If this is something I have to do alone, so be it. All I know is that Wilhelm Frankenstein somehow found a way into the spirit world, and who knows what else he found? He might've made all sorts of incredible discoveries. Maybe he even knew how to bring the dead back to life. If he did, there must be some record of it.'

'The Dark Library is ash now,' said Henry.

This stopped me for a moment, and then I realized something.

'Only in our world,' I said with a grin. 'In the spirit world it's still there. Every book that ever came into this house will still be there, unburned, unblemished.'

'Books,' said Henry wearily. 'Our last adventure was filled with books, and—'

'It ended with failure, yes. Alchemy and science, prim-itive and modern, they failed us. But clearly the occult holds more wisdom than I gave it credit for. There will be a great many books to read . . .' I looked over at Henry. 'For someone as clever as you, it would not be nearly so great a chore.'

'Your flattery's shameless,' Elizabeth said. 'Henry's too sane to help you with such a mad plan.'

I sighed, nodding. 'It's too bad, though, Henry. Inside the spirit world there's such total . . . *vitality*. Elizabeth felt it too. Somehow it makes us more of what we are. It gave me my fingers back. What might it give you?'

I saw him chew at his lip.

'It's remarkable.' I watched his face, trying to gauge if I were swaying him. 'You'll find what's best about you, what's most powerful. It allows you to be the self you always wanted to be but kept hidden, or thwarted. I felt I could do anything—'

Henry laughed sarcastically. 'That's nothing new!'

I chuckled. 'No, maybe not. But inside it just might be true.'

'I've had enough of this blasphemous talk,' said Elizabeth. 'Good night, both of you.'

'Don't forget your prayers,' I said before she shut the door.

'That was a bit sharp,' said Henry.

'But funny,' I replied, and we both laughed.

Henry looked at me, intent. 'What else?'

'Inside it's simpler, truer.' I thought of Elizabeth, how our feelings for each other had been raw and uncomplicated, animal in their urgency. 'There's nothing stopping you from doing anything you might like.'

He looked away, as though afraid of betraying some secret. 'Truly?'

'Truly.'

He blinked and pushed his wispy blond hair back from his forehead. 'When you next go, I'll come with you.'

I woke early the next morning, dressed, and waited in the music room for Elizabeth to pass by on her way to breakfast. When I heard her footsteps in the hallway, I trilled a few notes on the piano – the same melody that Konrad had played the night before – and heard her stop. Hesitantly she entered the room.

I improvised a tune on the keys and quietly sang, 'I don't think someone's quite ready for the convent yet.'

'Shhh!' she hissed, closing the door and coming closer.

'Were you planning on pretending it never happened?' I asked. 'That bit at the end?'

For a moment she said nothing, and I wondered if she would refuse to speak of it altogether.

'Thank you for not writing it down in your account,' she said finally, then cleared her throat. 'It would seem that our behaviour in the spirit world is . . . uncensored. All our base impulses are given free rein—'

'*Base* impulses,' I said. 'You make it sound like they're evil.'

'Just because one has feelings doesn't mean one has to act on them.'

'What a prig you are! Why's it so hard for you to admit your feelings for me? You had no trouble showing them last night.'

'Do you know what distinguishes us from animals, Victor?'

'Yes, but I think you'd like to do the explaining—'

'They know only instinct. No knowledge of right or wrong. They have no self-control. Humans do. And we're meant to exercise that control.'

'So is this the real reason you won't go back inside?' I asked her. 'Because you're worried you might be overcome with passion for me again?'

'I won't go back inside because it's a wicked endeavour, and if you were smarter, you wouldn't go back either.'

'I don't believe you.'

'I'll be blunt, Victor. I am not in love with you.'

This stung, but I pressed on. 'You're just angry because I was the one to end the kiss.'

Her cheeks reddened. 'Rubbish.'

'You would've had us kiss until our bodies died. Hah! You feel rejected by me!'

'If you must know the cruel truth, Victor, I kissed you only because I couldn't kiss Konrad.'

And she turned and left me there, wondering whether it was true.

Mother was not at breakfast again, and our morning lessons were subdued. Father seemed dispirited, and dismissed us early. I needed to be alone with my thoughts, and went for a long walk into the foothills.

The clouds that had oppressed us the past week were thinning, and by the time I paused to catch my breath, the sun had broken through. I took off my jacket and looked back across the lake, glad to see some colour returned to it. My gaze lifted to the mountain peak where the Frankenstein family crypt was carved into the glacial rock. Inside lay Konrad in his icy sarcophagus.

In that sunlit moment it seemed madness to try to bring him back, no more possible than stopping the turning of the earth. What if . . . What if I were to let life simply take its course? Surely it was a form of madness, what I had in mind.

But I couldn't stop my thoughts from straying back to the spirit world, its lustrous colours and textures, the surge of life in my veins, my healed, painless hand. I'd opened a door, and it had revealed all kinds of possibilities, all manner of power.

And perhaps it would allow me to keep the promise I'd made to myself, to unlock every secret law of this earth, to bring Konrad back.

A jolt of pain in my missing fingers made me curse. I turned from the mountain, looking back at our chateau poised on the lake's edge like a powerful and brooding sentinel. I imagined myself a malign spirit, whirling about the house, trying to get in.

There was a second promise I'd made not so long ago – to stop coveting what was my brother's. If I brought him back, would I have to surrender any chance of winning Elizabeth?

Hadn't I sacrificed enough already for Konrad? I'd given my fingers, dared to enter the spirit world, and might face even greater trials to give him back his life.

In the spirit world Elizabeth had kissed me and pushed herself against me with a passion that seemed impossible. Surely some part of her had to love me. She denied it, but

I didn't believe her, and if I could get her to spend more time with me in the spirit world, maybe that ardour would grow even stronger and I'd be able to unlock it in the real world. How could such a pursuit be deceitful if she herself wanted the same thing as me?

I will bring my brother back, I thought.

But I'd keep Elizabeth for myself.

As I made my way back home, I saw a fine carriage I didn't recognize near our stables. Inside the chateau I found my father's manservant, Schultz, and asked him who our visitor was.

'Professor Neumeyer from the university,' he told me. 'He came to examine the caves.'

'Is he there now?' I asked, eager to have another chance to explore.

'No. He's speaking with your father. I believe they're in the west sitting room.'

'Thank you, Schultz,' I said, vaulting up the stairs.

I found them on the balcony, Elizabeth and Henry, too, standing against the balustrade, the professor pointing at something along the shoreline. He was not at all my idea of a professor. I'd expected someone bespectacled and papery, but this fellow was built like a bear. He wore clothes that looked better suited to hunting than studying, had a bearded ruddy face, and hands that could break bones with ease.

'As you see,' he was saying, 'the site of your chateau is most desirable. Access to fresh drinking water and easy transport routes across the lake. It commands a view in all directions and is backed by the mountains, both strategic advantages. You're by no means the first people to have lived here. The Allobroges Celts had settlements as far back as five hundred years before Christ.'

'Did they make the drawings in the caves?' I asked.

'Ah, Victor,' said my father, turning. 'I'm glad you're back. Professor Neumeyer has been kind enough to take a look at our recent discovery.'

'All too briefly,' he said, shaking my hand in a grip that was almost painful. 'And, no, young sir, the Celts did not make those paintings. I believe they are altogether older.'

'How much older?' Elizabeth asked.

The professor shrugged his powerful shoulders. 'I've never seen anything like them. They were made no doubt by an ancient hunting culture. Look here.' He pulled something from his pocket. 'Their tools were primitive but ingenious as well. This stick of carved bone is stained with pigment at both ends – an early brush, I believe.'

'There were strange geometric symbols,' I said. 'Did you see them?'

The professor's bushy eyebrows lifted. 'Indeed I did.'

'They had language,' I said.

'Ah, now there's a question. Those markings seem purposeful, so I say yes. But it's a codex I've never encountered. I made a transcription and mean to send it to a colleague of mine in France who discovered something similar in caves near Lascaux. I'm hopeful he'll be able to translate them for me.' He looked at my father. 'Alphonse, you've got a true treasure here. There are surely chambers and galleries yet to be discovered. I'd like to bring some artists to make a record of the paintings, and some colleagues to help make a thorough examination of the site.'

My father nodded. 'I'd never hinder such an undertaking. The house is open to you.'

'I'd like to go to Mass,' Elizabeth said as we were finishing a late lunch after the professor had departed.

I knew that she only ever asked to go to Mass during a weekday when she was distraught. The last time was when Konrad was very ill and she'd wanted to light a candle for him. I had a fair idea what was bothering her, but it irritated me she was drawing attention to it. I looked over at Father, wondering if he suspected anything.

But all he said, somewhat distractedly, was, 'Of course. Victor and Henry can take you.'

Before Konrad's death it had always been his job to take Elizabeth to and from Mass in the nearby village of Bellerive, and he'd used this time alone with her, I later learned, to woo her. And she'd also used the time to slowly and secretly start converting him to the Church of Rome.

As I drove the horse and carriage down the lake road, I couldn't resist asking her playfully, 'So are we leaving you at the church permanently? Have you chosen your wimple yet?'

She tried to give me a withering look, but I could see the mirth behind her eyes.

Sitting between us, Henry turned to her in genuine alarm. 'You're not serious! That's not happening today, is it?'

Elizabeth and I laughed together.

'No, Henry,' she said. 'I won't be joining the convent just yet.'

'Thank God,' murmured Henry.

'Any day now, though,' I said, and then a worrying thought halted my chuckling. I looked at Elizabeth sternly. 'You don't mean to confess anything, do you?'

'That's really none of your business,' she said. 'And even if I did, the priest is sworn to secrecy.'

'This is true,' Henry said.

'Still,' I said through gritted teeth, 'it would be best if you didn't go whispering our secrets to anyone else.'

'Well,' said Elizabeth, unable to restrain a smile, 'why not come right into the church with me, to make sure I don't go on a whispering spree.'

'I think I will,' I said as I guided the horses into the churchyard.

'Good. Henry, you're most welcome to join us too.'

'I'll wait outside, thank you,' said Henry, who worshipped at the Calvinist church.

'Better hurry, Victor,' she said tauntingly over her shoulder as she lifted her skirts and ran towards the entrance. 'I'm feeling very contrite. Who knows what I might confess!'

I ran after her. During the service I waited at the back, watching Elizabeth like a hawk, to make sure she didn't try to duck into a confessional booth. But she seemed intent only on her own prayers, and after a while I wandered into a side chapel where, above the altar, there was an oil painting of Jesus raising Lazarus from the dead.

The Bible was not a book I was terribly familiar with, but this story I did know.

In the picture Jesus radiated light, his hand outstretched towards Lazarus, whose body was still partially wound in burial linens. Yet his eyes were open, one arm flexed to help push himself upright. All around, people were staring in amazement. Some swooned; others wept in joy, or perhaps terror.

I stared so long I didn't notice that parishioners were leaving the church, and that Elizabeth was at my side.

'I might've slipped into confession without you knowing,' she said mischievously.

'Did you?' I asked sharply.

'No. It's very moving, isn't it?' She nodded at the painting.

'Do you really believe such a thing can be done?' I asked her.

'Of course. By God.'

'Then why not ask Him?'

She said nothing.

'Have you asked?' I persisted.

'Please don't be disrespectful, here of all places.'

I wasn't trying to be disrespectful. I was genuinely curious. 'Surely you want Konrad back as much as the rest of us. More, maybe. So why wouldn't you ask, if you believed in such astonishing power?'

'Miracles were rare even when Jesus walked the earth. Lazarus was a friend of His, and people needed to believe, to know He was the son of God.'

I stared back at the painting, at the power emanating from Jesus's body like a corona.

'Is it because you don't really believe it can be done?' I asked.

She sighed. 'When Konrad died, I prayed for his soul to go straight to heaven. Death is part of life, Victor. I hate it, but I've accepted it.'

'When he died,' I told her, 'I made myself a promise at the crypt. I promised myself I would bring him back.'

'That was not a good promise.'

I pointed at the painting. 'What if I can achieve the same thing?'

She put her fingers to my lips to stop me.

I grabbed her hand. 'Please come and help me.'

Slowly she shook her head.

'Henry and I will go alone, then,' I said with a sigh, releasing her hand. I looked down, forlorn, but watched her from the corner of my eye. 'Konrad will miss you. When I think of him in there alone . . . Well, he's got Analiese, of course. She must be a great comfort to him.'

'Can't you see I'm at war with myself?' she whispered, her eyes wet. 'I want him back! My memory of him is so intense, it mocks reality.'

'Then help me make a new reality.'

The church's stained glass darkened briefly as a cloud passed over the sun.

'God is the sovereign master of life, Victor, not us.'

'Rules, and then more rules,' I muttered savagely. 'They can all be broken. You love him too much to let this chance pass!'

Her breath slipped out of her, and I sensed her resolve falter.

'You don't know what it cost me, going in just that once,' she said, and then with resignation added, 'I may already have eternally damned myself.'

I grinned. 'In that case what have you got to lose?'

CHAPTER SIX

THE STONE BOOK

A drop upon the tongue and we are here, all three. I sit up on my bed and turn to Henry, seated in the chair at my desk, hands in his lap, eyes just opening. Here is my oldest friend, and yet it takes me a moment to recognize him. His frame seems more substantial, the lines of his once slender face wider, his wispy hair more abundant, the jaw harder.

'Why're you staring at me?' he asks.

Because you're transformed, I think. But instead I say, 'How do you feel?'

His nostrils flare and he smiles. 'Fine.'

He opens his hand and regards his talisman – a bit of folded paper. An odd choice, I think, and a mysterious one, for he wouldn't show us what was written on it. He slips it into his pocket, and when he stands, he stands taller.

I look over at Elizabeth in my armchair, radiant with beauty. As she pulls her hair bracelet over her slender wrist, she looks at Henry, surprised and intrigued – and with a sting I know that she too has noticed his change. Her hazel eyes swing over to me, appraising, then slide away.

The faint ticking in my hand draws my eye to the spirit watch, and I see the fetal sparrow limb jerk slightly to the right. Outside my window the eerie white mist coils and moans, and the glass shudders. Henry looks over sharply.

'This is the evil spirit?' he asks.

'Don't be afraid. It can't come in,' I say.

'I'm not afraid,' he says, so calmly I believe him.

'Good,' I say, but I'm not at all sure I'm happy with this new, more confident Henry.

We leave my bedchamber, and as we walk down the hallway, I notice that Elizabeth lets Henry walk between us, as if she's trying to keep me at a distance. Is she afraid we might touch and become overwhelmed once more? But any pleasure this thought gives me is tempered with jealous anger. I don't want her to be able to control her attraction to me here. I smile to myself. We will see how long she can resist me.

All around us the house seems to pulse, remembering itself. As we make our way down the hallway, we check for Konrad and finally find him in the library. Analiese is with him, and they sit side by side at a table, their heads practically touching as they look over a book. Her fingers stroke absently at her earlobe. I sneak a glance at Elizabeth and see an expression I've never before seen on her face – undisguised jealousy.

And then Konrad squints and turns towards us, a hand shielding his eyes.

'You're back!' he calls out. 'And, Henry? Is that you?'

'It is,' our blond friend says.

Konrad stands, takes an eager step towards us, forgetting for a moment our searing heat that keeps him at a distance of some five feet. 'I'd clasp hands with you if I could,' he says. He gives a chuckle and adds, 'I must say, Henry, I'm amazed that Victor bullied you into coming.'

'I didn't need so much bullying,' Henry replies amicably, but with an uncharacteristic firmness. 'I wanted to see you, Konrad, and this place for myself.'

'Hello, Konrad,' says Elizabeth.

'Hello,' he returns, and then almost guiltily adds, 'I've been teaching Analiese to read.'

'How wonderful,' says Elizabeth with a smile so sincere, it's almost frightening. 'Is he a good teacher, Analiese?'

'Very good, miss. No one ever taught me my letters, and he's very patient with me.'

'Nonsense, you're learning splendidly,' Konrad says. 'And it passes the time. It seems an age since you were last here.'

Swiftly my eyes move about the room, and I see his sabre resting atop a shelf of books.

'You've been safe?' I ask him.

He nods and adds quietly, 'But the sounds are getting more frequent.'

'Sounds?' asks Henry, looking at me. 'You didn't mention anything about strange sounds.' His expression is somewhat accusing, though nowhere near as alarmed as I'd expected.

'Just a rather noisy houseguest,' I say lightly.

'Where?' he asks.

'No one knows, sir,' says Analiese.

'Look, butterflies!' Elizabeth says, head tilted up.

I turn and see three of them. They flit among us expectantly. Henry inhales sharply when one lands upon his arm, and watches, enthralled, as the creature's wings begin to radiate colour.

'Incredible,' he murmurs as it flutters away.

One grazes Elizabeth's hair, glowing amber, and then moves on.

The third one circles over me and then settles on my shoulder. At the exact moment of contact, I feel my mind sharpen.

'Yours doesn't fly away,' Henry says, with what I think is a hint of envy.

'I'm naturally attractive,' I say, and then turn to my brother. 'I was hoping I might enlist your help.'

Konrad squints over at me, a smile tugging at the corner of his mouth. Even separated by death, my twin knows me well. 'What is it you're planning, Victor?'

I take a breath. The butterfly still sits on my shoulder, and somehow its mere presence speeds my mind, as though I can see deeper into the future. 'I'm planning on bringing you back to us.'

A small gasp comes from Analiese. Konrad sinks back down in his chair, head bent.

'Victor, don't—'

'Please, just listen—'

'Victor!' he shouts, looking up angrily. 'This isn't fair. I was resigned to my fate. And then, seeing you . . .' His gaze strays to Elizabeth and remains so long that he winces, a hand flying up to cover his eyes. 'I'm not sure if it's a blessing or a curse. I *see* your lives, blazing from you like you're gods! But I can't share that light. I can't even touch you!'

'Soon,' I tell him.

'No. This is like dangling a rope to a drowning man who can't quite reach it. It's too cruel. We've chased after mirages before, Victor. Don't make me any more promises.'

'I have nothing to promise,' I tell him. 'But you have nothing to lose.'

This silences him for a moment, and once more I see his eyes stray to Elizabeth, his heart's desire.

'So what exactly is this plan of yours?' he asks.

'It begins,' I tell him, 'in the Dark Library.'

Elizabeth, Henry, and I sit at the same table where we once pored over alchemical tomes, trying to find a miraculous cure for Konrad. Only, this time he is with us, at a far table where our heat and light will not blind and sear him.

Analiese is not here. She said she'd be of no help to us, as she can't read. But I sense she's afraid, and perhaps disapproving. When I opened the secret panel to the staircase, she drew back and said she never knew such a place existed. She is even more pious than Elizabeth.

Within the Dark Library the shelves sag under the weight of books. Every volume that ever resided here is now present, though not all are visible at first. The very oldest ones – those that weren't here in my time, or perhaps even my father's – are hidden at first. But stare long and hard at the shelves, and phantom tomes shimmer before your eyes. Touch them, and they gain substance. I show Elizabeth and Henry how to see through layers of time, and together we gather armloads of books and pile them high.

'This will be a great deal of work,' says Henry, blowing air from his cheeks. 'We can't achieve it all in one visit.'

'We'll see,' I say, drawing the spirit clock from my pocket.

As if anticipating my plan, the butterfly, which for some reason has refused to leave my shoulder, flutters down to my hand.

'What are you doing?' Henry asks.

With my finger I touch the glass above the fetal sparrow leg. I close my eyes, focusing my mind's energy into a column of power, as dark and thick as ink.

Slower . . .

I lift the clock to my ear.

Tick . . . tick . . . . . . tick.

. . . *and yet slower still* . . .

Tiiickkk . . . . Tiiiiiickkkkkk . . . .

And then a long silence in which I count many beats of my own heart before the clock gives another languorous tick.

'Hah!' I cry exultantly, holding it out to Elizabeth. 'I've slowed it even more than last time. It scarcely moves now!'

'How is this possible?' Henry demands, taking the clock from Elizabeth and listening.

'It's possible,' I tell him.

I feel suddenly bereft as the butterfly lifts from my hand and circles about the room.

'Is it safe, though?' Henry says. 'Our bodies are waiting for us, and they need—'

'Our bodies will be fine!' I say dismissively. 'I did it last time. Elizabeth saw it.'

'You were a second longer than the first,' Henry says. 'I timed it exactly.'

'A second!' I scoff. 'What does it matter? Time is completely different here, and I have mastered it! As long as we stay only one full revolution, we're safe!'

Henry glances at Elizabeth.

'If you're worried, Henry Clerval,' I say, 'you can always go back.'

'No,' he says, rolling up his sleeves. 'Let's make use of all this time you've bought us.'

'Excellent!' I say.

Konrad catches the books I toss to him, and he sets to work as well, searching like us for any writings about raising the dead.

'There are many accounts of revenants,' says Henry, paging through a volume, 'but they aren't promising stories.'

'What's a revenant?' Elizabeth asks.

'A mindless corpse that rises from its grave, stalks about town, eats livestock and people, and then gets hacked to pieces by the townsfolk.'

'Don't waste your time on that,' I tell him. 'That's not what we want.'

'No,' he replies, 'but we'll not *find* what we want unless we read everything carefully.'

He's right, and it irks me that he's moving through the texts faster than I am, but this spirit world makes us more of what we are, and Henry has always been very clever with languages. I return to my own book, struggling with the Latin and the crude Gothic lettering.

A butterfly – is it the same one as earlier, or different? – suddenly alights on my hand. I look at its rainbow-hued wings and then past them to the text beneath my fingertips, and—

I feel a coursing of language through my head, the Latin translating itself with such speed that my breath catches and I cough, as though I've swallowed too much water.

The butterfly does not flutter away but remains poised upon my hand, wings folding and opening serenely.

I touch my hand to the page again, and once more a torrent of knowledge fills me. Hurriedly I turn the pages, sweeping my fingers across entire paragraphs at a time, my eyes scarcely focused on the book but rather on the chamber of my own mind, where all this arcane knowledge is presenting itself to me.

'You're going too fast, Victor,' I hear Elizabeth say, as from another room. 'You'll miss something.'

'There's nothing of use here,' I say, shoving the book from me and grabbing another. Greek, Latin, Aramaic, lost dialects, I surge through all of them one after another.

I look up briefly. Henry and Elizabeth are both watching me strangely.

'It's the butterfly, isn't it?' Henry says.

I nod in amazement. 'It's helping me read more quickly, like some new form of energy that speeds my mind.'

'How do you know you aren't deceiving yourself?'

Yet he holds out his finger and clicks his tongue, as if summoning a cat. The butterfly, however, does not leave me.

'Well, we all want one now,' Elizabeth says with a laugh.

'It's unbelievable,' I murmur, and with my empowered hand I inhale another book's contents in a matter of seconds, and toss it to the floor.

'All nonsense,' I say. 'I wouldn't trust any of it.'

Across the room Konrad says, 'How can you tell? All these books are filled with arcane spells and incantations. Why is one any less reliable than another?'

'The butterfly. It seems to know what I seek, and helps me sift the gold from the dross. But there's no gold, not here. There's something else,' I say, surprising myself.

'What do you mean?' Henry demands.

'Something I, we, should be looking for.'

'A different book?' Konrad wants to know.

'It's hidden somewhere. I'll know when I see it . . .'

The butterfly flies from my finger, and I give a cry of dismay. 'Not yet!'

Henry immediately reaches out to lure it to him, but it avoids both our hands and settles instead on my temple, and in that same instant I see an arrangement of strange symbols in my head. I hardly dare breathe.

'I know these,' I mutter, closing my eyes, concentrating harder. They're not symbols upon a page but cut into stone. Abruptly I stand.

'Where are you going?' Elizabeth demands.

The butterfly still rests on my temple, and I don't want to lose it. 'There's writing in the caves.'

'What caves?' Konrad exclaims in frustration.

'Ah,' I say, 'we forgot to tell you. We Frankensteins have the caves of an ancient culture under our chateau.'

'Are you mad?' I hear Konrad call out as I hurry down the stairs.

'No, it's true,' says Elizabeth, following me. 'Come and see. It's remarkable.'

'Anything else I should know about?' Konrad asks, exasperated. 'In the few weeks I've been dead?'

I hurry to the bottom of the stairs and peer down into the fake well. I take hold of the ladder jutting up from the depths and swing myself onto its rungs.

'It was never a well?' Konrad asks in amazement as I climb down.

I reach the bottom. The giant horses painted on the wall have an even greater force and dynamism, as if at any moment their muscular flanks will heave, their hooves kick up a cloud of grit. With my hand I reach up to make sure the butterfly is still poised on my head, but stop myself – I can sense it's there, can feel the quiet, potent power it's ready to bestow upon me.

Elizabeth is first to arrive. She looks about the cavern, but instead of wonder on her face, I see unease.

'What's wrong?' I ask.

'Don't you feel it?'

I shake my head, bewildered.

'She's right,' says Henry, stepping down and making room for Konrad to descend. 'There's a vile atmosphere it didn't have before.'

'That sounds like the old Henry,' I say. 'You can always wait in the library, if you like.'

'Don't be an ass, Victor,' my brother says as he looks about the cavern. I notice his sabre is in his belt. 'There's something not right about this place.'

Truly I feel no sense of foreboding, only a fierce impatience. 'They're just ancient, dank caves.'

'No. There's something down here,' says Konrad.

'Yes, something we need.'

'That's not what I meant,' my twin says, his hand on his hilt.

I think of the ominous sounds he's heard from deep within the house. But fear does not touch me.

'All of you,' I say, 'you have too much valour to hang back now! And we have nothing to fear.' I look at Henry and Elizabeth. 'We're the living! Light and heat pour off us. Nothing can harm us here! Trust me.'

With some reluctance they follow me through the high-vaulted galleries and chambers. This journey is a far cry from the first one we made in the real world, when we were giddy with the wondrous bestiary galloping across the walls. Now we proceed more warily. There are times when, from the corner of my eye, the luminous animals seem to move – a quick dip of the head, an eye flashing with predatory light.

When we reach the image of the sabre-toothed tiger, Henry points to the nearby line of symbols we discovered before on the wall. 'Are these the ones you mean?' he asks.

I swallow and, full of hope, put my hand to them. The pads of my fingers trace their sharp contours, and before my mind's eye the dashes and circles swiftly, miraculously, shape themselves into language.

I exhale. 'No. This isn't what I want. It's just an account

of a hunt, a tally of kills. There must be more writing somewhere.'

'This is as far as we went,' Elizabeth says, looking at the branching of the passageway.

A cool pulse of knowledge travels through my temple. 'I know the way,' I tell her, already walking on ahead.

'Wait,' says Henry. 'Do we have time for this?'

I fish about in my pocket and pull out the spirit clock. 'Not even half a revolution. Catch!' I toss the clock at Henry. 'You can be the timekeeper, Henry, since I can tell you don't trust me.'

'What if we get lost down here?' he demands, catching me firmly by the sleeve.

In all the time I've known him, I don't think he's ever tried to restrain me, and I don't like it. I jerk my arm free.

'I said I know the way.'

'Your butterfly will guide us, I suppose,' he says. 'And what if it decides to fly away; what then?'

I search about on the floor, staring hard, until I find an ancient piece of charcoal. I snatch it up and slash an X on the wall.

'There. We have our turning marked.'

'The house changes,' says Elizabeth. 'We've both seen it happen.'

'Not these caves,' I say with utter certainty. 'They've

been the same since time began. There's nothing to change.'

I start walking again. Thrice more the passageway branches, and I mark each one. The wall paintings become less frequent, and I'm scarcely aware of them, drawn deeper by supernatural instinct.

'There's only a quarter revolution of the clock left,' Henry says behind me.

'Victor,' Konrad says, 'you're going too far. You'll have trouble getting back to your bodies in time.'

'Almost there,' I say. And I'm right, for the passage abruptly opens out into a high-domed cavern.

'Good Lord,' Henry exhales.

I am staring up at it too, a crude but vast image drawn in bold black lines. It stands tall on two legs, has a head, and an outstretched arm from which emanates jagged lines that convey immense power.

'Is it a man?' Konrad asks from behind us.

'What else could it be?' says Elizabeth.

'How odd, though,' remarks Henry, 'that the animal pictures are so realistic but this one is . . . so primitive.'

As I stare at it, I think of the painting in the Bellerive church – Jesus standing over Lazarus.

'Look here!' I cry, for underneath the image is a vast text of strange lines and dots and shapes. 'This is the book! A book in stone.'

From far away a noise unlike any I've ever heard comes wafting into the cavern – a quick, fevered series of gasps, and then a slow moan that dissipates like the last vapour of breath.

'*That* is the sound!' Konrad cries. His sword is suddenly drawn, his eyes fixed on a passageway that slants downwards so steeply that it is more like a chute. 'It came from down there!'

'What in God's name was it?' Henry says.

'Something forgotten by God,' Elizabeth whispers. 'It sounds like a soul in torment.'

'A bit dramatic, don't you think?' I say with a snort. 'A portal to Hell just below our house?'

Henry forces out a nervous chuckle. 'Yes, that might be a bit ambitious, even for the Frankensteins.'

Only silence wells up from the steep passageway now. I walk closer. Unlike the others, I feel no fear, no presence of evil. I taste only power. I want to see what's down there.

But my gaze, as if gently directed by forces beyond me, turns back to the writing on the cave wall.

'Whatever's down there is a long way away, and no concern to us,' I say. 'This text is what we came for.'

'Be quick about it, please,' says Henry, his eyes still fixed on the passageway.

As I near the wall, the butterfly lifts from my temple

and settles on my hand, and I put my fingers to the symbols. Behind my eyes I feel a great pressure building, words and images and ideas assembling themselves, and then in a blinding torrent I see—

A body lying on the earth, its flesh corrupted. I see the legs of many living men encircling the body, standing over it. I hear their rough voices joining in a chant. Some kind of scythe comes down and severs the foot at the ankle. I feel my stomach rise. I see things in little bursts of light. Blades dividing the body again and again, and then—

Pain blooms through my head, and with a cry I pull back my hand.

'Victor!' I hear Konrad call out behind me. 'Are you all right?'

'It comes so hard and fast . . .' I wince, pushing through the pain. 'It's like pictures in my head.'

'Stop this!' Elizabeth implores me.

'No. There's more.'

I thrust my hand against the wall, and suddenly it's as though it is welded there, and I see—

A severed foot cast into a long damp hole like a grave. Someone kneels beside it and carefully unties an animal bladder. From the opening scuttles something darker than shadow. At first I think it's a beetle, but the shape is more fluid, altogether more disturbing. The human steps back as the shadow leaps onto the severed foot, burrowing hungrily into the rotted flesh—

I stagger back once more, retching.

Henry has his hand on my shoulder. 'Victor, you need to—'

'No!'

'Our time's running out!' he shouts at me, holding out the clock. I squint at it in disbelief, for the leg has nearly made a full revolution. Surely not so much time has passed. I hold it to my ear.

Tick . . . Tick . . . tick . . .

I don't understand. It has slipped back into its normal tempo, but I don't have the energy or concentration to grapple with it right now. I need all my faculties to complete the stone translation.

'I must finish,' I gasp. 'I'm almost done!' I put my fingers to the wall, and—

A pair of human hands reaches into the damp hole and covers the severed foot swiftly and completely with mud, and adds still more, patting it into a rounded shape, little bumps that can be only arms, legs, a head. A stick makes two pricks for eyes.

'Victor, what do you see?' Elizabeth demands, but I block her out and return to the searing image before my mind's eye.

Light sweeps over the little mud man, as though the sun were racing through the sky, and then darkness, soon chased away by the light. I am dizzy watching, time speeded up. The little mud man trembles and begins to grow, the torso elongating, gaining definition, and muddy features appearing on the face.

Animals draw close, sniff, and cringe back. A feral cat's hackles rise; rats squeal and turn away. Nothing will go close to it, inert and defenseless as it is.

Faster and faster the creature grows, looking more human by the second. His skin is no longer muddy but the colour and texture of proper flesh. And then, stretched on the ground is a man, the very same man I first saw dead and decaying – but now whole, reborn.

His eyes open.

I fall back from the wall as if pushed, and land hard on the ground.

'Victor, are you all right?' Elizabeth is asking. She reaches towards me but then stops, as though remembering what happened when our flesh last touched.

'What did you see?' she asks.

'Our time's very nearly up!' says Henry urgently, extending his hand to me. Gratefully I take it, and he hauls me swiftly to my feet. I touch my head, which throbs like an overworked muscle.

'Go!' says Konrad. 'Don't wait for me!'

From the steep passage comes another distant moan, and I turn once more in its direction, drawn.

'*Now*, Victor!' Elizabeth says, and I take the lead back towards the entrance. I smile, suddenly giddy. I feel as though I'm bounding through a dream. I gallop past stags and bulls, ibexes and horses. I smirk at the crouching tiger.

'Slow down,' Elizabeth tells me sharply. 'We're leaving Konrad too far behind.'

Heedless of my supernatural speed I turn to see my twin in the distance and can't help laughing, for I remember all our childhood races where he outstripped me, and now he cannot even hope to keep up with me.

'Our time's almost out,' I reply, noting that I'm not even out of breath.

'And whose fault is that?' Henry says, just behind me.

'We're fine!' I say, my mind still throbbing with the cave writing. The things I've seen.

'He might get lost!' Elizabeth says.

'We blaze a trail of light for him,' I retort, 'and we've marked the turnings.'

She stumbles on a rock, and I reach out to take her hand. It's impulsive, yet I also know full well what I'm doing, and even before my fingers close around her wrist, our eyes meet, and I feel desire spark between us, see it in her face, like a hunger.

But Henry catches her first, steadying her.

I exhale in disappointment, and then anger, and start to reach out for her again, when I hear Konrad calling out, closer now.

'I said don't wait for me!'

And we begin running again, though at a pace that allows my twin to keep up. When we reach the ladder, Henry says, 'The claw's tapping the glass! What happens now?'

'We still have time,' I assure him.

I feel my body in the real world tugging me back towards it. There is no arguing with it. I swiftly climb the rungs.

'Victor!' Konrad calls out to me from below. 'Did you find what you wanted? Tell me what you saw!'

'I found it,' I tell him over my shoulder with a triumphant smile. 'The way to bring you back.'

CHAPTER SEVEN

A CRITICAL INGREDIENT

'The way you tell it,' said Henry, 'it sounds a bit like the Egyptian cult of Osiris.'

We were on the water, bathed in sunlight, sailing close to the wind on the twenty-footer. The day had dawned with all the warmth and promise of a summer morning, and after our lessons and lunch, we'd asked our cook to prepare a picnic hamper, and we'd taken the boat out. At the tiller, leaving the chateau in our wake, I'd finally had the chance to tell them in full detail what the writing on the cave walls had shown me.

'Someone murdered Osiris,' Henry continued, 'I forget who, and cut his body into fourteen pieces and scattered them. His family found the pieces and buried them, and he came back to life as the god of the underworld.'

'A myth,' said Elizabeth. 'How do we know these cave writings are any different? They were made by primitive, superstitious people. Do you really think they knew how to bring people back to life?'

'Ah,' I said, 'they didn't bring him back to life. That's

what's so interesting. They *grew* him a new body. Prepare
to come about, please.'

I pushed the tiller hard over. At the front of the
cockpit, Elizabeth and Henry busied themselves with the
foresail. Henry, never the most confident mariner, was sure-
footed now and winched in his sheet with a confidence I'd
never seen before. And Elizabeth, I couldn't help noticing,
seemed to have regained the weight and bloom she'd lost
in the past few weeks. There was enticing colour in her
cheeks and a new lustre in her windblown hair.

The boom swung overhead, and the mainsail filled
with a satisfying *whoomph*. I adjusted the tiller and turned
my face into the breeze, inhaling happily. From the
moment I'd woken this morning, I'd felt remarkably well –
bursting with energy. Hopeful, even. For the first time
since Konrad's death, I'd actually *wanted* to get up and face
the day. And I hadn't yet had a single jolt of pain in my
maimed right hand.

It seemed our visit to the spirit world had helped all of
us in some way.

'A body part and a bit of mud,' said Elizabeth
reflectively.

'Surely creating life can't be so simple,' Henry added,
pushing his spectacles back on his nose but looking at me
with a hint of challenge.

Elizabeth surprised me with her quick reply. 'Is it so different from the way God created Adam, fashioning him from the mud?'

'Well, no,' Henry said. 'But you're also forgetting the black liquid Victor described. That was one of the ingredients.'

'It wasn't liquid,' I said. My mind still felt seared by the ancient words and images, as though I'd stared too long at the sun. 'What came out of that sac was alive. It didn't just flow; it moved of its own will.'

'Right,' said Henry, 'so all we need is mud, a body part, and a magical liquid we don't have.'

I shook my head, suddenly realizing something. 'No. Even then it wouldn't make life. The body's just a shell. It has no *spirit*. The body must first be grown in our world until it's ready for Konrad to inhabit.'

'This was all in those writings?' Henry asked, incredulous.

I nodded. 'In the end it all came in such a rush.'

I saw Henry glance at Elizabeth before returning his gaze to me. 'And you're certain, absolutely certain, that this is what you read – or saw in those cave symbols? It can't have been an easy translation, even with the butterfly's help.'

Firmly I said, 'I'm sure, Henry.'

'And you're already imagining going ahead with this?' he asked. 'It seems a primitive, barbaric thing.'

'What other choice do we have, Henry?' Elizabeth said to him impatiently, and I was startled – and delighted – by her fervour. 'If I'd merely read it in a book, yes, I'd say it was outlandish. But we've entered the land of the dead, all of us, and seen what it holds. And we need to get Konrad out of there as soon as possible. That noise . . .'

I saw Henry suppress a shudder as he remembered the weird moan lifting to us from the depths. But I also remembered how Analiese had said she'd never seen anything – which meant that, whatever was down there, it hadn't stirred for a long, long time. I didn't see why it necessarily had to be evil. A greater part of me wanted to know more about it. But if Henry and Elizabeth feared it and thought it would harm Konrad, all to the good. It would keep them focused on the urgency of our endeavour.

'Yes,' I said. 'I don't think we should waste any time.'

'That liquid,' she said, 'or whatever substance it was. We need to know how to get it.'

'Why didn't the hieroglyphs tell you?' Henry asked.

'There may be other writings in the cave,' I suggested. 'Or elsewhere. We'll need to go back.'

She nodded reluctantly. 'Though, I don't like the place.'

'Henry does, I think,' I said.

Henry leaned back with the look of someone remembering a fleeting and guilty pleasure. 'I can't deny it,' he said. 'There was something . . . Can "liberating" be the right word?'

'You're the expert with words,' I said, and grinned.

'I'm different when I'm there,' said Elizabeth. 'I don't like myself.'

I laughed. 'You are *more* yourself. That's the wonder of it. We all are.'

She blushed and set her gaze on the shoreline. 'Well, if that's true, I'd be very worried if I were you. You're even more reckless and arrogant inside.'

I was indignant. 'How so?'

Henry snorted. 'With those butterflies on you, you carry on like you're a demigod. And what you did with the spirit clock—'

'Didn't we all return safely?'

'Well, yes,' he said.

'And how long were our bodies without us?'

'A minute and two seconds.'

'An extra second only!'

'There are limits to what the human body can endure!' Henry exclaimed.

'I think you'd be amazed, my friend.' They clearly had no idea of the kind of power and vitality I felt in the spirit world, how my senses and experiences there seemed even more real than the sunlight and wind and water that surrounded me now. I realized that, more than anything, I wanted to return.

'Victor.'

I was expecting Henry to chastise me further, but I saw him staring fixedly at the tiller. He pointed.

'There's something on your right hand.'

I glanced down quickly and in amusement said, 'That, Henry, is called a *shadow*.' I was remarkably glad to see that familiar look of worry etched upon his pale brow. He was not yet so transformed by the spirit world.

'No,' he said, moving closer. 'Where your fingers *used* to be.'

I looked and gave a rueful grunt, for, by some trick of the light, it did indeed look as if I had a fourth and fifth finger, gripping the tiller.

'It's just shadow, Henry. Look.' And I moved my hand along the tiller. The two phantom fingers elongated and then seeped back beneath my hand with a fluid speed that was not at all shadowlike.

I jerked my hand off the tiller.

'It's still there!' Elizabeth cried, pointing.

I turned my hand over and saw something dark and slick against my flesh.

'What is it?' gasped Henry.

'Some kind of beetle!' Elizabeth said.

I gave my hand a violent shake, but it clung. I swiped it off with my left hand. 'Where'd it go?' I said, looking about the cockpit floor.

'It's on your other hand now!' shouted Henry.

I saw it slyly squeezed into the fold between my thumb and palm. In growing alarm I stood, striking at it.

'I can't get it off!' I cried. 'I can't even feel it!'

Unmanned, the boat strayed into the wind, and as the sail luffed, direct sunlight washed over my hand, and instantly the shadowy insect seeped up my shirt sleeve.

Horrified, I tore off my jacket, threw it to the deck, and desperately began ripping open my shirt, popping buttons.

The boat swayed, and the swinging boom nearly brained me.

'There it is!' cried Elizabeth, and I caught just a glimpse of something scuttling into my armpit.

'Gah!' I lifted my arm high, staggering off balance, and turned to the sun so I could see better. The thing oozed from the tangle of my underarm hair around to my back so that I lost sight of it.

'Where's it gone?' I demanded, lurching about so Henry and Elizabeth might spot it.

'It doesn't like the light!' Henry said. 'It rushes to hide.'

'Just get it off me!' I cried.

'It's too quick!' Henry protested, hands slapping at my skin. 'It flows like mercury!'

I was in a near frenzy to rid myself of this pest, and whirled about, looking back over my shoulder.

'Victor,' Elizabeth said with frightening solemnity, 'it has gone down your trousers.'

I tore my waistband loose even as I kicked off my shoes. I yanked one leg free and saw the shadow crawler dart down my second trouser leg. When I finally rid myself of the trousers, the diabolical little creature stretched towards my underpants and disappeared.

I hesitated only half a second before dragging my underpants off. I was stark naked now and didn't care one bit, so frenzied was I.

'Get a jar from the picnic hamper,' I shouted, 'and catch it!'

Elizabeth's eyes travelled all over me, tracking it. I didn't care. All I could think was, *Would it get inside me somehow?* I clenched my buttocks tightly together.

As the boat swayed and turned, sun and shadow played across my body, and the shadow creature now bolted from my privates to the back of my thigh.

'On my right leg!' I cried.

Henry dumped out two jars of water and tossed one to

Elizabeth. I turned my front to the sun to keep the thing behind me.

'Can you see it?' I bellowed.

'Yes, it's on your back now. Try to stand still, Victor!' Elizabeth said, drawing closer.

I felt their jars buffeting me as they tried to catch the thing.

'I've got it!' cried Elizabeth as she drove the jar into the small of my back with such force that I yowled in pain. 'It's caught! Henry, where's the lid?'

'Here, here!' he said.

I watched over my shoulder as Elizabeth very swiftly tipped the jar away from my skin, slipped the lid over the top and screwed furiously.

'There!' she cried triumphantly.

My relief was immense, and yet immediately, bizarrely, I also thought: *I want it back. Now.*

I felt a stab of pain return to my hand. Forgetting my nakedness, I turned to look at the thing, battering itself against the glass in vain.

Henry cleared his throat. 'Victor, you need clothes.'

Elizabeth, I noticed, seemed to have no trouble with my nakedness and merely smiled, her gaze level with mine, holding out my underpants.

After I'd hurriedly dressed, I grabbed the jar and held

it to the sunlight to get a better look at the little fiend. With no shadow to offer it refuge, the thing hurled itself hysterically about the jar, and I feared the glass would shatter.

'This is no normal animal,' I said. 'Where is its head, its limbs? It changes shape every second!'

As if exhausted, it retreated into a corner and made itself as small as possible, a dense black ink splodge.

'It's getting fainter!' said Elizabeth.

'I think you're right,' Henry agreed.

The thing was fraying at the edges, unravelling into smoky tendrils.

'The sunlight harms it,' I murmured.

'Let it die!' Henry said.

As it continued to diffuse, it became butterfly-shaped, and I caught, just for a moment, a glimpse of miraculous colours on its wings.

'Wait!' Immediately I sheltered the glass jar with my body, and then wrapped a napkin around it.

'What're you doing?' said Henry.

'It's one of the butterflies! From the spirit world!'

'But how?' Elizabeth demanded.

'The one that was helping me in the caves. It must've come out with me. It *came out* with me!'

Very slowly Henry said, 'How could something from

the world of the dead come into ours?'

I looked into the jar. Protected from the sun, the creature had composed itself and regained some of its intense blackness. It poured itself around the inside of the glass. I inhaled sharply. It was unmistakable.

'Do you know what this is?' I said, grinning up at the other two. 'This is the last ingredient we need to grow Konrad.'

CHAPTER EIGHT

MUD

I touched the handle of Konrad's bedchamber, leaned my forehead against the wood. A deep breath, and then I entered and shut the door soundlessly behind me. It was almost completely dark, for the curtains were drawn tight, with only a faint penumbra of light around them.

For a moment I imagined the other world beyond this one, the one in which Konrad resided. Briefly the room seemed to shimmer, about to reveal itself to me in all its guises through history, but then it solidified into the undeniable truth of here and now.

We hadn't changed anything in his bedchamber. No one could face it, not yet, that final resignation. And if this endeavour of mine was successful, there'd be no need of it.

I needed some part of Konrad. Neither Elizabeth, nor Henry, nor I had been able to contemplate venturing to his crypt and desecrating his body. But then I'd realized we wouldn't have to. The cave writings had told me that all that was required was some part of him that had once been living. Surely it wouldn't matter how large or small.

On his chest of drawers I found his brush, and from the

bristles I began to pull as many of his hairs as I could.

I heard the bedchamber door slowly opening, and I whirled, the brush still clutched guiltily in my hands.

On the threshold stood my mother, a hand lifted to stifle a scream.

'Konrad?' she gasped.

'Mother, it's me, Victor. I'm so sorry to startle you.'

I rushed over to her, pocketing the brush, and helped her to the nearest chair. She was still in her night robe, even though it was near noon.

'I mistook you . . .' It took her a moment to regain her breath.

I didn't like to look upon her, for my beautiful mother's cheeks were hollowed, and her normally lively eyes dulled.

'Let me help you back to your bedchamber,' I said.

'Your father thinks it only makes me worse to come here, but I need to. I still need to. And you do too, clearly.'

She took my maimed hand and placed it between hers. Her skin had a papery feel to it, her bones and tendons more prominent than I recalled. I was terribly worried about her but dared not say anything. Voicing my fears aloud would, somehow, make them far too real and frightening.

'Does it still pain you, your hand?' she asked.

'Not very much at all,' I lied.

She looked about the darkened room. 'Almost every night I dream of him. And sometimes we talk. What I would give for just one more real conversation.'

Before I could stop myself I said, 'If I could bring him back for you, I would.'

'I know, Victor. You try so hard.'

'Father thinks—'

'Your father thinks you're rash and headstrong, but he told me he'd never known anyone show such love and devotion to a sibling.'

'He said that to you?'

She nodded. 'Every day I'm thankful for you, and Elizabeth, and William and Ernest, and one day I won't wear this grief so heavily, but that day . . . seems a very long way away.'

I kissed her on both cheeks and hugged her. 'You should rest,' I said.

'All I do is rest,' she replied wearily, and then formed her face into a brave smile. 'Are you taking Konrad's hairbrush as a keepsake?'

I swallowed uneasily. 'Yes. I want it for my own.'

And I need it, to bring him back, for all of us.

The work cottage stood on the farthest reach of our property, at the edge of an unused pasture that bordered forest. Beyond the crude door was a dirt floor, plank walls, no windows – a place to give labourers shelter in bad weather, a place for unused stone and fence posts, shovels and rusting saws.

On the crude wooden table we placed the lanterns we'd lit, and closed the door. Carefully I set down the jar containing the butterfly spirit. It had spent a day and night in my room, carefully hidden, like some strange insect a guilty boy keeps from his mother. It swam along the inside of the glass, then grew legs and scuttled about, then sprouted black wings and fluttered, batting itself against the lid, its entire being bent on escape. *Soon enough,* I thought. *Soon enough you can come out and start your work.*

From my breast pocket I took the vial of Konrad's hair and set it on the table.

I looked at Henry and Elizabeth. 'We will do this,' I said.

Henry nodded. 'Yes.'

I saw Elizabeth take a deep breath, but her gaze was steady as she nodded. In the church that day, before the painting of Jesus and Lazarus, she'd made her decision, and she'd never been one to back down. 'What do we do first?'

'Well, it's . . . fairly straightforward,' I said. 'First the hole.'

I passed Henry a shovel, and plunged mine into the dirt floor behind the table. Working together it was a quick enough job. The hole was shallow, no more than a foot deep, and six in length. *A crib*, I thought.

But it looked more like a grave.

At its bottom the earth was moist and claylike. Elizabeth pushed back her sleeves and knelt. She took several handfuls of thick mud and started working away, fashioning a torso, pinching off a head, then arms, then shaping the lower half into two legs. She used the tip of her little finger to make indentations for the eyes and then traced a mouth. Watching, I had a sudden memory of her as a little girl, sitting in the courtyard garden, making shapes in the soil with a stick, her brow furrowed with concentration.

I couldn't help laughing. 'I can't see you taking such care over me,' I said. 'Two splats of mud, and away we go.'

When she looked up at me, her eyes were wet.

'You've done a fine job,' I told her, my voice softening. I knelt down beside her. 'Here.' I helped her smooth the outlines of the little mud creature, as though this would give it a greater chance of becoming perfect, of becoming Konrad. Our fingers touched and, for just a split second, lingered, as though remembering something. Then she pulled back her hand to continue her work alone. I stood and watched.

'How long will it take, before it grows to its proper size?' Henry asked.

I conjured up the stone book's searing chain of images – the sun chasing the darkness across the twitching body of the mud man. 'I'm not sure. It was a good number of days. Six, perhaps?'

'And then?'

'We'll give the body a drop of the elixir and enter the spirit world.'

'But wouldn't the body appear in the spirit world too?' asked Henry. 'And then we'd have two Konrads?'

From the floor Elizabeth shook her head, frowning. 'The body won't enter. It has no spirit, and it's our spirits that inhabit the land of the dead.'

'Precisely,' I said, though it had taken me some time to puzzle this out myself. 'The body will wait in the real world for Konrad's spirit to claim it.'

'But how will Konrad find his body without a talisman?' Henry asked.

This I'd already considered. 'Before we enter, we'll put some talisman in the creature's fist, and when we enter the spirit world, the body won't be there but the talisman will be. I'll need your help now, Henry.'

We returned to the table.

'We need our butterfly spirit to bind with Konrad's hair,' I said.

Henry took up the jar with the spirit and peered inside. 'The moment we unscrew this lid . . .'

I nodded. 'It'll try to escape onto one of us, me most likely. It seems to prefer me.'

'Your irresistible charm,' said Henry.

I chuckled nervously. Everything suddenly seemed unreal. Were we really doing this?

'Is our mud creation complete?' I asked Elizabeth.

She nodded and came to the table.

I handed Henry the vial of Konrad's hair and took hold of the jar with the butterfly spirit. 'I'll slide open the lid just a touch, and you jam the end of your vial inside and shake out the hair – quickly, mind.'

'I'm ready,' he said, removing the small cork from the vial.

The moment I put my hand on the lid, the spirit became still at the bottom of the jar, attentive, coiled. I unscrewed the lid and held it firmly in place for a moment, while Henry positioned the vial. He nodded, and I slid the lid an inch to the side.

Henry darted the vial into the gap but didn't even have time to shake out the hair. In the blink of an eye the spirit sprang into the vial, where it stretched itself long and spiralled in a frenzy round and round the strands of Konrad's hair.

'What do I do?' whispered Henry.

'Stay still, stay still,' I hissed. 'Elizabeth, the cork!'

She snatched it up from the table. I pulled back the jar's lid so she could reach inside with her slim hands and jam the cork hard into the inverted top of the vial.

'Thank goodness,' I breathed. Trapped inside, the spirit hungrily twined with Konrad's hair until it was difficult to tell them apart. Henry's hands were shaking slightly.

'What's the best way to put this inside the mud creature?' he asked.

'Let's do it now while it's occupied,' I said. The spirit was still ecstatically entangled with Konrad's hair.

Swiftly we moved to the hole, where Elizabeth knelt and pressed her thumb deep into the centre of the little mud creature's torso.

I seized a small handful of clay, ready. Henry held the stoppered vial against the cavity in the mud man's chest.

'Look at it,' Elizabeth said, pointing. The spirit had bundled itself and Konrad's hair into a small compact ball. It pulsed darkly.

'Open and pour,' I told Henry.

He yanked out the cork, shook the vial, and the hair and

the spirit rolled out and into the mud creature. Instantly I pushed some clay over the top, sealing the cavity. Elizabeth added a little more, smoothing it. Then we pulled back our hands and just stared.

It was only mud, just a sad little mud baby made by children.

'Will this work?' Elizabeth whispered.

'Yes,' I said fervently.

After a few minutes we left the cottage, secured the door with a padlock, and started the walk back to the chateau, all our hopes and fears carried silently within us.

We'd just entered the main hall, our hands still damp from washing them at the stable pump, when Dr Lesage appeared, coming down the main staircase.

'How's Mother?' I asked.

'Oh, her spirits seem improved today. She said she had a nice chat with you earlier.'

'May we visit her?' Elizabeth asked.

'She's taking the rest she needs right now,' said the doctor. 'Don't look so grave, Miss Lavenza. She has no disease of the body. Time will be her cure, I have no doubt.'

'Well, I'm glad to hear it,' said Elizabeth.

The doctor turned to me. 'And I'm glad to catch you

before I leave, young sir. Your parents wanted me to have a quick look at you.'

'But I'm not ill,' I blurted, and regretted it, for I'd sounded almost guilty.

'I merely want to examine your hand,' the doctor said with a reassuring smile. 'Your father said he still sees you wince from time to time. Is it giving you pain?'

Elizabeth and Henry left us. We went into the empty dining room, and I sat by the window while the doctor bent his head to examine the ugly stumps of my severed fingers. His forehead bore liver spots, and there was dandruff among his thinning hair. He seemed older than I remembered. His hands were pleasantly warm, and I felt my shoulders relax.

'The wounds are healing well. There is no sign of infection or disease.'

'It was never the wounds that hurt,' I told him.

'No. You feel the pain where the fingers once were, yes?'

I nodded.

'And the pain, how is it?'

'It comes and goes.'

'It is not so unusual as you might think. I have heard of cases where the severed limb continues to give phantom pain for some time. The body remembers its injury.'

'Time will be my cure too, then,' I said. 'Mother hasn't been worrying about me, has she?'

'No, no,' he said. 'How is your sleep?'

I almost smiled. If he only knew how deeply I had lately slept – as deep as death itself.

'Fine,' I said.

His elderly eyes regarded me kindly. 'I'm not concerned only about your hand, Victor. Your grief is another matter.'

I looked out of the window. I did not want to appear weak. I did not want to give anything away.

'I have no doubt,' he said, 'that you will heal. But there are things that might speed it. You appear to me pale and run-down. Your father says you've been skulking about the house.'

'I've just been out for a long walk,' I protested.

'Excellent. I recommend more of the same. Summer seems not ready to leave us quite yet, and I advise you to take full advantage of it. Daily outings. Plenty of fresh air. Walk. Ride. Row. Sail. Take your meat bloodier. And I will leave you an opiate, with instructions to take it only sparingly, and for no longer than three weeks. It will ease your pain, and help you sleep.'

'My sleep is . . .' And I stopped myself with a sigh.

'Good,' he said, clapping me on the shoulder. 'I'll let your father know we've spoken, and remind him to keep you out of doors!'

'Thank you, Doctor,' I said with a smile, for he didn't

know how well his prescription would aid my plans.

The next morning, after delivering a brief lesson, Father released Elizabeth, Henry, and me to the outdoors, with firm instructions to exert ourselves and breathe deeply. Cook had packed us an enormous picnic hamper, and we set off on foot in the direction of the far pasture. The day, as the doctor had predicted, was truly beautiful, a return to summer.

Henry and I, the hamper between us, perspired lightly in the early October sun as we hurried to keep up with Elizabeth. Throughout our morning lecture it had taken all my effort to concentrate on Father's words, and Elizabeth had seemed so agitated, I'd feared Father would notice.

No one spoke, though my own head was noisy with hopes and questions about what awaited us inside the cottage. When we reached it, I pulled the key from my pocket and hoped no one saw the slight tremble in my fingers.

What will I behold on the other side of this door?

I pushed it wide. The place was completely silent, though filled with a strange, expectant humidity. Elizabeth and Henry moved inside, already lighting lanterns. I closed the door behind me, and the serrated shadows of saws and shovels leaped about the walls like goblins.

The huge work table blocked our view of the hole we'd dug, and as we walked around the table, gooseflesh prickled up my arms. Step by step we drew closer, our lanterns high. In the swinging light I made out a dark lump at the bottom of the hole. We kneeled.

Right away I saw this was no mere lump. It was bigger, unmistakably bigger, and it had changed entirely. What we had fashioned yesterday with our hands – a muddy, plumped-up gingerbread man – had transformed itself into the fully formed shape of a baby.

'It's working,' I whispered.

'He's flipped himself over,' said Elizabeth.

Already to her it was *he*. I was mute with wonder, staring. It had moved. We had formed it and left it on its back, and it had *moved* on its own. Many times I'd seen William sleep just like this, on his stomach, knees drawn up, rump raised in the air.

'It's miraculous,' whispered Henry.

Its face was turned from us. Its body was mud-coloured, chafed in places. I noticed the straight, knobbed line of its spine, its tiny feet and toes. We hadn't fashioned those toes. They had developed overnight of their own accord.

Henry and I turned to each other, shaking our heads in

awe. I looked now at the hairless head, which seemed large in comparison with the rest of its body.

'Is it normal?' I asked. 'The size of the head?'

'Of course,' said Elizabeth. 'Babies' heads always seem larger than the rest of them. But I'm going to turn him over. I'm worried he can't breathe properly with his face in the dirt like that.'

'What makes you think it needs to breathe?' I asked.

She looked over at me in surprise. 'Of course he needs to breathe.'

'I'm not sure it's properly alive,' I said, recalling the searing torrent of images from the cave writing. Had the mud man breathed, even as it had grown?

Elizabeth reached down with her hands.

'Wait, wait!' I said. 'You shouldn't touch it!'

Elizabeth sighed impatiently. 'Why ever not?'

'In the images I saw it was never touched. It . . .' I couldn't put it into words, the sense that the mud body was a thing of the earth and neither needed nor wanted human intervention. 'I just think—'

But I was too late, for Elizabeth had already reached down and taken gentle hold of the mud creature. I felt myself tense as her skin touched its skin. One hand supported its head and neck as she tenderly turned it onto its back.

'He's warm,' she breathed. 'And the skin feels like real skin.'

I'd expected her only to adjust its position, but she lifted it clear out of the hole and cradled it against her body.

Once more, unaccountably, I tensed. 'Elizabeth, you should put it down.'

Blissfully ignoring me, she said, 'Look at him, you two. Just *look* at him.'

For the first time I saw its face. Its finger-poke eyes had become serenely closed eyelids. The pinch of mud that had been its nose was now a smooth button with two delicate nostrils. The mouth that had been hastily traced with a fingernail was now a sweet bow-shaped pair of lips, parted slightly.

I willed my shoulders to drop, my stomach to unclench. Why had I not wanted Elizabeth to touch it? Was I afraid it would break? Was I afraid of what I might see in its face?

I looked down to its chest. At the place where we'd buried Konrad's hair twined with the butterfly spirit, there was a faint blemish, like scar tissue.

The chest flinched once, then again and again, rhythmically.

A heartbeat!

Last summer in my makeshift dungeon laboratory, when

I'd made my first alchemical substances, I'd felt a surge of accomplishment and pride, but that was nothing compared to the fevered exhilaration I now experienced. I'd helped create this with my bare hands. But even so, a rogue thought shouldered its way into my head.

I've helped create a rival for Elizabeth's affections. Am I insane?

I watched, mesmerized. Was it breathing or not? And then it came, a slow gentle rise of the chest, and with the exhalation a supremely contented sigh issued from its little mouth.

With sheer delight Elizabeth beamed at us.

'It's working,' she said. 'It's Konrad, growing.'

'Do you see what this means?' I exclaimed. 'That butterfly spirit, it must be some kind of vital spark, the stuff of life itself! We've used it to create life!'

'Will it just sleep and sleep as it grows?' Henry asked.

'That seemed to be the way,' I replied.

I had the strangest sensation, watching Elizabeth hold it, seeing the raw love and tenderness in her eyes. She would never look at me like that. Perhaps she'd never even looked at Konrad quite like that. This was something else, something I remembered seeing on Mother's face when William and Ernest were babies. And then, with a small shiver, I wondered if this made me the father of this mud creature.

Elizabeth and I had made this odd little baby together, both our hands shaping him in the earth. Eyes, nose, mouth, heart. We'd fashioned it from the clay. What a strange little family we were.

Its nostrils flared as it drew in breath.

'Does it look like Konrad?' I asked.

She gave a soft laugh. 'Can't you see it?'

'No.'

'You don't even recognize yourself, then,' she said in gentle mockery.

As though I'd inhaled some strange ether, I was suddenly aware of Elizabeth's potent new womanliness, and it caused a hungry stirring in me. My body hadn't forgotten how she'd pressed herself against me in the spirit world. I looked at the mud creature still cradled in her arms.

'You should put it down,' I told her.

Elizabeth lifted an eyebrow. 'You just don't like me holding him. Admit it! Only Victor's allowed to be the centre of attention.'

'Don't be ridiculous. It needs to be in the earth.'

'Does he really? Or are you just making that up?'

I tried to rein in my temper, never easy at the best of times. 'I was the one who read the cave writing. And I'm telling you, the mud man was never touched, and it stayed in the ground the whole time.'

Disconsolate, she looked at the hole in the floor. 'It seems too cruel.'

More gently I said, 'It can't grow otherwise.'

I gave a small jerk of surprise as the creature's little arms flexed suddenly. Its head wobbled from side to side, its eyelids squeezed tighter, and its mouth turned down with displeasure.

'It's waking,' I hissed. 'Put it down, now!'

Elizabeth hesitated, and I angrily reached out to take it. But she held it tighter against her.

'He's hungry, Victor. Look!'

It was blindly nuzzling against her blouse.

'You can't feed it,' I said irritably, for I found the sight both embarrassing and arousing. 'It doesn't need food.'

'Clearly he does,' said Elizabeth, for the creature was even more agitated now, and from its mouth came a small unearthly cry. I'd heard many babies cry in my life, and each one was uniquely different, but there was something about this sound that raised the hairs on the back of my neck, a keening rattle, like the wind blowing through naked branches.

'Poor little thing. He's parched!' Elizabeth said. 'There's milk in the hamper. Hold him a moment, Victor.'

'This wouldn't have happened,' I muttered, 'if you'd put it back sooner.'

'Just take him,' she said, and I was acutely aware that I did not want to hold it. I'd held William many times and knew how to do it properly, but the moment this mud creature was in my arms, it began to wail. I felt its little body tense, and its limbs flailed about in fury. Its eyes remained closed, for which I was strangely grateful. No doubt it would urinate all over me shortly.

'Ah, Victor, he has your temper,' commented Henry wryly. 'What a surprise.'

'Care to hold it?' I snapped.

Henry hesitated for a moment, eyes wide, and then surprised me by nodding. I gratefully deposited the thrashing thing into his arms, and stood back to enjoy Henry's suffering. He had no siblings, no experience dandling babies and jollying them along as I'd had. But the moment the mud creature left my arms, its wails quieted. Henry held it well, I must admit, snugly against his chest, swaying it gently from side to side while mumbling something that sounded like *Shoo-ba-labba-shoo-ba-labba-shoo-shoo.*

'*Shoo-ba-labba-shoo-shoo?*' I said mockingly.

'I don't know where it came from,' he replied a bit sheepishly. 'Perhaps my mother sang it to me.'

'It did the trick,' Elizabeth said, shooting me a withering look as she returned with a jar of milk. 'You have a father's touch, Henry.'

The pleasure at this compliment blazed from Henry's face like a beacon. Elizabeth unscrewed the jar of milk, dipped a rag into it, and then pushed a sodden corner between the creature's lips. It grunted and proceeded to suck hungrily. While Henry held it, Elizabeth fed it until its lips grew lazy and its body limp.

In silence I watched this whole scene, and then noted the way Elizabeth smiled up at Henry, how Henry smiled back, as if they'd just shared something profound and immensely satisfying.

'It's asleep,' I said tersely. 'It needs to go back now.'

Biting her lip, Elizabeth looked down at the hole. 'At least let me put a nappy on him.'

'You brought a nappy?' I asked.

'And a blanket.'

I sighed. 'Honestly.'

'He might get cold,' she protested. 'He's just a little baby. How can you be so heartless?'

'There's no point pinning on a nappy,' I said. 'It'll be too small within hours. It'll only hurt it.'

'Oh,' she said. 'I suppose you're right. May I?' she said to Henry, reaching out for the baby. She took it carefully in her arms, smiling. Then, with great reluctance, she placed it back in the hole. Even I had to admit it seemed a pitiful sight. Henry must have gone to the hamper for the blanket, and he gently tucked it around the baby.

'Is it even safe to leave him here?' Elizabeth asked worriedly.

'Yes. No harm will come to it.' I closed my eyes to better remember the images from the cave. 'Even animals wouldn't go near it. They were . . . afraid.'

She still knelt by the hole. 'Maybe we should bring him inside the chateau.'

I looked down at her in horror. 'We can't risk it! Someone'll see!'

'But what if he wakes up and cries?' She looked truly distressed. 'I'd want to be there to comfort him.'

'It woke only because we disturbed it.' I scratched at my forehead, feeling somehow that we'd made a mistake, but it couldn't be undone now. 'All it's meant to do is sleep and grow. It doesn't need food. It doesn't need us.'

'Why do you keep calling him "it"?' she demanded angrily. 'This is your *brother*, Victor.'

Not yet, I thought.

'We'll come and check on . . . *him* . . . tomorrow,' I told her placatingly. 'And every day. He'll be fine. I promise.'

I offered her my hand to help her up, and she took it.

'I'm sorry I snapped at you,' she said with an apologetic smile. 'I'm just a bit . . . overwhelmed by all this.'

I gave her hand a quick squeeze, and she squeezed back before releasing me.

'Tonight we'll have to return to the spirit world to tell Konrad all is well,' Henry said.

I looked at him, saw his eagerness, and grinned. I was glad I wasn't alone in craving the spirit world. In Elizabeth's face I saw hesitation.

'You must come,' I said to her. 'It'll ease Konrad's mind. Time moves so strangely there. It might seem to him an age has passed and we've abandoned him.'

This melted her hesitation. 'Yes, all right. Tonight, then.'

And we left the cottage, and our strange sleeping mud creation.

CHAPTER NINE

A CELEBRATION

'Your body's growing!' Elizabeth tells Konrad, exultant. 'It's working. We'll have you back!'

'You're a bit odd-looking at the moment,' I say with a cheeky grin, 'but I'm sure you'll turn out just fine.'

'You're already completely adorable,' Elizabeth reassures him. 'I can clearly see you in the shape of the face.'

'It seems he grows with great speed,' Analiese remarks.

'By tomorrow he'll no doubt be much bigger,' Henry adds.

Here we all are – three living, two dead – in the music room.

'Ancient writings have led us astray before,' Konrad says. He's trying to stay calm, but I can see the excitement in the angle of his shoulders.

'This was like no other writing I know,' I reply. 'Reading it was like *witnessing* the event itself. It was real, Konrad.'

He sighs, in wonder or sheer desperation, I can't tell.

'I hope you're right. When will . . . When will it be ready, then?'

Strange, all these sidelong conversations we're forced to have. He can never meet my eyes. I can gaze upon him, but he can only guess at me. I feel this inequality, but no pity. Our whole lives together, I was unequal to him, but when he returns, when I bring him back to life, things will surely be changed. The chessboard of our lives will forever be rewritten.

I'm bringing you back, Konrad. Don't forget that.

'I can't say,' I reply. 'But not long.'

Then he surprises me by turning in Elizabeth's direction and asking, 'You're sure you're not opposed to this enterprise?'

She shakes her head.

'You should see her coddling the baby,' Henry says. 'You'll be spoiled when you return to us.'

Konrad gives a laugh. 'I can scarcely believe it will work.'

'It will work,' I say, watching the numerous black butterflies flitting from person to person, showing off their colours briefly before darting off. There is such power in these things, so much knowledge to be unlocked.

'Have you heard any more of those noises from below?' Elizabeth asks with concern.

'From time to time,' says Konrad, and I can tell from his face he's trying to be brave for her. 'But no louder than before. Whatever it is, it's not moving.'

'Let's not worry about that,' I say. 'Tonight's for cele-brating! I've slowed the spirit clock. We should have music and dance. I'd play piano, but—'

And with a grin I remember: I have all my fingers here. I'm so delighted, I rush to the piano and sit down. I was never as accomplished as Elizabeth or Konrad, but my hands have a new confidence as they command a waltz from the keys.

When I look up, Henry is dancing with Elizabeth. Circling them like their own little solar system around the sun is Konrad with Analiese. Laughter mingles with my music, and I play faster. I cannot remember the last time I felt so heedlessly happy. Not for months; maybe not ever. Everything I desire is right here, right now.

'I wish I could dance with you as well, Konrad,' Elizabeth calls out to him.

'Me too,' he says, and then politely adds, 'though I'm most pleased with my current partner.'

'You're very kind,' Analiese replies. 'I'm a terribly clumsy dancer.'

'Not at all. But it might go smoother if you let me lead,' Konrad says with a chuckle.

I wonder how their touches feel to each other. Are they cold and dewy, or do they have a human heat to them? I also wonder how much time they've spent together here.

Surely they must constantly seek out each other's company, and maybe more. She is very beautiful. Is this truly the first time Konrad has held her?

I feel a thrill of pleasure course up through my arm, and look down to see that a butterfly has settled on my right hand, riding with my fingers as they cavort across the keys, no doubt enhancing my playing.

Beyond the windows I see the mysterious white mist, slowly churning, as if taking an interest in our doings. The glass shudders faintly, but I play louder to drown out the noise.

When I next look up, I almost trip over the keys. Dancing, Henry and Elizabeth fit perfectly in each other's arms, and I have never seen Henry look so straight and commanding. With every turn on the floor, Elizabeth seems to surrender to him. She smiles, and he says something that I can't hear, and Elizabeth laughs, a sound so lovely I want to lock it away so only I can hear it.

Can she actually be trying to make me or Konrad jealous? Is she punishing him for dancing with Analiese? I look at my brother and can tell he's distracted. Not even death can divide me from his thoughts. Although he cannot look directly upon them, he seems to sense the strange gravity between Elizabeth and Henry. A furrow appears in his brow.

My feelings of loyalty to my brother are quickly vanquished by my own jealousy. When I catch the look Elizabeth now gives Henry, my heart coldly compresses, for it reminds me of that look she gave me, on our first visit to the spirit world. Is the touch of another young man, *any* young man, enough to win such a look from her here?

I want that look upon *me*, and I want what followed – the animal abandon when we but touched.

I will dance with her myself.

I stand, and even though my fingers leave the keys, the piano still plays. In amazement I see, through the propped-open top, several butterflies flitting from string to string, continuing my song.

I laugh in delight and seize a violin from its shelf, taking up the bow. I've never studied the instrument properly, but a butterfly comes and settles on my bow hand, and when I stroke it across the strings, music soars from them.

'Ha! Look at this!'

Elizabeth glances over with a laugh. 'You're a prodigy, Victor!'

Is she complimenting me, or mocking me? I cannot be sure. After a few moments I set down the violin and grab a flute from its rack. A butterfly hovers over the stops, and the moment I exhale into the mouthpiece, the most delightful sound flows through it.

Elizabeth does not even react to this new feat, only whispers something into Henry's ear. He gives her the secretive smile of a man who has received something precious.

I can stand it no longer. I must put an end to their dance. I set down the flute and start to walk towards Henry to cut in. The waltz still careens from the piano, picking up speed. Everyone dances on, laughter and music swirling crazily around me. The very walls of the room seem to colourfully pulse in time to the beat, or to my racing heart. When I take her in my arms, what will happen? Will she pull free? Has she learned to master her desire for me, even here? Or will we embrace and kiss in front of everyone?

I do not care.

I tap Henry on the shoulder. 'May I?'

With a maddening confidence he steps back with a bow. I stretch out my hand and see Elizabeth hesitate, fear and desire intermingled in her hazel eyes. Her hand lifts towards mine.

'Take care of the music for us, will you, Henry?' I say dismissively.

'Of course. You'll need their help dancing, no doubt.'

I turn, an eyebrow raised. 'Henry, you envy my accomplishments?'

'Accomplishments? It's not your own doing. You're like

Wilhelm Frankenstein, painting his portrait with the help of those butterflies.'

I shrug. 'They choose their own master, Henry.'

'Why do they choose to help only you?' he demands, and I'm surprised by the anger that transforms his face.

'I had no part in it, Henry—'

'No doubt you think it's yet another sign of your brilliance?'

I'd meant to placate Henry, but his insult quickly erases any such intention.

'Why not? They seem discerning little fellows, so why not pick the most able master?'

'Your arrogance knows no bounds, does it?' says Henry, taking an aggressive step towards me.

Instinctively I shove him back. 'I didn't know you had such a temper, Henry Clerval!'

Music hurtles from the piano, heedlessly loud and out of rhythm. The whole room seems to tilt slightly.

'You need taking down a peg!' Henry says, furious.

I think I hear Elizabeth laugh. I feel reckless, drunk. Konrad and Analiese have stopped dancing and are staring at us in confusion and alarm.

'A fencing match, perhaps?' I shout at Henry.

'Excellent!' he hollers back. 'But you fence alone, without your little winged friends.'

'Fine by me! To the armoury!'

'You two, stop this!' says Konrad. 'What's got into you?'

But I scarcely hear him, and Henry and I stride angrily out into the hallway. The very walls pulse and flare their history as we pass, paintings and tapestries and coloured plaster, as though reacting to our wild moods. We race each other down the great stairs and along the main corridor. Several times a new wall thrusts itself before us, or an unfamiliar passageway beckons, but each time I hold out my hand and shout, 'I will pass!' and the familiar house materializes before me.

As if transported, we're suddenly in the armoury. My blood is up. With a puff of breath I dislodge the butterfly lingering on my finger and seize one foil, tossing the other to Henry.

He is much my inferior; it will not be a fair fight, but I don't care, so eager am I to scourge that look of contempt from his face.

'Victor, stop this!' I hear my brother say again.

'If Henry wants to reconsider—'

'En garde!' Henry shouts.

'Whatever happened to our mild little Henry Clerval?' I ask in feigned amazement. 'He's become a fearless warrior!'

'Sirs, please,' Analiese protests. 'We're meant to be celebrating.'

I glance over at Elizabeth, surprised I've heard no objections from her, no cries of dismay, and am taken aback to see her watching, silent, her breast rapidly rising and falling, and in her face is the unmistakable look of animal excitement. I almost don't recognize her.

It unnerves me enough that Henry strikes me against the chest with his bated foil.

'You see! Without the butterflies he's nothing special!'

The very walls of the armoury flash with all the weapons they've ever held – the maces and halberds and sabres – and all that cold hard steel ignites me.

'En garde!' I snarl, and strike him, in the chest. Then, before he can even parry, I strike him again, and again, the rules abandoned, my only goal now to humiliate him.

'Come on,' I say, knocking his parry out of my way. 'Strike me!'

'These are not the rules of play!' he shouts.

'Then make your own!' I dare him, and stab him once more in the chest.

Enraged, he throws down his foil and punches me in the face, sending me staggering to one knee.

Slowly, furiously, I stand. He is waiting, his fists raised before his chin like a pugilist, eyes burning. He is a jacket filled with fury, and I've never seen him like this before. All I know is that I want to hit him. Butterflies flutter over my head, as if offering help, but I wave them away. In my mouth is a taste like venom.

Konrad's voice is anguished. He is standing as close as he dares to us, one hand outstretched. 'Henry, Victor! Enough!'

But his words are of no consequence – we are untouchable to him, like gods – and I come at Henry with a yell. He ducks and punches me in the ear. The pain has a sound, as piercing as a scream. Instinctively I clutch the side of my head, raising my arm to fend off another of his blows.

'I've been taking boxing lessons,' he says with a wicked smile, 'and it turns out, I'm rather good at it.'

I try to strike him, but he nimbly steps back.

'But I had to work at it, Victor. It wasn't just handed to me by little butterflies.'

He hits me in the shoulder, the stomach, my right flank, until I topple to the floor. I check my face for blood, but there is none.

'Behold how the mighty have fallen!' Henry cries out.

And as he smirks down at me, two winged spirits land on my shoulder, and a terrible power courses through me.

'I have worked too, Henry, and *risked* for what I have.'

He sees the butterflies, and all the swagger leaves him. 'This isn't fair!'

But I will not be humiliated, and I stride towards Henry, whose confidence crumbles even as he raises his fists. He strikes at me, but I smack away his hand as I would a bug, and with my right arm deliver a blow so powerful that his feet actually leave the ground. He flies backwards and hits the floor.

Elizabeth rushes to his side. 'Are you all right?' she asks, and in her voice is not just concern but also admiration. Has she mistaken him for the victor?

Henry raises himself on his elbows and glares at me. 'You *coward*!' he bellows.

'Coward?' I exclaim.

I don't know whether it's the insult or the sight of Elizabeth kneeling at his side, but I am completely undone with rage. My head is pure noise – the mad discord of the piano still playing upstairs, the sound of rattling window-panes, and, from deep beneath the chateau, an agonized moan that might as well be my own.

'I will not be called a coward!' I roar, and snatch up my rapier from the floor, yanking the guard from its tip.

I rush towards Henry. He sees me coming and tries to scramble up, but I put my foot upon his chest and point my sword at his throat. The fear in his face thrills me.

I am invincible here!

'Take it back!' I spit.

'I–will–not,' he returns through gritted teeth.

With a yell I draw back my rapier, ready to thrust deep.

'Victor!' screams Elizabeth, and I turn to see her with Henry's rapier in her hand, unbated, aimed at my heart. 'Put down your sword!'

'You wouldn't strike me,' I say.

'Try me.'

I laugh and step back, lowering my weapon.

'Come now,' I say. 'This was just play. If it got a bit rough, so what?'

Elizabeth won't meet my eye, and I feel a keen sting of betrayal, and anger. How dare she try to congeal my power and satisfaction into something cold and shameful.

It takes me a moment to realize that the vibration in my pocket is the spirit clock. It seems as though a long time has passed.

'Our time's up,' I say, holding the clock up for the others to see.

Our goodbyes are subdued. I feel the tug of my talisman, urging me back to my bedchamber, where our bodies await. We hurry along the corridor to the grand staircase, the house strangely placid after its earlier shape-shifting riot. In my bedchamber I recline, my spirit body adjusting itself with supernatural certainty to its counterpart in the real world, and—

Returning, I rubbed at my face and neck, anticipating bruises, but there were none. When I stretched, there was no soreness in my ribs and stomach, either. Injuries in the spirit world, it seemed, did not cross over.

I glanced over at Henry and Elizabeth, and an uncomfortable silence stretched out as the three of us avoided one another's eyes.

'It seems,' I said after a while, 'that we got a little carried away.'

Henry scoffed.

'I'd just like to remind you, Henry Clerval, that you punched me in the face during a *fencing* match.'

'You told me to invent my own rules.'

'You two were both brutes,' Elizabeth murmured. 'You especially, Victor.'

'And what about you?' I countered. 'You had a sword pointed at my heart!'

'Only to stop you from killing Henry!'

'You didn't really mean to stab me, did you?' Henry asked.

'Of course not,' I said, hoping my uncertainty didn't stain my voice.

'You were both completely out of control,' Elizabeth said.

'Strange,' I said, 'I didn't see you objecting. In fact, you seemed quite *thrilled*.'

Her only reply was an impatient sigh, but I knew I was right. She'd observed our duel with the tense anticipation of a wild animal watching the brawl of prospective mates.

This brought me up short. Was that what it had been? Had Henry and I been *displaying* for her, so she could choose the finer specimen? The very idea made me indignant. Surely I didn't need to *prove* myself, especially alongside Henry? It was unthinkable that Elizabeth could harbour romantic feelings for him. In all the years he'd been our beloved friend, he'd been bookish and nervy and faintly ridiculous. Elizabeth had never shown the slightest amorous interest in him – to my eye, anyway, which, I had to admit, was often dim to such matters. I'd been virtually blind to her love for my own twin.

My certainty began to crumble. Henry was very fine with words, and Elizabeth prized that. And I'd not forgotten his aura of paternal strength when holding the mud creature. Then there had been the speed and hardness of his newly trained knuckles against my body. I looked at him anew. Could he truly be my rival?

'Are you really taking boxing lessons?'

He nodded. 'After our encounter with Julius Polidori, I thought it wise to learn how to defend myself without a sword.'

'You're already skilled,' I said grudgingly.

He raised his fists. 'Shall we spar again?' He gave a shy laugh, and for a moment he was the old Henry again. But when we shook hands, his grip was firmer than I remembered, and I wondered if it would truly be so easy to forgive the words and blows we'd exchanged.

'I'll not go inside again,' Elizabeth said. 'The place makes all of us mad, bad and dangerous to know. I shudder to think what we might do next. Let's all of us make a pledge. Until the baby's grown and ready to be reunited with Konrad's spirit, none of us will go inside again.'

With reluctance Henry nodded. 'I think that's for the best.'

'Victor?' Elizabeth said.

'I don't think it's fair to Konrad,' I objected. 'You know how erratically time passes there. You two do as you wish, but I'll go in from time to time, to give him the latest news and keep him company, just so he doesn't despair.'

Elizabeth looked at me, thoroughly unconvinced. 'How noble of you, Victor.'

That night as I slept, I dreamed I was in my room, having

just woken. The chambermaid had already been. She had left me fresh water, pulled open my curtains and opened the window, for it was a fine, fragrantly warm day.

As I lay back with a contented sigh, hands folded behind my head, I noticed a sparrow perched atop my bedpost. I watched it. It watched me. Suddenly I was frightened of it, what it might do. Then it darted towards me and flew right under the collar of my nightshirt. I felt its busy compact shape settle just below my left collarbone. It stayed very still, and so did I, for its tiny claws were sharp against my bare flesh, and I knew that if I moved or tried to grab the bird, it would struggle and its beak would peck and its claws would clench.

I lay frozen, not knowing what to do, this little sparrow at my breast like a second heart.

CHAPTER TEN

THE PIT

I t was very early when I woke – my clock said five in the morning – yet I felt completely rested. More than that, a tremendous sense of well-being coursed through me. I clenched my right hand tightly. Not even a ghost of pain lingered in my missing fingers.

I wanted to be up. I dragged my nightshirt off, and a small shadow darted across my chest and disappeared round my back. Hardly daring to breathe, I sat very still.

There is one on me.

It must have clung to me unnoticed when we returned last night. Unease gusted across my mind but was quickly overwhelmed by a blaze of excitement.

Hurriedly I dressed and made my way to the west sitting room, which Father had stocked as our temporary library. I lit a lamp and took down the thickest, most obscure tome from the shelf.

I opened it at random and peered down at the page of tiny script. Greek, by far my weakest language. Leaning close, I touched the text with my fingers. Within my calm and ordered mind, line after line translated itself for me, telling me of the exploits of the great hero Odysseus, returning home from the Trojan War.

I withdrew my hand and sat back, breathing quickly. It was incredible! It was just like in the spirit world, when the butterfly had helped me in the Dark Library. Restlessly I closed the book and stood, pacing. I could not stop smiling. The spirit sharpened my mind. It healed my hand. What else might it do for me?

Impulsively I made my way down the grand staircase and let myself out into the courtyard. The air was pungent with the earthy smells of night-time.

Standing still was impossible. I ran out of the courtyard and down the curving drive. As I turned onto the lake road, my energy was boundless. My strides lengthened, knees lifted high, arms knifing the air. The sky was gaining colour. The road stretched out ahead of me, and I never wanted it to end. My breath was deep and tireless. I could go for ever.

I lost track of how long I ran, but when I stopped, I realized I'd already reached the village of Bellerive, a good ten-minute trip by horse and cart! The sun cleared the eastern peaks, and light glittered across the surface of Lake Geneva. I began laughing with sheer joy.

With this spirit upon me, I was invincible.

* * *

Returning to the chateau, I stopped short at the entrance to the courtyard, for I recognized the low murmur of voices from within. I peeked around the stone wall and saw Elizabeth and Henry taking a stroll together.

My exhilaration cooled. Had Henry noticed she was an early riser and come down hoping for a few moments alone with her? I'd hardly forgotten the looks she'd bestowed on him the night before, and the way she'd rushed to his side during our duel. Could Henry actually think he had a chance at winning her?

As I watched, he passed her a folded piece of paper and said something I couldn't hear. Elizabeth nodded and put it into her pocket, and then Henry went inside.

I waited until Elizabeth too went inside before entering the courtyard. My body had a keen appetite for breakfast, and my heart felt an altogether different kind of hunger.

'There's something we need to discuss,' I said later, as the three of us walked towards the cottage with our picnic hamper, to check on our mud creation.

'What's that?' Henry asked.

All morning I'd detected a slight coolness from him. No doubt he was still wary of me after our duel. And Elizabeth too had seemed more reserved than usual during breakfast and our shortened lessons with Father.

'What will happen when Konrad comes back?' I asked.

Elizabeth frowned. 'How do you mean?'

'How will everyone react? Konrad walks in and says, "Oh, hello. I'm back," and . . . I have trouble imagining what follows. But it involves screaming and horror.'

Elizabeth took a deep breath, and I knew she hadn't yet allowed her thoughts to explore this uncomfortable question. 'There'll be surprise at first, certainly—'

'Surprise?' I said with a laugh. 'They'll think him a ghost or demon!'

'Your parents don't believe in such things. You know that.'

'I wasn't thinking so much of my parents. They'll be shocked at first, but their joy will blot out whatever doubts they might have. What mother wouldn't welcome her beloved son back, whatever the means? No, I was thinking more of our servants, and the people of Geneva in general.'

'They won't be so open-minded,' Henry said. 'When news gets out, we'll be accused of consorting with the devil.'

'Maybe not,' said Elizabeth hopefully. 'Those with faith will see it as a miracle. Those without will see it as a . . .

wonderful mystery. And after a few weeks . . .' She trailed off, at a loss.

'Our family will be reviled,' I said firmly. 'It wouldn't surprise me if a mob came to burn our home and us within it. We'd have to flee Geneva altogether, abandon our ancestral home, and try to start a new life in some far-flung barbaric place.'

Henry looked over at me sharply, alarmed no doubt at the thought of Elizabeth being torn from his life.

'That's a drastic plan,' he said.

I almost smiled. 'Indeed.' I waited a moment before saying, 'There is one other plan that might work.'

The solution had presented itself to me this morning at breakfast, gleaming and perfect in my enhanced mind.

'What is it?' Elizabeth asked eagerly.

'We need to send him away at once. It's not so draconian,' I added hurriedly, seeing the surprise and hurt on her face. 'When we bring him back from the spirit world, we'll let Mother and Father know but keep it secret from all but the most trusted servants, if any. He'll be sent away under an assumed name. To Italy. Or even farther, preferably. Greece, perhaps, where he'll be amply provided for, housed, schooled. He'll grow a beard and bleach his hair and become tanned, and then when some months have passed, he'll return to us as a distant cousin.

He'll have a new name, of course, but he'd still be Konrad and he'll live with us happily ever after. And no one but us will know the secret!'

Neither of them spoke for a moment. Then, sadly, Elizabeth remarked, 'It seems too cruel, to send him away the very moment we bring him back.'

'But it's only for a short time, so he can return to us *for ever*.'

'Oh, I can see the cold logic of it,' she replied, looking at me with a suspicious tilt to her chin.

She knew me well, but I governed my temper. Gently I said, 'I know it's hard. But after all we've already suffered, it's only a small sadness, and it's the only practical way of guaranteeing that Konrad can rejoin us properly. Unless, of course, either of you have a better plan.'

She nodded reluctantly. 'I can't think of any better. You're right, Victor. It seems to be the only way. Thank you.'

When I unclasped the lock and opened the cottage door, I heard a small, furtive sound, then a guilty silence. Quickly we moved inside with our picnic hamper and closed the door. I lit a lantern. What would my mud creature look like today? We walked around the table. In the hole was nothing but a tangled blanket, spattered with blood.

'Where is he?' Elizabeth gasped.

Henry swung his lantern high, splashing light around the cottage.

'What if some animal got him?' Elizabeth cried.

'Impossible,' I said, looking all about. 'Animals are frightened of it.'

'Then, where is he?' she demanded, near hysterics.

'It's moved, that's all. It's just woken up and crawled . . .'

Could I have been wrong? Could a fox have taken him in the night?

'You said he wouldn't wake up!' she cried, peering behind timbers.

I heard a noise from a cluttered corner and rushed over, instinctively grabbing a pitchfork. My lantern swung wildly. A pair of eyes eerily flashed back the light. Something small and swift scuttled on all fours behind a broken wheelbarrow. Cautiously I stepped closer, lantern held high, pitchfork at the ready. Cringing against the wall was the naked mud creature, its tiny face ghoulish with spattered blood.

'He's been hurt!' Elizabeth cried at my side.

'No,' I said dully, 'it's been eating.'

Scattered all around in the dirt were the gory carcasses of small animals. Several mice had been devoured, fur and all, with nothing left but their crushed heads. A rat had been chewed open and most of its innards consumed. In the mud creature's hands was still clutched the red and sinewy remains of what must have been a chipmunk, judging by the tail.

'Good Lord,' murmured Henry, looking distinctly ill in the lantern light.

'He was hungry!' said Elizabeth. She stepped closer and said soothingly, 'Konrad, it's all right. Don't be frightened.'

It was the first time she'd named it, and my skin unexpectedly crawled. She hurriedly dragged the wheelbarrow out of the way, and knelt.

'There, there, my little one.'

It made a small whimper and crawled towards her. She enfolded it protectively in her arms and stood up.

'Could someone please get me a cloth and some water?' she said.

Immediately Henry went to the hamper and returned with a damp cloth. I was left the task of holding the lantern so the two of them could gently wash the clotted gore from the mud creature's face and hands.

'There now. That's better, isn't it?' said Elizabeth.

It had grown to the size of a three-year-old. Its skin had lightened to the colour of clay fired in a kiln, but there was no longer any hint of mud about this creature. Its skin was as soft and supple as any human's, and it looked to all appearances like a normal toddler. It yawned, and I wasn't surprised to see that its baby teeth had come in.

'Incredible, that it could catch so many,' I said, my eyes straying back to the slaughter behind the wheelbarrow. Had it hidden and lain in wait for them as they'd sniffed about, flashing out a little fist to squeeze the life out of them? Or had it actively pursued them, crawling with supernatural speed, pouncing upon them, jaws wide?

'He was starving, Victor,' Elizabeth said impatiently. 'I was afraid he might be.'

'It wasn't supposed to wake up.'

'Well, he did.'

'This is what comes when you interfere with things,' I snapped back.

'It's pointless to argue about it now,' she said. 'We have a child that's growing very quickly, and he's hungry.'

'I'll bring some milk from the hamper,' said Henry. 'He must be thirsty, too.'

I exhaled in exasperation, angry with Henry for playing such a perfect nursemaid – and angry with myself, too, for I hated being proved wrong. I'd been so certain the creature wouldn't wake again. Nor would it have, if Elizabeth hadn't meddled with it.

At the sight of the milk bottle, the creature greedily reached for it with both hands, seized it, and pulled it to its mouth. A good deal slopped over its face and body, and Elizabeth's dress, but it drained the bottle in short order and then looked about pleadingly for more, making an anxious whine.

Henry spread our picnic rug and hamper on the dirt floor, and Elizabeth sat down with the child on her lap. She wrapped it in a blanket and began to set out the food. From her fingers Elizabeth fed it morsels of bread, cooked ham, salted fish – and it devoured them all.

I examined it carefully, this creature formed from mud, this being I'd helped create. In the space of a single day and night, it had transformed from a baby to a toddler. It was hard to comprehend the speed of such growth, the stretch of bone and flourishing of vein and sinew and muscle. Already this creature was much larger than our little William.

Most unnerving of all, it was getting more difficult for me to think of this creature as an *it* when I could now see myself and my brother in its features. Mother had had a portrait of Konrad and me painted when we were three, and the resemblance was striking.

The child gave a belch, spitting up some milk and food, and pushed away the bit of apple Elizabeth was offering. I winced at the sour odour, but Henry showed no distaste as he mopped up the child's mouth.

'Apple,' said Elizabeth, bobbing one before it. 'Apple.'

The mud child's eyes followed the piece of fruit, but there was a curious blankness to its gaze.

'It's nothing but appetite and impulse,' I said. 'There's no point trying to teach it anything.'

Elizabeth frowned at me, as though I might have hurt the creature's feelings. 'He has every part a person should have, except a soul. Learning will help him, surely. And I don't see how it can hurt.'

She sang a silly nursery song to it, and its dark eyes widened slightly.

'This is a rather good one,' said Henry, and recited a nonsense poem I remembered from my own childhood.

The child seemed suddenly restless, and squirmed from Elizabeth's lap. In a second it had crawled over to Henry and was reaching up for him. Henry laughed with un-disguised pleasure.

'He appreciates fine verse,' he said.

'As do many of us,' Elizabeth said, and chuckled.

Henry took hold of the child's hands, and it pulled itself up to standing.

'Its legs are strong,' I said, though it should have come as no surprise. This same strange child had chased down mice and rats and killed with its tiny fists.

'He'll be walking soon,' Elizabeth said proudly.

'Very soon,' I agreed, wondering if it would occur to the mud child to try to escape the cottage.

'You still think it humane, or safe, to keep him here?' Elizabeth asked me, with her chin at a challenging tilt.

I looked at the child carefully, at the lack of expression in its eyes, and I truly thought it was an empty vessel. 'It seems it wakes only to eat,' I said. 'We'll leave all the food and water beside the hole. If it wakes again, it'll have more than enough to keep it going until we visit tomorrow.'

As if to corroborate my claim, the child's eyelids were already drooping with fatigue, and it crumpled asleep into Henry's arms.

'I'll settle him, then,' said Henry, placing the child's naked body carefully back in the hole.

Elizabeth was ready with the blanket, and tucked it carefully all around. Then she went back to the hamper and returned with an old doll of Ernest's, a uniformed man made of soft felt.

'It doesn't need that,' I said.

She knelt at the edge of the hole and slipped the doll under the blanket, against its chest.

A small crease appeared in the mud child's forehead as its nostrils twitched, then flared, inhaling deeply. Then it exhaled and slumbered blissfully beneath its blanket.

As we entered our house, our housekeeper Maria was scudding like a storm cloud through the hall.

'Is anything the matter?' I asked.

The corners of her mouth turned down. 'It seems they've discovered something else beneath the house now. I heard one of the workers muttering something about bones. I don't know why your father allows this, now of all times.'

'Where's the professor?' I asked.

'Upstairs talking to your father, I believe,' she said.

We hurried to his study and knocked on the door.

'Ah,' said Father, admitting us, 'your timing is uncanny. You'll have an enthusiastic audience, Professor.'

The professor's face was blanched with grit, but through the chalky dust I could see a brushstroke of high colour in each cheek. He was pacing, and his bearlike chest swelled with barely restrained enthusiasm.

'What's been discovered?' I asked.

'Something momentous,' he said. 'I was just about to escort your father.'

My stomach was knotted with excitement as we made the descent into the caves. It was an altogether different world from our previous visit. The place was lit as brightly as a Geneva street. As we ventured through the wondrous galleries of horses, bulls, and stags, we passed artists at easels, sketching.

'They're in heaven,' the professor said with a laugh. 'They say they've never seen images so vital. Their work could fill the Louvre already.'

Farther along one young scholar tapped at the rock with a small hammer, collecting shards, while another stood upon a ladder, examining the soot marks upon the ceiling. We passed the bear and the sly tiger, and when the passage branched, I felt an eerie lack of surprise when the professor chose the same route I had taken in the spirit world. I noticed that a rope had been staked into the wall, guiding us, turning by turning, to the high-domed chamber in which towered the giant brushstroke man.

'Extraordinary!' my father exclaimed, and I made sure to make a gasp of amazement, to conceal the fact that I had visited this chamber before.

'A human figure at last,' the professor said proudly, 'and what a colossus he is!'

The chamber was brightly illuminated, and yet when I glanced at Elizabeth, her expression was uneasy, and Henry's eyes were fixed intently on the passageway that slanted steeply downwards.

'Who was this fellow, do you think?' my father asked.

'Clearly someone held in great regard,' the professor replied. 'Those markings underneath no doubt have a tale to tell.'

'Have you any better idea of their meaning?' I asked.

'Alas, no word yet from my colleague in France.'

From the slanting passageway echoed a moan, followed by the slow, gritty scrape of heavy footfalls. I swallowed and took a step back.

'Dear God!' Henry said in a choked voice.

All at once an enormous shadow unfolded itself from the passageway, and Elizabeth stifled a scream. A large man stepped out into the chamber, rubbing his head.

'Very sorry to have startled you, miss,' he said apologetically. 'Just banged my head on the way up. It's wickedly steep.' He walked to Neumeyer and handed him a notebook. 'The measurements you asked for, Professor.'

'Thank you, Gerard. You left some lanterns burning?'

'I did.'

'What's down there?' Elizabeth asked hoarsely.

'Ah. Most wondrous of all,' said the professor. 'Though, if you're of a delicate sensibility, perhaps it's best you wait here.'

'I'm sure I'll be fine,' said Elizabeth, and I could tell she struggled to keep the annoyance from her voice.

'Very well.' The professor took up his lantern and handed another to Father. 'The way's steep and dark, but there are crude steps cut into the floor. They're slippery, though, so please be careful.'

In me was a ravenous curiosity. Since hearing that unearthly noise emanate from the passageway in the spirit world, I'd craved more knowledge of it. The way down was indeed perilous, the walls moist with dew, the shallow steps slick. Deeper into the earth the atmosphere grew decidedly more humid and carried an earthy hint of freshly turned soil.

'Are you all right?' I heard Henry ask Elizabeth.

She nodded, and I smiled to myself. I knew she was made of sterner stuff than Henry supposed.

From below I caught a faint flicker of light, but it was several long minutes before the passage levelled out abruptly and we found ourselves in a long narrow chamber.

Skeletons were laid out on crude shelves cut deep into both sides. Our lantern light blazed off the bones, ghoulishly animating them. Near the ceiling some skeletons had become calcified, almost overwhelmed by a blanket of white mineral moss, their gaping jaws disgorging strange spiky blossoms.

'A burial chamber,' said my father quietly. His voice was

subdued, and I couldn't help wondering if the sight reminded him, as it did me, of our own family crypt, and the body we had recently left there.

'It's quite a find,' said the professor. 'I don't think there's been anything like this discovered on the continent.'

'How old are these bones?' I asked, and I touched one with my fingertips. Instantly I had in my mind a sense of immense age, too old to fathom.

'Very old indeed,' said the professor, 'based on the strangeness of their skeletons.'

'How are they strange?' Elizabeth asked.

The professor stepped up to one of the best-preserved skeletons and held his lantern close. 'Take special note of the knee joints, and here, the skull. The thickness of them. I have never seen the like on any human being.'

Coldness ghosted over my skin. 'You're saying this fellow here was a giant?'

'This fellow is actually a woman,' he said with a grin made eerie in the swinging lantern light. 'And, no. Though brutishly built, they're roughly the same height as us. But I wonder if those buried here were actually human.'

'What else could they be?' Elizabeth asked, startled.

'It's very controversial,' the professor said somewhat uncomfortably, turning to my father, 'but I know that you, Alphonse, are a man of wide and liberal beliefs.'

'Speak freely,' Father said.

'There are theories, unpopular still, that we were not always as we are. Some think that before man was man he was something else. That over thousands, if not millions, of years we changed from one thing into another. These skeletons here may be what we once were. Before we became properly human.'

'The first Frankensteins, perhaps,' said Henry with a nervous attempt at laughter.

'Would this have been the tomb of an entire clan?' Father asked.

'Possibly,' said the professor. 'But these skeletons here are merely a prelude to something else.'

'Why do you say that?' Elizabeth asked.

'You will see.'

He led us farther along the chamber until it opened into a much larger one. At its very centre was a raised mound, encircled and entirely covered by a profusion of ornaments carved from stone and bone. As we drew closer, I saw that some were fist-size figurines of men or women. Others were carvings of animals – all the great beasts depicted on the walls. In wonder I knelt down to see them better.

'In many ancient cultures,' said the professor, 'it is common for a chief or shaman or king to be buried with family members or dignitaries who were chosen to share the tomb.'

'Those skeletons in the passage?' Henry asked.

'Precisely. But given their sheer number, and the profusion of ornaments here – and that wall image in the chamber above – I believe whoever was buried beneath this mound was considered a god.'

CHAPTER ELEVEN

A DOOR OPENS

I'd meant to wait till after midnight before making my entrance to the spirit world, and must have fallen asleep while reading on my bed. I woke with a start. The candle had all but burned down. Quickly I stood, walked to my shelves, and opened my chess set. Nestled beside the queen was the key to the bottom drawer of my desk. As I crossed the room, I faltered. Lingering in the air, like the memory of some spectral perfume, was the sense that someone, not long ago, had just been here.

Uneasily I opened the drawer, and stared in panic. The spirit clock and the green flask of elixir were both gone. Had we been discovered? Had Father stolen into my room and seized these things?

I took several deep breaths. No. Not Father.

Silently I crept out into the hallway and made my way to Elizabeth's bedchamber. What right did she have to confiscate my elixir, to try to control my actions? Inside my head angry words tumbled one over the other. Her door was locked, but I'd anticipated this and took from my pocket a slender two-pronged device I'd mastered at the age of twelve. In four seconds the door was open and I walked inside, my angry speech already rehearsed.

She was lying fully dressed on her bed. Her eyes were shut, each of her hands holding something. In her right I caught sight of the outlines of the spirit clock.

She was inside!

After all her talk of never going in again, she'd gone inside – and without me!

On her night table was the green flask. Hurriedly I drew out the dropper and let it drip once upon my tongue. I replaced it and sat down in an armchair. I pulled off my family ring to grasp in my hand. I had only a few seconds to wait before—

—I open my eyes in Elizabeth's empty bedchamber. At once I see a colourful butterfly launch itself from my body, and with a grunt of dismay I realize that this is the spirit, *my* spirit, that has been upon me all day, giving me such strength and mental agility. I stand and follow it out into the hallway, lifting my hand, but it flutters high out of reach.

'Come back,' I whisper, feeling a flicker of panic within me.

But almost at once it crosses paths with a black butterfly that spirals gracefully down towards me, its musical wings softly thrumming as it lands upon me. At once I feel the familiar pulse of energy and calm.

I hear voices, and pad silently down the hallway to Konrad's bedchamber. The door is ajar, and I peer inside. Konrad and Elizabeth are sitting as close together as they possibly can, talking tenderly. My brother has his head lowered to avoid her glare, and he certainly hasn't noticed mine. I open the door and stride in.

'You hypocrite!' I say to Elizabeth.

They both turn in alarm, Elizabeth with her hand to her chest.

'Victor! I thought you were fast asleep.'

'No doubt you stole them for my own good,' I say mockingly.

The surprise on her face becomes defiance. 'I did nothing of the sort, though it would've been good for you! You're not one to resist temptation easily.'

'Nor you, clearly.'

'And why do you get to keep them locked up in your room as if they belong to you alone?'

'I found them.'

'No more than Henry or me.'

'They're mine. And how did you know where I kept the key to my drawer?'

'You've been keeping it in your chess set since you were

204

twelve years old! I was going to return them as soon as I was done. Anyway, is it so wrong to want some time alone with the person I love most in the world?'

'Not at all,' I say dismissively, though her words sting. 'We had the same idea.'

She laughs. 'No, we didn't. You've come to see what's in that burial mound.'

'Well,' I say, taken aback at being caught out so swiftly, 'I'll admit to being slightly curious. So you told Konrad about what the professor found?'

From the moment I'd heard the moan from that slanting passage and had felt the strange energy wafting up from it, I'd known it was only a matter of time before I made the descent to find its source.

'Don't go, Victor,' Konrad says.

'You needn't come, either of you, if you're afraid,' I say, knowing this will light a fire under both of them. 'But I'll need to slow the clock, to buy myself more time.'

Reluctantly Elizabeth hands it to me, and I urge the supernatural gears to slow until they are scarcely turning.

'Victor,' my brother says, 'whatever's down there is dangerous.'

'We don't know that yet,' I insist. 'But if it's true, surely we ought to know about it.'

'True enough,' Konrad says with difficulty.

But I'm also thinking, *There's a power in that place, and I need to know what it is.*

At the threshold of the slanting passage, Konrad falters.

'I don't know if I can do it,' he says when I look back to see if he's following me and Elizabeth.

'You're safe with us,' I tell him. 'We're the living. Nothing can hurt you while we're here.'

His fear is etched deep into his face, but he takes a determined step after us, sword in hand.

Not a single menacing sound have we heard during our descent. Indeed, the caves have seemed eerily peaceful, the paintings muted. Now, as the slanted passage begins to level out, I see the skeletons on either side of the narrow chamber, exactly as they are in the real world. But when I enter the larger chamber, gone is the burial mound heaped with ornaments. Instead, in the room's centre is a huge open pit. A silent energy hovers over it.

'The skeletons are the same. Why isn't the mound?' Elizabeth asks.

I step closer. 'I don't know.'

I have no idea what to expect. At the edge of the pit I look down and down. It is extremely deep. At the bottom lies a vast hunk of whitish stone.

I stare harder, trying to peer deeper into time, to see

what was once here, but for some reason, even with a butterfly upon me, this thing defies my scrutiny.

'It's nothing,' I say, strangely disappointed. 'It's just a piece of rock.'

'No,' Elizabeth says in amazement. 'Look closer.'

She's right. Chiselled lightly into the stone's surface is the vaguest outline of a curled-up human figure, as though a sculptor had carelessly marked out his work and then abandoned the project.

Warily peering down, Konrad says, 'It reminds me of those pictures Father once showed us of the victims of Pompeii, fossilized by volcanic ash.'

'Only this is much, much older, if the professor's right,' I say. The stone seems so heavy and inert that it's difficult to imagine this is the source of the strange noises we've been hearing. And yet, from this object emanates an unmistakable aura, like heat off a hot paving stone.

'If it's so old, why is it still here?' Konrad says. 'Why hasn't it been gathered?'

'It's like it's been abandoned down here,' Elizabeth says. 'There's something pitiable about it. See how its knees are pulled up. It's like a baby in a stone womb.'

'Babies are meant to be born,' says Konrad numbly.

The huge stone jerks slightly, as though something within has moved. At the same moment a tortured moan wells from the rock's pores and rises to engulf us. I'm aware of Elizabeth and Konrad stepping back from the edge, but I'm frozen in place – not with fear but with fascination.

'It means to wake,' Konrad says. 'That thing will wake!'

And he's running up the passage.

'We must go with him,' Elizabeth says, hurrying after. 'He might get lost.'

With reluctance I turn from the pit and follow them, so I can lead them out of the caverns.

Emerging from the secret stairwell into the library, we find Analiese waiting for us.

'I saw the door ajar,' she says, 'and thought I heard your voices from below.'

'It must be killed,' Konrad says, still frantic. 'Is there any way to kill it? Victor, you have special strength and power. Can you kill it?'

'What have you seen?' Analiese asks, her eyes wide.

Konrad paces. 'There is a thing, a monstrous thing, in the caves beneath the house, trapped in stone. It needs to be destroyed.'

'Why do you assume it's evil?' I ask calmly.

'The thing positively reeks of malevolence!'

'I don't feel it,' I tell him honestly. 'We don't even know who or what it is. Who's to say it can even *be* killed?'

'It could simply be a soul waiting to be gathered,' Analiese says. 'Only, it's been here a long time to atone for a very great wickedness.'

'Yes, wicked enough to be here for thousands of years!' Konrad says. 'I shudder to think what it will be like when it's birthed from that stone womb.'

'You'll be long gone by then,' Elizabeth says reassuringly. 'Your new body will be ready in a matter of days.'

Konrad sags, momentarily calmed, but then shakes his head in distress. 'But what of Analiese? What if it wakes before she's gathered?' My brother looks in my direction. 'Victor, can you grow a new body for her as well?'

'Oh, no, sir,' Analiese says humbly. 'I would rather leave my fate in God's hands.'

'Ana, we can't just leave you here!'

'Ana,' I hear Elizabeth murmur, surprised by this endearment.

'No doubt it will seem old fashioned to you, but my faith in God is absolute,' the serving girl says. 'In any case too many years have passed. I have no place in the world now, no people of my own. Where would I go?'

'Well, we'd make sure you got a position in our household,' says Konrad impulsively. 'It's easily enough done, isn't it, Victor?'

All this time I'm watching Elizabeth, seeing the

jealousy that in the real world she would have ably concealed. But here it blazes on her face. She turns away and walks restlessly towards the library's French doors.

And I see that Konrad has given me a gift, all the more wonderful because I'm not sure I would have thought of it myself. He wants me to create a rival for Elizabeth.

'Well, I hadn't thought about any of this,' I say. I try to appear reluctant. 'It's no easy thing to achieve, but if you feel so strongly about it, I could find her grave and take—'

Analiese gives a blood-congealing scream, and I see her staring at Elizabeth. I whirl, and in shock see that Elizabeth seems to have tripped, grabbed hold of the door-knob of one of the French doors, and pulled it open.

At once crackling white mist pours itself into the room and resolves itself into a thick tentacle. With astonishing speed it slithers along the floor, aimed directly at Analiese. Thrice it winds itself around her ankle and jerks her off her feet, dragging her towards the open door. Shrieking in terror, she kicks frantically, clawing at the floorboards.

Impulsively I rush towards the open door, where Elizabeth stands frozen, watching, and throw my whole weight against it. I feel a strong, almost fleshy resistance and have to heave once more before the door squishes shut. Outside comes the shrill, enraged howl of a gale. It pounds at the glass, making the door shake.

At my feet the white tentacle thrashes about, its severed end spraying out an eerie vapour. But the thing still has abundant life in it and continues to whip Analiese about on the floor as she screams.

Konrad stabs at the middle regions of the thing repeatedly with his sword, but the tip scarcely pierces its misty skin.

'Let me!' I cry, and after only a moment's hesitation he tosses me his sabre. I seize it with both hands and drive it into the tentacle. Again and again I impale it, and quickly its thrashing weakens and it begins to dissolve before my eyes. Its tentacle grip on Analiese releases, and with a gasping sigh it all at once disintegrates.

Analiese tries to push herself from the floor but gives a whimper as her arms fail her. For just a moment her black dress flickers, and in that one blink of an eye, her beautiful figure frays and distorts, as though her spirit has forgotten its former bodily shape altogether. Even her mane of fair hair darkens, shrinking back as if burned. But she takes a deep breath, squeezes her eyes tightly shut, and is immediately herself again. It all happens so quickly, I wonder if anyone else has seen it, or if I merely imagined it.

Instantly Konrad rushes to her side and puts his arm around her shoulders to help her sit up.

'Thank God,' he says. 'Are you all right, Ana?'

Shakily she replies, 'Yes, I think so. Thank you, sirs . . . for saving me from that vile thing.'

'What happened?' Konrad looks over at Elizabeth in confusion, and I catch an almost accusing look in his eyes.

'I grabbed the doorknob to steady myself,' she says defensively. 'The door just sprang open . . . I'm sorry.'

'No, no, miss,' says Analiese. 'It was an accident. You mustn't blame yourself.'

We all look out through the glass and see the mist coiling and uncoiling, restless, predatory.

'Such malignant power,' mutters Konrad, helping Analiese to her feet. 'You're sure you're all right?'

'Quite fine, thank you.'

'You see how dangerous this place is, for both of us,' Konrad says pointedly. 'You must make Analiese a body as well.'

'No!' says Analiese with uncharacteristic force. 'I don't want my grave defiled. It's not right.'

'But—' Konrad begins, looking pained.

'I prefer to wait till I'm gathered,' the serving girl says, more mildly now. 'Though, I'm very grateful to you for such kind thoughts.'

In my pocket I feel the vibration of the spirit clock and pull it out.

'Our time's up,' I say.

'Goodbye,' Elizabeth says curtly to Konrad, and quickly leaves the room.

'I'll return tomorrow night,' I tell my brother, and wish, as I have so many times before, that we could embrace. In hopes of comforting him I say, 'Whatever that pit thing is, it's been here thousands of years and will be here thousands more. There's nothing to fear from it.'

He hurries after me to the library door. 'Victor, wait just a moment.' He lowers his voice so Analiese cannot hear us. 'Elizabeth seems distraught. What's wrong?'

I almost smile at how thickheaded he is, but I cannot bring myself to lie outright. 'She's jealous, Konrad. She thinks you have feelings for Analiese.'

I expect him to scoff at the absurdity of it, but he looks saddened, and slightly guilty.

'You've no idea how lonely it can be here,' he says quietly.

I nod understandingly. 'She's very lovely.'

He looks stricken. 'No, listen to me. No one could ever replace Elizabeth in my heart.'

But it sounds to me like he's trying to reassure himself. 'Of course not,' I say. 'I must go now. I'll see you again soon.'

I hurry down the hallway after Elizabeth. Along the way I see a second black butterfly and hold out my hand.

As if summoned, it lands upon my palm. I close my fingers gently around it.

Feeling slightly drunk, I enter Elizabeth's bedchamber and find her lying back on the bed. The very walls pulse with my surging emotions. For a moment I'm giddily confused. I am her lover, on a midnight assignation. Our eyes meet. I start to walk towards her, my desire for her an urgent drumbeat in my ears, but she tears her gaze away from mine and disappears.

With a sigh I check to make sure my butterflies still rest upon me, one on the shoulder, the other in my hand. I take my place on the armchair and—

Returning to my body, I found Elizabeth already sitting up on the edge of her bed, her eyes fierce in the candlelight.

'Did you see the way the spirit went straight for her?' she demanded.

'I hadn't thought of it,' I replied, perplexed. 'Perhaps it sensed our living power and—'

'But it showed no interest in Konrad!'

I frowned. 'What are you suggesting?'

'I don't trust her. From the moment I first met her. All her talk about an evil spirit. How do we know *she's* not evil?'

'Elizabeth—' I began, but she cut me off.

'Why's she still there at all? Why hasn't she been gathered?'

With sudden force a thought came to me. 'You didn't open that door on purpose, did you?'

'Of course not!' she said with too much vehemence. She looked away and shook her head. 'Honestly, I can't remember . . .'

'You might have destroyed us all!' I exclaimed. Even I was awed by such recklessness.

'I *wanted* to destroy her,' Elizabeth said with the dull incredulity of a dreadful realization. 'I can't control my passions in there, Victor. I was an idiot to go back. All I wanted to do was visit Konrad, on my own, without any distractions.' Her eyes flashed accusingly at me. 'I needed to see him, especially after that terrible night with the dancing and fighting, and the way I behaved. And it was wonderful to talk, just the two of us, and I felt so close to him, and then . . . when he started calling her Ana . . .'

'You mustn't be jealous of her,' I said.

'Always stroking her ear, to make sure he notices how pretty she is. She's been trying to win his heart. And I think she already has.'

'Don't be ridiculous,' I said with a surge of guilty joy.

'Isn't it obvious? He wanted to make a body for her! Bring her into our home!'

215

I exhaled, as if thinking hard. 'He was just being kind. And it does seem horrible, to leave someone behind.'

She nodded bravely. 'Kindness has always been one of his most lovable virtues.'

'Exactly,' I agreed, but not wanting her to feel too comforted. 'And remember, they've been each other's only company for weeks – and to them it might seem like much, much longer. I mean, one could hardly blame him if . . .'

I bit my lip to stop myself.

'Has he said something to you?' she demanded.

'About what?' I asked innocently.

'He loves her, doesn't he?'

Slowly I shook my head. 'Elizabeth, I don't know how anyone could love a person more than you. It would be madness.'

In the candlelight I could see that her eyes were wet.

'Please go now, Victor. I'd like to sleep.'

'Of course.' I stood, but before leaving I took hold of the spirit clock and flask of elixir. 'Good night, Elizabeth.'

And I left her bedchamber, knowing her heart was heavy, while mine was buoyant with unexpected hope.

CHAPTER TWELVE

TEETH

In my bedchamber I lit a single candle and stripped off my clothes. I set an empty flask upon my desk and sat down. I breathed calmly, my gaze drifting across my naked body, waiting. Before long I saw two small, compact shadows glide over my ribs and pause in the ridges of my abdominal muscles.

Slowly I closed my left hand around the open flask – then struck. It took me three tries to trap the shadow against my tensed flesh. I swiftly sealed the flask, the spirit's fluid darkness seeping up the inside of the glass.

I smiled.

That makes two.

'Victor? Victor!'

With a jerk I looked up, annoyed at having my concentration broken. Elizabeth stood over me, staring in bewilderment at the collection of books I'd piled around me at the table in the west sitting room. Judging by the light now filling the windows, I'd lost track of time.

Once again I'd woken very early. Hungry to fill my

mind, I'd come here to read. I'd been concentrating on the wonders of human anatomy, tomes in all languages under the sun. As I'd devoured the pages, I'd been scribbling occasional observations and questions in a small notebook. I closed it now, put down my quill, and looked back at Elizabeth pleasantly.

'Is it time for breakfast yet?'

'What are you doing?' she asked, and I saw her eyes take in my ink-stained hand, and the lamp I'd lit when I'd first arrived in darkness. 'You were turning pages like a madman.'

I shrugged. 'Just looking at the pictures.'

'Don't lie to me, Victor. You have one on you, don't you?'

I nodded. I saw no point in insulting her.

'Since when?'

'Two nights ago. It must have clung to me as I was leaving.'

Henry stuck his head into the room. 'Ah, there you are, Victor. If you want breakfast, you'd better hurry. They're starting to clear.' He must have seen Elizabeth's grave face, for he walked in and, more quietly, asked, 'What's wrong?'

'Victor has a spirit upon him,' Elizabeth whispered.

Henry looked at me uneasily. 'Is that wise?'

I laughed. 'It heals the pain in my hand! And it sharpens

my mind. These books, I can understand them so easily, and so quickly, just as I did in the spirit world!'

'And how do you know it won't also make you behave as you did in the spirit world?' Elizabeth asked.

I lifted my hands impatiently. 'Can't you see it? These things are little packets of vital energy. Just one of them has the power to grow a new body for Konrad. Life from death! Who knows if there's any limit to what they might help us achieve.' I paused. 'You and Henry could have one as well.'

Perhaps with one upon her Elizabeth's supernatural passion for me would be rekindled in the real world.

I saw Henry chew at the inside of his lip. He was tempted. But Elizabeth shook her head.

'They're powerful, I agree, and you're right. We don't know what they might be capable of. But for *that* reason we should be very cautious. Who's to know what they might do in the real world?'

'Ah, I see,' I said. 'You're happy enough for them to bring your beloved Konrad back, but not help me.'

'We all agreed to bring Konrad back. We made no further pact. On this you're acting alone, Victor.'

'So be it,' I said. 'But I don't intend to let this opportunity pass.' I looked at the books piled around me. 'There's too much to learn.'

'This is what worries me,' she said. 'You're too ambitious. And the spirit world has too strong a pull on you.'

'And you as well, it seems,' I replied. 'Have you told Henry what happened there last night?'

Henry looked at her in surprise, clearly hurt. 'You went in last night? *Both* of you?'

My stomach rumbled loudly. 'Elizabeth will tell you all about it,' I said, enjoying her obvious discomfort. 'Now if you'll excuse me, I'm off to have some breakfast before it disappears.'

It had grown.

The day before, we'd left a three-year-old, and now, entering the cottage, I beheld a child of six or seven. It was asleep in the hole, the blanket tangled about its torso and legs. Its skin had lightened still further and looked like human flesh in every way. It even had the characteristic Frankenstein pallor. The only hint that this creature had been birthed from mud was the clay-coloured scar in the centre of its chest.

The food we'd left had been devoured, none too neatly. And scattered among the remnants was something that took me a moment to understand.

'They're teeth,' I said, kneeling down and picking one up.

'His baby teeth,' Elizabeth said. 'He lost them all in one night.'

For some reason the notion made me slightly queasy, and I let the tooth drop back to the dirt.

'Let's leave the food and milk and be on our way,' I whispered. With luck we could just let the body sleep and grow until it was ready.

Yet Elizabeth looked at me askance, as if I were suggesting putting the creature in a reed basket and floating it out into the lake.

'Is that your idea of taking care of him?' she asked.

'What more can we do but shelter and feed it?' I replied.

I was trying to be quiet, but Elizabeth spoke in her normal voice, and it seemed to me she was hoping to wake the child up. I was glad to see that it showed no signs of rousing. I did not want to spend time with it. I would much rather have been back in the library, reading.

'Let's be off,' I said to Henry, and touched Elizabeth on the shoulder, but it was futile. Henry made no move to leave, nor did Elizabeth – and, sure enough, the little creature stirred, sniffing, and then its eyes opened. They locked first onto Elizabeth. For a moment it only stared, as if trying to remember her. She beamed down at it.

'Hello, little one,' she said.

It sniffed again and looked down at the doll she'd given it yesterday. Its eyes widened, and it grabbed the doll, sniffed it, pushed it against its mouth as if tasting it, and then pulled it away, peering at its miniature human features. Surely such a thing made no sense to the child, and I wasn't sure if it looked puzzled or if I was simply superimposing a feeling onto its blank face.

'It's just a doll, a toy,' Elizabeth said gently.

The child looked up, and when it crawled towards her, it tucked the doll under one arm. Elizabeth settled the child on her lap, wrapping her arms around it.

I wondered if she was trying to comfort herself, clinging to this facsimile of Konrad's young body, when she felt she might be losing Konrad's love.

'He should have some fresh air,' she said.

'That's a fine idea,' Henry seconded.

I shook my head. 'Are you two mad? What if we're seen?'

'Out here? No one comes this way,' she said.

'It's almost in sight of the chateau,' I told her. 'Justine might be taking Ernest or William for a walk—'

'He's seen nothing but the inside of a dark cottage,' Elizabeth cut in. 'He needs the sun, and sky.'

'No, it doesn't,' I said.

'I can't see how it could hurt,' said Henry. 'Just for a few minutes.'

I glared at Henry. I knew he was agreeing with every-thing Elizabeth said regardless of what he thought. Did he think he would impress her by being a little lap dog?

I looked at the child and offered my last defence. 'It's naked,' I said.

'I brought some old clothes of Ernest's,' Elizabeth replied cheerfully, and went to the hamper to pull them out. The child sat obediently while she pulled them on. It was quite a transformation. Clothed, it looked so much more like Konrad – and me – that I was startled, and a bit ashamed of myself. I knew full well this creature was not properly human yet, but to all appearances it was a fine seven-year-old boy, locked away in a windowless cottage like a prisoner. And yet I could still not think of it as *him*.

'What a handsome little fellow you are,' Elizabeth said. 'And heavy.' She grunted as she hefted it onto her hip.

I made them wait inside while I opened the door and took a good look outside the cottage. I saw no one in any direction.

'Just a short outing,' I said.

In the sun we spread out the picnic blanket. Still possessively gripping its doll, the child pressed it to its nose and inhaled. Then it turned its head to look in the precise direction of the chateau.

'Did you see that?' I asked.

'What?' said Henry, taking some food from the hamper.

'It sniffed the doll and then looked towards the chateau. It's like it could smell our home.'

'He probably just heard a noise,' Elizabeth said, and passed the child some ham, which it ate with great enthusiasm.

'He's surely strong enough to walk,' Henry remarked. Henry, I noticed, had no trouble referring to the child as a he, instead of an it.

He took the child's hands and pulled gently. Swiftly the child pulled itself up into standing. Henry stood and, stooped over, encouraged it to take a step. I was reminded of a puppeteer cajoling a marionette. For a moment the child did nothing, but then it lifted its left foot, planted it, and then, swaying, did the same with its right.

'Hah!' said Henry. 'His first step!'

'Well done, Henry!' said Elizabeth.

'Hurray,' I muttered distractedly, keeping a keen lookout, trying to think up some explanation in case we were surprised by someone.

The child took more of its grotesque steps, but ever more quickly and confidently. As Henry guided it over to Elizabeth, she stretched out her arms and caught the child up, kissing it on the head. But the child seemed restless and wriggled from her embrace. Standing, it turned to look at the forest that bordered the pasture. Perhaps something caught its attention, a squirrel in the branches, a bird taking flight, but it started walking, completely on its own, wobbly but determined.

'Look at this!' Elizabeth cried proudly.

Fearful it would wander off and be spotted, I stood and kept pace with it across the grass. It stumbled but kept going, more and more quickly. What a little bundle of impulse it was.

'Shall we turn around now?' I said when it neared the trees. I stepped in front of it, barring its way. The child's usual look of blank passivity was suddenly replaced by one of outrage. I'd seen Ernest and William in a temper when you crossed their wills, but they were still themselves. What startled me now was the utter transformation of this strange child's face. In its eyes something old and intelligent kindled, and a low growl rattled in its throat. Its brow creased, and its lips pulled back to reveal a quick glimpse of teeth, one of which seemed oddly shaped.

'Come back, Konrad,' said Elizabeth, approaching from behind with her hand outstretched.

At once the child's face resumed its usual expression.

'What's wrong?' Elizabeth asked, looking at me strangely.

'Nothing,' I said. Had I imagined it?

But that flash of teeth, and the split-second image of fury and intent on its face, unsettled me.

That night Father invited Professor Neumeyer to dine with us.

'We're proceeding very slowly on the burial mound,' he said, pausing to take a drink of wine. 'I'm allowing my colleagues to use only small spades so that we don't risk damaging the remains. We've excavated some four feet, and nothing yet. Whatever was buried, they buried it deep.'

'And the curious markings on the walls?' Father asked. 'Any progress deciphering them?'

'Ah, yes, indeed,' he said, and I forced myself to look away, for I feared my gaze was too intense. I avoided looking at Elizabeth and Henry, too, and concentrated instead on my roast beef.

'I still haven't heard from my friend in France,' the professor continued, 'but today my colleague Gerard, who specializes in languages, thinks he managed to puzzle out some patterns, using other primitive writings as a template.'

'So he's been able to translate some of it?' Elizabeth asked with an excellent imitation of detached interest.

'It's educated guesswork, mind you,' the professor said. 'But it seems to invoke some kind of ceremony involving the dead.'

I swallowed dutifully, and brought another forkful to my mouth.

'A primitive burial rite?' Father asked.

The professor shook his head. 'Resurrection.'

'Ah,' said Father, and he turned and looked directly at me.

I held his gaze as long as I thought natural. 'Fascinating,' I said, and lifted my glass and drank. My confidence returned.

He can suspect nothing, I thought.

What we are doing is beyond belief.

After dinner I put on a coat and walked out along the jetty. One of our rowboats was tied up alongside, and I stepped into it and stretched out to watch the sunset fade and the first stars appear. It had always been a favourite thing of ours, Konrad and me.

My mind sped me away from the chateau and up into the sky's vault. I used to imagine greatness for myself, but now I no longer needed to imagine it. With the spirit butterflies upon me, it was within my grasp. There was no knowledge that would remain hidden from me. All I'd ever desired would be mine. I would have Konrad. I would have Elizabeth. And more.

Planks creaked, and I turned to see Elizabeth walking

out along the jetty, reading something. It was quite dark by now, and she went right past without noticing me, so engrossed was she in the piece of paper. As she made her way slowly to the end of the jetty, she read aloud. Her voice was low, almost hesitant, as if afraid of revealing too much:

'She walks in beauty, like the night
Of cloudless climes and starry skies;
And all that's best of dark and bright
Meet in her aspect and her eyes.'

'Very pretty,' I remarked, sitting up in the boat.

She gave a small gasp as she turned, and guiltily began folding up the paper.

'Why do you put it away?' I said, stepping onto the jetty. 'Read on!'

'I—' She faltered, and then her eyes narrowed. 'What are you doing, lurking out here?'

'I didn't realize Henry was writing you little rhymes now.'

'Don't be absurd. Henry and I just critique each other's work.'

'No. It was written for you. *About* you.'

I knew this with absolute certainty. Those few simple

lines had captured her. But as jealous anger began to pump through my veins, I wondered how Henry could know her so well. Yes, he'd been her childhood friend for nearly a decade, but I'd thought only I comprehended her dark and light. And all along there was wispy Henry Clerval, observing and loving her from afar with his ink-stained thoughts.

'It would be presumptuous to think it was written *about* me,' Elizabeth said primly.

'Oh, please. He's completely smitten. He's wooing you. Let me read the rest!'

She clasped the parchment protectively within both hands.

'That good, is it?' I asked sarcastically.

'It's extremely accomplished.'

'Meaning *romantic*.' Damn Henry! His skill with a pen was immense. Just this past summer I'd asked him to write some words for me. How stupid of me not to realize he'd eventually start using them himself. And I knew how much Elizabeth valued poetics. I'd racked my mind earlier, urging its new sharpness to concoct some romantic phrases, but nothing had come. Matters of the heart, it seemed, would always elude me.

'I never thought Henry such a scoundrel.'

She laughed. 'That's rich, coming from you.'

'Well, he can hardly be blamed,' I said. 'After all the encouragement you've given him.'

'When have I encouraged him?' she demanded angrily.

'Oh, not in this world maybe, but in the other, when you danced with him. You're a veritable *temptress*.'

'If you were closer, I'd slap you,' she said.

'Let me help,' I replied, and stepped closer. She promptly slapped me, which surprised me only a little.

We glared at each other in the near dark, and then she looked away.

'I'm sorry I slapped you,' she said.

'That's all right. I quite enjoyed it.'

'I know how I behaved that night. That's why I needed to go back alone, to make sure I hadn't hurt Konrad.' She gave a bitter laugh. 'Of course, it seems it's *his* affections that have strayed.'

'No, no. I'm sure that's not the case,' I said half-heartedly.

'So why shouldn't I let *my* affections stray?' she said with a flare of defiance.

To this I made no reply.

She turned away with a sad shake of her head. 'The truth is, when I read Henry's poem, it's not Henry I think of.'

'Poor Henry,' I murmured. Not even his beautiful words could help him. 'He seems emboldened, though. He genuinely thinks he has a chance at winning you. If you let him write you poetry, you'll only hurt him.'

'I suppose I miss being admired,' she said.

'I admire you,' I told her impetuously. 'And I wish I could write you romantic things.'

There was silence, and I regretted my words. She turned round to face me. 'You don't love me, Victor,' she said gently. 'You fool yourself.'

'Don't tell me what I feel.'

'To you I could only be a possession, another thing to be mastered.'

'That isn't so,' I objected. 'I may not be able to pen you pretty verses. And I'll never be as reliable and kind and graceful as Konrad. I'm not perfect. But neither are you, and I love you all the more for it. You're wilful, and you have appetites bigger than you care to admit. But you're beautiful and intelligent, and I can't think of anything on this entire earth I more desire.'

She was looking at me the whole time I spoke. A small swell from the lake made the jetty tilt, and we both took a step closer. It was almost dark now, and I remembered how once, in total darkness, I'd tricked her into thinking I was Konrad and stolen a kiss. But right now she knew exactly who stood before her, and I was certain that if I bent my head to hers, I would not be stealing.

'I want you to be mine,' I said.

'I will be yours,' she whispered.

I knew I'd never hear four more thrilling words in my whole life. My body was alight as I leaned towards her mouth.

'But first,' she said, gently drawing back, 'you must make me a promise. Promise me you'll have nothing more to do with the spirit world. Rid yourself of the spirit butterfly. And never go back, except to return with Konrad. Do that for me, Victor, and I'll be yours.'

She stood before me, unutterably beautiful, patiently awaiting my reply.

'Why is it necessary to make such a choice?' I demanded.

'If you love me so much, it should be an easy one.'

'I can't make that promise.'

A sigh escaped her parted lips, and she shook her head, as if rousing herself from a daydream. She laughed softly, almost ruefully.

'Victor, I believe there is something on this earth you desire more than anything, and it isn't me.'

CHAPTER THIRTEEN

SLOWLY WAKING

A colourful butterfly rests upon my temple, a second on my hand. Knowledge flows into me in an unstoppable torrent. I am unquenchable.

In the spirit world library I sit amidst piles of books, mastering their secrets one after the other. I've slowed the spectral clock to an occasional meek tick. Perhaps I'll never be a poet or lover, but here, I am an engineer, an explorer, an architect of wonders.

An intricate passage on metallurgy stops me. I read it once more, but not because I don't understand it. Quite the opposite. I understand it perfectly, and a huge excitement builds within me. I stand abruptly, open the secret passage, and hurry down the steps to the Dark Library.

Inside I swiftly scan the shelves and find the slim green volume of alchemy by Eisenstein. It takes me only moments to locate the right page. My eyes sweep the text, my spirit heart skips a beat, and I smile.

'Victor?'

From the top of the stairs comes Konrad's voice.

'Yes,' I call back.

'How long have you been down here?' he says when he enters the Dark Library. He looks hurt. 'Why didn't you tell me you were here?'

'I was just on my way to find you,' I say guiltily, for I realize I've completely forgotten about him. But almost at once I resent feeling guilty. In a matter of days he'll live again – *my* doing! – and in the meantime there's so much to learn. 'There was something I needed to check.'

'Down here?' Konrad asks.

'Catch!' I toss the green book in his direction. 'Recognize it?'

He glances at the spine and starts paging through it. 'Didn't you use this to make the flameless fire?'

I nod. Last summer, during one of our adventures, we'd had to descend in a perilous cave system, and this particular tome had given me a recipe for a waterproof substance that burned without fire. The flameless fire had saved our lives.

'But it contains an even more beguiling recipe,' I say. 'Keep turning.'

I know from his surprised frown when he's found the right page.

'Is this Father's writing in the margin?'

'He tried to turn lead into gold, one of the oldest alchemical quests of all.'

'Father dabbled in alchemy,' Konrad says in amazement. 'More than dabbled, by the looks of it.'

'But he didn't succeed.'

Konrad looks up. 'How do you know all this?'

'I confronted him. I thought, since he'd used alchemy, he might help us complete the Elixir of Life. I was wrong.'

'Why didn't you ever tell me this?' Konrad asks.

'He asked me never to tell another living soul.' I can't help smiling. 'And I'm keeping my word to him. He was a young man when he did it; he was facing financial ruin. So he made a substance that *resembled* gold, and managed to sell it in foreign parts.'

'I wish you'd not told me this.'

'It's the truth. You should know.'

'So why's this little book so important, then,' he asks, 'if it contains gibberish like this?'

'It is gibberish. Riddled with fancies and mistakes. But I know how to fix them. Upstairs I was reading modern metallurgy and chemistry, and look—'

I hurry to a table, take up some paper and a quill, and begin scrawling out numbers and symbols, my thoughts assembling themselves so quickly that my hand can scarcely keep up.

'If you combine alchemical aspiration with the rigour of modern science, miraculous things are possible.'

When I finish, I slide the paper down the table to Konrad. He takes it up and shakes his head in wonderment. 'This makes no sense to me, Victor.'

'This formula,' I tell him, 'will make us gold!'

'How can you be so sure?'

'The butterfly spirits have thrown open the treasure vaults. Things that would've taken me weeks or months to learn, I absorb almost instantly with their help. And not just inside the spirit world. Outside, too.'

'You've taken them *outside?*' he asks in alarm.

I nod. 'They've healed the pain in my hand, quickened my mind, given me boundless energy. There's one waiting for you when you return to us.'

He says nothing.

'Trust me. Once it's on your body, you'll have no reservations. Didn't we always talk about having adventures? Imagine what we can do together, the places we'll go! We'll never fear being poor, like Father did. But gold's just the beginning. With these spirits aiding us, we don't need to fear even death. The entire world will be our dominion.'

'You talk as if we're a nation going to war,' he says uneasily. 'You're too passionate for your own good sometimes.' His eyes actually meet mine and hold their gaze. 'Your light's not as bright as it used to be,' he says, and then adds wonderingly, 'and your heat's less intense too.'

I shrug. 'You're just getting used to them, maybe.'

'Are you sure you feel well?'

'Don't worry about me,' I tell him firmly.

From the depths of the chateau comes a terrible gagging cry. Konrad's body tenses.

'That's a new sound,' I murmur.

'Yes, and they come more often,' my brother replies anxiously. 'I can't help worrying that it's . . .'

'Escaping?' I shake my head. 'From all that stone? I don't think so.'

Konrad nods, unconvinced, and I feel a rush of pity for him. I'm awash in power, and he is so helpless.

'Look, let me go and check,' I say. 'I'll come back and tell you.'

'Find me in the armoury,' he says. 'Practise helps clear my mind. Be careful, Victor.'

I set off, eager to calm my brother's worries but also impelled by the familiar curiosity. I want to gaze upon this thing again.

I check my spirit clock to make sure I have time, and then climb down into the caverns and run, streaking through the animal galleries. I pass the giant painted man and start down the steep passage to the burial chamber. At the pit's edge I peer down, and swallow back my surprise.

The huge mass at the bottom now looks less like stone

than a cocoon made of dense fibrous material. As I stare, the entire thing shudders. Beneath the surface I see a faint, confusing shadow. A segment of the grey cocoon bulges outward, revealing the shape of a hand – but a hand with fingers longer and larger than any normal hand. A heartrending wail blasts past me, sounding like a creature enduring unspeakable torture.

It has changed. There's no denying it. What was once stone has now softened. And whatever's inside seems more awake.

Suddenly from its surface a strange dark shoot erupts. As I watch in silent awe, it unfurls like some supernatural plant to a height of several inches. Then it thickens and becomes fleshier, almost like a pustule.

Within seconds it bursts, releasing a black butterfly. Timidly it circles about, slowly but surely rising with each stroke of its fledgling wings. In amazement I stare, my excitement mounting with every beat of my heart.

I have discovered their source.

I find Konrad in the armoury, practising his lunges against a dummy. For a moment I watch as his unbated sabre savagely pierces the dummy's shoulder, its gut, its heart.

'There won't be anything left of him before long,' I say.

He turns, tries to grin, and then just looks at me expectantly.

'It's a little changed. Not much,' I say.

'You're lying. I know you too well, Victor.'

'The stone doesn't seem quite as . . . thick,' I admit.

He paces, restlessly swiping his sabre back and forth.

'My new body, is it all right?' he asks.

'Of course. It's growing quickly.'

'How long till it's ready?' he demands.

I've seen fear in him before now, but this is desperation, crackling in his voice.

'Three nights.'

'Who's to say that thing won't get free before then?'

'I can't see how—'

'I want to *kill* it, Victor!' He strides over to the racks of weaponry and pulls down a crossbow and a leather quiver of bolts.

'How do you know you can kill it?' I ask.

Frantically he pulls down a halberd, a long sword, a shield. 'I don't know if I have the power. But you do.' He looks at me, a child's need for reassurance etched across his features. 'You killed that evil spirit when it was strangling Analiese. You can kill this. Kill it for me, Victor.'

My heart aches. 'I can't,' I say.

'Of course you can. You're the living. You have light and heat and—'

I stammer out an excuse. 'I – I don't think it deserves to be killed. I couldn't do it.'

I refuse to do it.

But I don't tell him this. That creature in the pit, whatever it is, is *birthing* butterflies, and I crave the power they give me.

'Then, I'll do it myself,' Konrad says, shouldering a crossbow and heading for the doorway.

'I can't let you do that,' I say, blocking his path with my light and heat. 'It's not safe.'

He winces. 'Stand aside, Victor.'

From down the corridor comes the sound of Elizabeth's worried voice. 'Konrad, are you there?'

'I'm here!' he calls out, and we both move back in surprise as she bursts into the armoury.

'What are you doing here?' I demand. 'Did you break into my room?'

'No. I'm in my own.'

'Then, how did you get the elixir?' I ask.

'I thought to take a small vial for myself the last time,' she says, unable to hide her pleasure at my shock. 'Why should you have the only supply?'

'But you came in without the spirit clock,' I tell her.

'What if I hadn't been inside? Do you have any idea how reckless that was?'

'Since when has recklessness bothered you, Victor?'

'You might've lost track of time and let your body die!'

'I only mean to stay a short time,' she says defensively, 'though it took me long enough to find you, Konrad.'

'What's wrong?' he asks, looking more worried than ever. 'Is something the matter with my body?'

'No, no, you're fine. Is Analiese around?' Elizabeth asks in a lowered voice.

'I don't know where she is,' Konrad replies. 'Why?'

'After all that talk of making a body for her,' Elizabeth says, 'I decided to find out a little more about her. It turns out there are household accounts of every servant employed here, going back a hundred years.'

'Where did you find those?' I ask in amazement.

'Maria's office. I crept in about an hour ago.'

'And?' Konrad says.

'There's no record of any young woman called Analiese who worked here and died of fever in the house.'

My brother is silent for a moment. 'Well, someone made an error and left her out.'

'The records seem very thorough,' Elizabeth says.

Konrad frowns. 'You're suggesting she doesn't exist?'

I'm not sure I've ever heard him speak so irritably to Elizabeth.

'She's not who she says she is!' Elizabeth says.

'Why would she lie?' I ask.

'I don't know, but I don't trust her. She must have a secret.'

A small cloud of black butterflies flutters into the armoury. They land upon Elizabeth and me, and then dart away on their brilliantly coloured wings.

Konrad shakes his head. 'Elizabeth, I can't believe it. She's only ever been kind to me, my whole time here.'

'You talk about it like it's a lifetime.'

'It *feels* like a lifetime,' Konrad shoots back.

Elizabeth's eyes flash. 'Well, why don't we make a body for her, and when you come out, you two can spend *another* lifetime together!'

Konrad looks truly pained. 'Elizabeth, you're mistaken. I'm not in love with her. I only wanted to rescue her from this place – and from that thing in the pit, which is waking! Victor, tell her!'

'It does seem more active,' I concur, and touch my pocket, for my spirit clock is at long last tapping, lethargically at first, as though waking from a long slumber, and then with an angry insistence.

'Our time is up,' I say.

For the first time Elizabeth seems to notice the weapons Konrad holds. 'You were going to attack it?'

Konrad nods.

'It's too dangerous, too rash,' I say.

He gives a hollow laugh. 'I never thought I'd hear you call *me* rash.'

'I beg you not to do it,' I say. 'Please.'

My twin frowns. 'What are you not telling me?'

'Listen to me,' I say. 'That creature in the pit that so frightens you – it's the *source*! It creates the butterflies. I saw one grow from its very surface and fly!'

Konrad shakes his head angrily. 'Ah, I see. This is for you, Victor. I know how much you want these things for their power!'

'Yes,' I admit. 'But it's also for you, Konrad. One of these things is giving you a new body. If we destroy this creature in the pit, who's to say you won't also be destroying all the butterfly spirits it gave rise to!'

Konrad is silent, chest rising and falling heavily.

'I agree with Victor,' Elizabeth says, surprising me. 'We can't risk it. And you'll be out in just a few days. Promise me you won't try to harm it.'

Konrad looks at her uncertainly, then nods.

'It won't harm you,' Elizabeth tells him reassuringly, and before turning to leave adds, 'It's Analiese I'd watch.'

CHAPTER FOURTEEN

ADDICTED

When I woke the next morning, I was startled by the familiar throbbing pain in my missing fingers. Quickly I pulled off my nightshirt and sat with forced patience on the edge of my bed until I saw a quick fluid shadow move across my flesh.

The butterfly spirit was still upon me. So why was I feeling pain? For three blissful days I'd been completely healed, bursting with energy. But as I stood and opened my curtains, I realized I'd slept later than usual, and that my body felt weary. A first tendril of alarm spread through me. Was it possible the butterfly spirit, just like any earthly medicine, lost its effect after a while?

More. I need more.

I hurriedly unlocked my drawer and looked down at the flasks that contained my extra spirits, including the one I'd slyly collected last night as Elizabeth and I had left the armoury, and a very anxious Konrad.

I hesitated only a moment before opening the flask and thrusting my finger inside. At once the smudge of deep shadow swirled round the glass and was upon my skin. I took a sharp breath, feeling a bit light-headed. I withdrew my finger, and the spirit scudded coolly across my hand and up my arm, leaving behind it a blissful trail of well-being.

I sat for a moment, concentrating only on my breathing. Within seconds the pain in my right hand eased, then evaporated. My pulse slowed; my mind felt like some marvellous clockworks, its cogs and wheels meshed and ready for anything.

When I sat down at breakfast, Mother's chair was empty yet again.

'How is she?' I asked my father. He looked worn out.

'Her sleep's still fitful,' he said. 'And last night she had terrible dreams.' He rubbed a hand across his brow. 'I regret letting the professor begin his work in the caves. It's too morbid right now. But I have news that I hope will be more cheering.'

Elizabeth, Henry, and I all looked at him.

'I've decided we'll winter in Italy. There's a villa in Sorrento that's available immediately, and I plan to make the move as soon as possible.'

'When?' Elizabeth asked.

'Three days,' he said.

'So soon?' she asked, a quaver of surprise in her voice. I

knew immediately what she was thinking. Would that give us enough time? Would Konrad's young body have grown to the proper age by then?

'It's sudden, I know,' Father said. 'But I've conferred with Dr Lesage on this, and he agrees that a total change is what's needed for all of us. There are too many memories here. Your mother needs a new landscape and some Italian sun to help burn away her grief. And the two of you . . .' He looked now at Elizabeth and me. 'You look as if you could use a change too. Despite all these outings of yours, you still look pale and drawn. You especially, Victor. Have you been sleeping poorly?'

'Absolutely fine,' I said, studiously eating my boiled egg.

'You've lost weight, my boy.'

I shook my head. 'I feel very vigorous.'

'You look haunted. Dr Lesage will be here shortly to see your mother, and I'll have him check on you as well.'

'I'm absolutely fine,' I insisted.

My father just gave me a look that indicated his decision had been made. I hurriedly swallowed down my breakfast. I knew I had to get the two spirits off my body before Dr Lesage arrived. If he examined me, he might very well ask me to remove my clothes.

I caught Henry and Elizabeth looking at me worriedly.

No doubt the same thought had occurred to them.

One of our footmen came in. 'Dr Lesage is here, sir.'

'Very good. Please have Maria take him to Madame Frankenstein's reception room.' He turned to me. 'And, Victor, I'll have him examine you in your bedchamber directly afterwards. We'll postpone our lessons.'

I nodded, swallowing down my bread roll with some tea. 'If you'll excuse me.'

I walked serenely out of the dining room and then, several paces down the corridor, ran for my room at full tilt. I locked the door. Inside I ripped off my clothes. I took two empty flasks from my drawer and set them at the ready. Then, in the full light, I turned round and round, searching for the two shadow butterflies. It was as if they were trying to confound me, for I saw no sign of them.

'Come on,' I growled under my breath.

There was one, nestled behind my knee! I almost captured it first try, but it seeped from under the rim of the flask and shot to my back. I turned my backside to the window and forced both shadows to my front. One shimmied down my leg and lodged itself between my toes – virtually impossible to get the mouth of my flask around. This was devilishly clever. I began hopping about madly, trying to dislodge it.

There came a knock at my door. I froze. Dr Lesage already?

'Just a moment!' I called out. I careened about the room on one foot, grasping the other and trying to poke the spirit out from between my toes. I lost my balance and lurched against the chest of drawers. The washbasin crashed to the floor, shattering.

'Victor?'

It was Henry! I rushed to the door, unlocked it, and hauled him inside.

'You're completely naked,' he said, startled.

'Yes. I need your help.'

'I thought you might,' he said.

I thrust the flask into his hands. 'I need you to catch it. I'll face the window.'

Silently he took the flask, and I turned my back to him. After a moment I felt the rim of the flask slam hard once, twice, three times against my shoulders.

'Did you get it?' I demanded.

'Just.' He held out the sealed flask to me.

'Now the other one!' I said.

'What do you mean, the—' He stopped abruptly, and I knew he'd seen it. 'You've got *two* on you now?'

I seized the second empty flask and pushed it into his hands. 'Just catch it, all right?'

There was another knock on the door. 'Victor?' came Elizabeth's voice.

'Just a moment!' I sang out.

Once more I faced the window, wincing as Henry pummelled my body – with unnecessary force, I thought.

'It's in your armpit,' he muttered. 'Lift up your . . . No, the other one!'

I did as I was told and yelped as the narrow end of the flask rammed painfully into my flesh.

'Victor, are you all right?' Elizabeth asked worriedly from outside.

'You got it?' I asked Henry.

With a tight-lipped smile he waggled the sealed flask to show me.

'Victor, I'm coming in,' said Elizabeth, and I scarcely had time to yank up my undergarments before the door opened and she slipped inside. She saw Henry and nodded in relief.

'You got it off, then?'

'*Both* of them,' Henry told her.

Her eyes widened in astonishment. 'You have two now?'

'What of it?' I said, snatching up the rest of my clothes and dressing hurriedly.

'Why are two necessary?' she demanded.

'Because one wasn't enough,' I snapped irritably as a savage pain jolted through my missing fingers.

I saw her glance worriedly at Henry. 'Victor, has it

occurred to you that these things might be . . . addictive?'

'I am not *addicted* to them,' I said, buttoning my shirt.

She walked over to my desk and its open drawer. 'And you a have a third, I see.'

'I told you I was collecting them.'

She looked at me closely. 'I think your father was right, Victor. You do look haunted. I don't think you should let them on your body any more.'

'I'm touched by your concern,' I said with a laugh. 'But everything's fine.'

'It's not fine,' she said, anger creeping into her voice. 'We were only supposed to use their power to bring Konrad back. And now you've launched yourself on a completely different endeavour!'

'Both are possible,' I said, putting all the flasks back into the drawer and locking it. 'And when Konrad comes out, he might want one for himself, even if you don't.'

The child ran about on the grass, chased by a laughing, barefoot Elizabeth. Overnight it had grown again, and the set of Ernest's clothes it wore was too small on its frame.

We were in a pleasant clearing in the forest, not ten minutes' walk from the cottage. I hadn't wanted to stray so far, but Elizabeth had been determined to visit the place.

No doubt she and Konrad had taken romantic walks here together.

Sitting on the picnic blanket, the child had eaten its food eagerly, all the while clutching its doll. It seemed remarkably fond of the thing. And then it was up on its feet and charging off across the glade, Elizabeth at its heels.

Henry and I watched from the blanket, finishing our own meals. I had little appetite but forced myself to finish my cold breast of chicken. Dr Lesage had told me I'd lost weight. He'd asked if I was taking too much laudanum, and I'd shown him the bottle he'd prescribed, completely untouched. He'd said he could find nothing bodily wrong with me and told me the Italian sun would do wonders for my constitution. I'd thanked him and, after he'd departed, unlocked my desk drawer. With shaking hands I'd opened two flasks and let the spirits back upon me.

Sprawling on the picnic blanket with Henry now, I studied the child, my creation, carefully. Its appearance certainly reminded me of my twin. But while my brother Konrad and I had a lean frame, this new Konrad seemed built of sturdier stuff. Even though its body was that of a nine- or ten-year-old, I'd been surprised, when I'd first seen it today, at the firmness of its chest and arms and thighs. Even its stomach seemed taut with growing muscle.

I looked over at Henry, chewing meditatively on a

bread roll while watching Elizabeth across the glade.

'You've been writing her love poetry,' I said casually.

He swallowed in surprise, and coughed. 'Did she tell you that?'

I shook my head. 'I overheard her reading it. *She walks in beauty like the night.*'

'She was reading it aloud?' he asked, trying not to look pleased.

'On the jetty by moonlight. It's a very nice piece.'

He eyed me uncertainly. I knew he wanted to ask how we'd both found ourselves together at night, but he wouldn't give me the satisfaction. Instead he asked, 'Why are you telling me this, Victor?'

'She didn't think it was written about her. But it seemed perfectly obvious to me.'

He said nothing.

'I didn't know you entertained hopes of winning her. You once told me you felt like a feeble moth around her flame.'

'Moths dream of being butterflies too,' he said.

'I wish I had your gift with words, Henry.'

'You can't have everything.' He sniffed. 'Or maybe you can. Another trip to the spirit world and you can come out spewing sonnets.'

I chuckled. 'You've had your own gift from the spirit

world, I think. It's changed you, my friend. You're fearless now!'

'It merely showed me what I might be, and what I needn't be. Timid. Shy. Unattractive.'

When he said this last, he looked almost abashed, the old Henry, but then he met my eye boldly once more.

'I've grown up with her too, you know, and never even dared to think she might find me appealing. That she might love me. Why not? Why shouldn't I have my chance to win her?'

'Don't you feel disloyal to Konrad?'

'Did you, when he was languishing?'

I ignored his well-aimed barb. 'I'm just trying to spare you hurt. Her love for Konrad is like the foundation of the earth.'

'The earth sometimes shifts.'

I wondered if Elizabeth had told him of Konrad's request to have a body made for Analiese.

'Henry, listen to me. You have no hope of winning her. Konrad's coming back.'

'And then going away again, thanks to you,' he said, his blue eyes more piercing than I'd ever known.

'Ah. So that is your plan.'

Calmly he shook his head. 'No. That was *your* plan, remember?'

I mimed astonishment. 'Henry, *my* plan was to send him away so he could change his identity and return to us!'

'But in his absence you hope to win her. The plan bears your trademark genius, Victor. After all, anything could happen during Konrad's absence. He might fall in love with some beautiful Greek princess. Or Elizabeth, in her loneliness, might learn to appreciate the charms of another suitor. It's a fine plan. And it benefits me equally. Elizabeth can make her own choice.'

'Well, well,' I said. 'What do you reckon your chances are?'

'Just watch me,' he said.

And then we spoke no more, because Elizabeth, smiling and lightly perspiring, returned hand in hand with a very tired-looking child.

'I think the running's done him good,' she said. 'Did you see how sure he is on his feet?'

'Remarkable,' said Henry.

'He'll be ready in time,' Elizabeth said excitedly. 'He seems to grow at least three years overnight. At this rate he'll be ready the night after next.'

In the past few days I'd hardly given a thought to the actual mechanics of returning Konrad's body to the spirit world. But I now focused my spirit-sharpened mind upon the task, and a plan swiftly laid itself out before me.

'In two nights,' I said, 'we'll bring him inside the house . . .'

'Where?' Elizabeth wanted to know. 'His bedroom?'

'Certainly not,' I said. 'The dungeon.'

I wasn't surprised by Elizabeth's frown of displeasure.

'Just in case he makes noises, we won't be heard.'

'He's not likely to make any noise unless frightened,' Henry said.

I looked at the child's strangely impassive face. How much of what we said did it actually understand? 'We'll have to administer the potion to it, and it might not like that. What if it fights?'

'He'll do whatever I ask him to do,' Elizabeth said.

'Maybe. But the dungeon's the only place for it. Remember, we've got to keep Konrad hidden until we have a chance to tell Father and Mother. We can't have the servants seeing him. And we'll need to make preparations to speed him off to Greece.'

'Surely he could come to Italy with us, though!' said Elizabeth.

Henry and I exchanged a look.

I said, 'I still think it's better if he's properly separated from us – to avoid any suspicion.'

'How will you tell your father what we've done?' asked Henry.

255

'Or your mother,' added Elizabeth. 'I worry her health isn't strong enough to endure such a shock.'

I'd worried about the same thing. In her present weakened state, if Konrad appeared before her, would she think she'd gone mad?

'We'll tell Father first and let him advise us. But you two,' I added, 'are wordsmiths. Please, I need you to start scripting some calming speech to tell Father what we've done.'

Henry laughed nervously. 'I don't think such a speech has ever been written.'

'Yours will be the first, then,' I said. 'I've no doubt you can do it. The day after tomorrow I'll place the elixir and spirit clock in the dungeon, and all will be ready.'

'And we must pick a talisman for Konrad,' Elizabeth said.

'Of course,' I said.

At that moment a grey rabbit flashed across the glade, and the child's eyes locked on to it with a hunter's speed. In a second the child was up and after it, running for the forest.

I launched myself in pursuit, for I was, as always, afraid of someone spotting us. The child's speed was amazing, and when I entered the trees, I couldn't see it anywhere. Panicked, I turned in a full circle and then saw it, crouched low and absolutely still, eyes fixed intently on the rabbit witlessly nibbling in the distance.

I approached the child from behind. Before my hand even touched its shoulder, its head jerked round, and its face was not Konrad's but that same fierce and brutal mask I'd seen the day before – only larger and stronger. It all happened incredibly quickly. Its mouth opened, faster and wider than seemed natural, revealing teeth, including one serrated into four sharp points. When the jaws clamped down on my hand, the pain was enough to bring a curse to my lips.

'Did he bite you?' Elizabeth asked in surprise, hurrying over.

'Yes, he bit me!' I looked at the teeth marks on my flesh, two matching curves of short dashes, except for four little points, each of which welled with a tiny drop of blood.

'Konrad, you shouldn't bite,' said Elizabeth mildly, but the child's face had resumed its characteristic tameness. It yawned and rubbed its eyes with a fist.

'Little monster,' I muttered.

Elizabeth began to laugh. 'It hardly broke the skin.'

'I'm glad you find it so amusing,' I said.

'He takes after you.'

'What does that mean?'

'Your mother once told me what biters you and Konrad

both were, when you were little. Always chomping on each other. She was quite appalled by it.'

'Victor, you're pale,' Henry remarked, joining us.

'He has a tooth,' I said quietly, 'pointed like a saw.'

'Oh, that,' said Elizabeth carelessly. 'I noticed that yesterday.'

'It's not natural.'

'Likely it's just two teeth that've come in too close together. He's growing so quickly, I'm not surprised.'

'I've never seen a tooth like that,' I persisted, unconvinced by her remarks. 'And it wasn't just the tooth. Its whole face changed. It happened yesterday, too. You've never noticed anything odd about the child?'

'No.'

I looked over at Henry hopefully, but he too shook his head.

'There's something not right about it,' I said. The child was staring directly at me, and even though I knew it understood nothing, its gaze unnerved me. 'When its face changes like that, it's like another creature altogether. It's not Konrad.'

Elizabeth looked at me sternly. 'Of course it is.'

And certainly, at that moment, the child's resemblance to Konrad was uncanny.

'Look,' said Henry, 'his eyelids are already drooping. He'll not last the walk back.'

And with that he scooped the child up in his arms and headed for the cottage, Elizabeth at his side.

'Victor, will you gather our picnic things?' she called back over her shoulder.

'Oh, absolutely,' I said, watching them venture up the hill and into the trees, like some lovely family I was no longer part of. 'Please allow me to just clean up after everyone.'

Muttering under my breath, I returned to the glade and packed up the hamper. I was about to set off when I saw I'd missed the beloved rag doll. I scooped it up and was about to cram it into my pocket when something stopped me. I looked again at the doll. On the right hand the fourth and fifth fingers had been chewed off.

'You're making too much of it,' Elizabeth said as we locked the cottage behind us. 'Children chew on things all the time.'

'It doesn't strike you as eerie, or at least odd, that he chewed off the exact same fingers that I'm missing?'

We began our walk back towards the chateau under the unseasonable warmth of the October sun.

'He's very observant,' Henry said. 'Maybe he already recognizes the similarity between you and he's trying to imitate you.'

'You should be flattered,' Elizabeth added.

'Hah! I don't think it's kindly disposed towards me.'

She exhaled angrily. 'Well, no wonder, since you seem intent on denying him the least scrap of humanity!'

'Because he's not human, not yet!' I said, and then added, 'Maybe not ever.'

'What are you trying to say, Victor?' Henry asked with a frown.

'I wonder if this creature isn't . . . abnormal in some way. If you'd seen the way it looked those two times, you'd wonder the same.'

'Curious, that you're the only one who witnesses this,' said Elizabeth. 'Have you wondered if maybe you're seeing things? How many spirit butterflies do you have on you, by the way? Two, three?'

'Two,' I said.

'Maybe they're clouding your perceptions, like an opiate.'

'I see very well indeed, thank you,' I retorted.

'Well, you're certainly blind to your own jealousy,' she said.

'What do you mean?'

'I sometimes wonder if you've really accepted the fact that your brother is growing up and truly coming back!'

'Of course I have,' I said, wondering if she were right.

And then I stared, for I thought I saw something dark move across the nape of Elizabeth's beautiful neck and disappear beneath the collar of her dress.

'You have one on you too,' I murmured before I could check myself.

'What?' she said.

'There was . . . something on your neck. It looked like one of the shadow butterflies.'

'I have nothing on me.'

'Have you checked?'

'I would've noticed, Victor, when I undress at night!'

'You should check right now,' I said. 'Under the sun. It's easiest to detect that way!'

'Honestly, Victor, you've got cheek!'

'I did it on the boat!' I reminded her. 'Look, we'll turn away!'

'I have no intention of undressing in this field, thank you very much!'

Henry looked at me like I was a lunatic.

'You,' she said to me, 'have definitely been spending too much time in the spirit world. You've moved beyond megalomania and are well into paranoia now!'

And she walked on without saying another word to me, all the way back to the chateau.

CHAPTER FIFTEEN

NOCTURNAL VISIONS

I read at my desk, waiting for the church bells to toll midnight before I entered the spirit world. With scant nights until Konrad's return and our departure for Italy, it was all the more urgent to collect as many spirits as I could. I'd need them for the winter. But right now I was feverishly absorbed in my reading, looking up only to scrawl things in my notebook.

Suddenly, from within the house, came a staccato burst of quick screams and then a keening wail, all the more horrifying because I knew it was my mother's.

I was up and out of my door in a second, rushing down the hallway towards my parents' chambers. Elizabeth burst from her own room as I passed, and then, as we rounded the corner to the east wing, Father came hurrying towards us.

'Is Mother all right?' I panted.

He seized me by the shoulders, the intensity of his gaze terrible to behold. 'Where were you just now?'

'In my room, reading,' I said, feeling cold all over. What did he know?

He stared at me hard. 'You weren't out on the jetty?'

I shook my head. 'No.'

For a moment he held my eyes with his, and then his shoulders sagged and he released me. He closed his eyes, shook his head.

'I thought not. Your mother . . . she woke and went to the window and began screaming. She said she saw Konrad. I looked and saw nothing at all. It's not the first time she's had such nightmares, but she seemed so certain that I felt I had to check, to make sure it wasn't you.'

'Poor Aunt Caroline,' said Elizabeth, her eyes glinting with tears.

'She's badly off,' Father said. 'But she's strong; she'll rally. I just wish I'd taken her away earlier, all of us.'

Impatiently I waited for the house to settle, for the last of the servants to leave the hallways and take to their own beds.

Unlocking my desk drawer, I noticed that my hand shook slightly. I took out the spirit clock and the elixir, and as my candle backlit the tall green flask, I was startled to see how little liquid remained. I peered inside, tilting the container, trying to guess how many more drops it might yield. Why hadn't I considered this earlier? When the elixir ran out, I'd be cut off from the butterfly spirits for ever, unless – I found the recipe.

It was surely of Wilhelm Frankenstein's making, or if not, he'd learned it from some tome contained somewhere within the chateau.

The Dark Library was, as always, the obvious place to start.

Furious, I shove yet another pile of books onto the floor, to make room for the next.

I've lost track of how long I've been here, hunched over the table, scouring tome after tome, searching for the recipe. Damn Wilhelm Frankenstein and his mysterious ways! Why hadn't he written it down in his notebook with the other instructions? Or left it in the metal book with the spirit board pendulum? How many secret hiding places did the man need?

Even with three butterflies upon me, I'll never be able to read every single book in here in a single visit.

Maybe he liked to keep it close at hand.

The thought makes me look up, and a forgotten image flares in my mind.

When Elizabeth and I were leaving the spirit world together for the first time, my room revealed its former self as Wilhelm's very bedchamber, from three hundred years ago. His initials on the sumptuous pillows. And in the wall, a small cupboard in which had rested a single book.

As if the house had been trying to show me something.

At once I am running up the stairs, through the library, and along the hallway to my own bedchamber. Inside I fix my eyes on the wall.

Show me!

The walls pulse, the floor ripples, and my gaze burns through centuries of lathe and plaster and brick until I see a small secret recess. I reach out and seize hold of the shimmering book, which solidifies at my touch.

On the very first page is the recipe, written in a hand I recognize as Wilhelm Frankenstein's. I pass my fingers over it, committing all its ingredients to memory. It is simple, easy to replicate. I will transcribe it the moment I return to the real world. I turn the page to make sure I've not missed anything, and frown.

Across two pages are drawn various diagrams of some kind of hooded gown or robe. The fabric bears an intricate butterfly pattern. But when I turn the page, I see yet more drawings of the garment, closer and more detailed, and it appears that it's actually *made* of butterflies. Hundreds upon hundreds, sutured together by their wings into a tight dark weave.

As though sharing my strange repulsion at the image,

the three butterflies that have ridden with me now soar
from my body, brilliant with colour.

'Wait!' I say, for I want to bring them all back with me.

But they flutter across my bedchamber with such
purpose that, for the first time, I wonder where it is they
go. I hurry after them into the hallway.

They fly back into the deserted library, cross the room,
and slip through the seam of the secret door. I follow,
down the stairs, and then down the shaft to the caverns.

As I jog through the vaulted galleries, the ancient paintings are more luminescent than I've ever seen them. Several
times I turn quickly, for it seems a bison has just pawed the
ground or tossed its head. Every surface of my body is
alive: my fingertips taste the air, my nostrils inhale colour.
A strange sense of inevitability builds within me.

I'm curiously unsurprised when I'm led to the cave with
the image of the giant man. He towers above me, his stick
arm outstretched, generating such power that I can feel the
small hairs on the back of my neck lift, as though
anticipating lightning.

I follow the butterflies as they descend the steep
passage to the burial chamber. They fly directly to the pit
and then spiral down, as if drawn by a powerful current. I
rush to the edge and stare, stunned by what I see.

The strange, vast form at the pit's bottom is no longer

encased in stone or swathed in a cocoon but is now contained in a fleshy womb-shaped sac.

My three butterflies land upon it, and instantly all the colour drains from their wings and bodies and they become black once more. And at that very same moment the membranous sac trembles and becomes momentarily translucent. I see a quick, dark swirl of movement – limbs, a torso, and a glimpse of an enormous skull turning, as though looking up at me. Then the membrane is opaque once again and convulses violently as though pummelled from within by a thousand fists. A furious and frustrated wail rises up from the pit.

And for the first time in the spirit world, I feel terror, for I suddenly realize that even as the butterfly spirits have been giving, they've also been taking away. They give me speed of mind, instinct, but they drain me of something else, which they are bestowing upon this pit creature – life.

I take a step backwards, relieved by the trembling of the spirit clock in my pocket. I turn and rush from the caves, desperate to be away from the pit and the thing that rests there, fitfully waiting to be born.

I returned to the real world, my crippled hand pulsing with pain, for I had no spirits upon me now. In my panic to escape the burial chamber, I'd not sought out any. More than that, I was afraid of them now.

Wearily I exhaled. Outside, the wind thrashed branches, rattled the windows, and with a shudder I thought of the restless white mist encircling our chateau in the spirit world.

I replaced the ring on my finger, then swung myself off the bed to lock away the spirit clock and the flask of elixir. Halfway to my desk I heard stealthy footfalls pause outside my bedchamber. My door for some reason was not fully closed, and creaked open a hair's width.

For a moment I stood paralyzed, my skin chilled, for I'd had a nightmare about this moment, the certainty that someone was waiting just beyond the door. I dragged a deep breath into my lungs, my muscles tensed, my teeth clenched, and I rushed towards the door and wrenched it open, a roar ready in my throat.

Nobody was there.

But I heard a soft tread down the hallway. I hurried after it.

By the time I caught sight of her, Elizabeth had already reached the first landing of the great curving staircase, and I could tell at once from her eerily serene gait that she was sleepwalking. It had been her habit, since she was very young, to sleepwalk when anxious. I dared not call out to her now, for I didn't want her to wake and stumble in alarm. So I followed her silently as she walked with graceful ease down the stone steps towards the main entrance hall. She wore only her nightdress, and her feet were bare.

I kept pace with her. I wondered if her slumbering mind was worried about the child in the cottage and she meant to check on it. I couldn't let her wander out into the night like this. She surprised me with a burst of speed, turning away from the main entrance and rushing down the hall past the chapel and armoury. I lost sight of her briefly as she hurried down a side corridor, then caught up as she entered the cloakroom that exited near the stables.

In the near dark the coats and riding cloaks glowered from their pegs like mourners. The heavy door was bolted for the night.

Elizabeth stood directly before the door, arms at her sides, motionless.

Behind her I watched, wondering what she meant to do. Her posture was so expectant, I felt the hair on my neck bristle. Outside, the wind gave a moan. Within me swelled a terrible fear that someone was about to knock.

'Elizabeth,' I said softly, stepping closer. 'We'll check on him first thing in the morning.'

She gave no indication of hearing me. I drew alongside

her, and my heart skipped a beat when I saw the wide, oblivious smile on her face, as though she awaited the arrival of someone beloved.

I looked at the door, and my dread became a shrill sound in my head, a metallic taste in my mouth.

'Elizabeth, you should return to bed now,' I said, trying to keep the panic from my voice.

I put a hand on her shoulder, and at my touch she gave a shudder. Her smile evaporated and was replaced by wide-eyed anxiety. She gasped.

'It's all right,' I whispered. 'It's me, Victor. You've been sleepwalking. It's all right now.'

She looked all around her in confusion. Her breathing stuttered, and I saw her poor heart drumming its pulse in her throat.

'What were you doing, do you remember?' I asked her.

From outside came a horse's low whinny. A dog barked twice and then was silent.

Elizabeth frowned. 'I had a dream that—'

There was a single sharp knock against the door.

I felt all my breath dragged out of me, as if by hook and line. Elizabeth's arms clamped about me. Her mouth was against my shoulder, pressed hard to suppress a scream.

'He's at the door,' she said.

I fought against the weakness in my knees. 'It can't be.'

I felt her take a deep breath. She unlocked her arms and stepped away from me, calmly pushing her hair from her face. 'We need to open the door. It's Konrad.'

'The cottage is locked. And how would . . . It's never been here!'

'He's got out somehow,' she said with complete certainty, and reached for the bolt.

I grabbed her hand. 'You don't know what's out there!'

'Of course I do,' she said. 'Who do you think was on the jetty?'

Once more I felt a nightmare paralysis grip me as I watched Elizabeth unbolt the door and pull it wide. Cool wind washed over us. No one was there. On the doorstep was a snapped branch from the oak tree in our courtyard.

'There's the cause of the knock,' I said, pointing.

I moved to close the door, but Elizabeth quickly stepped outside.

'What're you doing?' I said, following her, but not without first grabbing a stout walking stick. I looked all about the courtyard in the fitful moonlight. Clouds scudded across the sky. Branches swayed. In her bare feet Elizabeth walked across the leaf-strewn cobblestones. From the stables came the reassuring smell of hay and manure. One of the horses nickered.

'There's no one out here,' I said, eager to get back inside.

'Maybe he's in the stables,' she said.

'Elizabeth, he's not—'

'We should've opened the door faster.'

I began to wonder if maybe she was still sleepwalking, and pinched her arm.

'I'm awake!' she said with a fiery look.

'We'll have the dogs up if we don't get back,' I said. 'We'll wake the household.'

But she insisted on entering the stables. The horses were familiar with the two of us, and softly snorted their greetings. After a night of phantasms I was comforted by their solid, friendly presence.

'No one here,' I said, quickly walking the length of the stable, looking into the stalls and tack room.

Elizabeth frowned and headed back out to the court-yard, squinting into the night.

'It was a branch against the door,' I said impatiently.

I took her elbow and steered her towards the door, but she pulled her arm free and walked on ahead. Inside, I closed the door and quietly bolted it.

'Victor,' she whispered, and something in the choked tone of her voice sent a chill through me.

She was pointing at the floor of the cloakroom.

Muddy footprints led down the hall into the house.

We said not a word, only followed the trail with all possible speed. My body felt strangely light, my heartbeat thudding in my ears. My left hand, I realized, still clenched the walking stick. The footprints led us to the base of the main staircase, and I looked up and thought I saw a shadowy figure disappearing from sight. I vaulted up the stairs, Elizabeth at my side.

The footprints were fainter now, little more than a smudge of heel and big toe. We passed Elizabeth's bedchamber, then mine. After that the trail disappeared altogether, but down the dark hallway I heard the telltale sound of a door opening. I rushed ahead.

The door to the nursery was ajar, and my pulse raged in apprehension as I slipped inside. A curtain had been left open. Frantic moonlight, filtered through the branches of a wind-whipped tree, filled the room.

There it was, leaning over little William's crib, reaching down with both hands. It had grown yet more and had the body of a strapping thirteen-year-old. It was completely naked, and in the turbulent light the silhouette of its face was not Konrad's. It was that same brutal face I'd seen in the forest – an aggressively jutting jaw, a low heavy brow. It was the expression of an animal sighting its prey. My pulse became a warrior's drumbeat, and I strode towards it, the stick raised over my shoulder. It saw me coming and whirled with a low whine that sounded to me like a hungry growl. Its muscled arm lifted to ward off my blow.

Elizabeth sped ahead of me and placed her body between us.

'Konrad, it's all right,' I heard her whisper as she took the creature by the shoulders. She looked back at me severely. 'Put that down. You've frightened him!'

I did not put it down but lowered it only slightly as I stepped hurriedly to the crib to check on William. My littlest brother was fast asleep. He looked completely unharmed, but I made sure his chest was rising and falling. Beside him in his crib was the soft felt doll Elizabeth had given the creature a few days ago.

My eyes met Elizabeth's. She'd seen it too but said nothing. The creature had wrapped its arms around her, and she was stroking its hair soothingly. It was now the same height as Elizabeth, and its resemblance to my twin was uncanny. It gazed at me with wide frightened eyes.

I heard a murmur and turned to see Ernest shift in his bed at the far end of the chamber. In the adjoining room was their nurse, Justine. Elizabeth lead the docile creature out, and in the hallway I closed the door softly behind me. We hurried away.

'What did you think he was going to do?' she demanded.

I said nothing.

'He was just giving William his doll,' she insisted.

There was not time for me to speak, or order the maelstrom of my thoughts.

'We need to get it out of here,' was all I said. 'Back to the cottage.'

For a moment I thought Elizabeth was going to object, but she nodded. We made our way downstairs to the cloakroom, found coats and boots for all of us, and stepped out into the windy night.

We walked with the creature between us. Even now, when it looked so much like my brother, so much like me, I didn't like to touch it. I did not take my eyes off it, for fear it would transform once more and lunge at me. But it only watched the moonlit clouds, the stars, the swaying silhouette of the distant wind-racked forest. When we were little more than halfway to the cottage, it began to stumble, and I realized it was falling asleep on its feet. It was still growing so fast that it couldn't stay awake for long.

When I finally made out the dark outlines of the cottage, Elizabeth said, 'It seems so cruel. He must've been cold, or lonely. Why else would he come all this way?'

By this time the creature was completely asleep, and we had to half carry, half drag it between us. When we reached the shed, I saw an untidy mound of dirt surrounding a ragged hole against one wall.

'It tunnelled out,' I said, taking the key from my robe and unlocking the door.

Inside we lowered the sleeping body into its earthen crib, which it almost entirely filled now. Elizabeth loosened its cloak – for its body would surely be growing even more before morning – and covered it with the blanket as the wind lowered outside.

I looked about and found a short length of rope. One end I tied snugly around the creature's ankle, and the other to a metal ring on the wall.

'Is that really necessary?' Elizabeth asked indignantly.

'You want it escaping again?' I seized a shovel and began filling in the hole it had dug under the wall.

The creature made a small whimpering sound, and one of its hands patted searchingly at the blanket.

'He's missing his doll,' said Elizabeth, distressed. 'We should've brought it with us.'

'*That's* how it found us,' I said, suddenly realizing. 'The smell of the doll.'

She looked at me dubiously.

'Remember, outside, I saw the way it sniffed it and

276

looked straight towards the chateau. He could smell it in the wind. Like a hunting dog.'

'That seems far-fetched.'

'Any more far-fetched than birthing a body from mud?'

We left and locked the cottage, and pulled the cloaks about ourselves, for the wind was at our faces now. As we hunched our way towards home, my words finally burst out of me.

'Did you see the way it looked in the nursery?' I demanded. 'The way it was staring down at William? That was hunger!'

'It was curiosity! He was giving him back his doll!'

'Or maybe the thing just dropped it so it could grab William!'

'What did you think he was going to do?'

My response was instant. 'Eat him!'

She stared at me as though I were a lunatic.

'You talk about him like he's a monster!'

'Elizabeth, you can't tell me you didn't notice this time. When we first entered, it didn't even look properly human! Its face was completely transformed, and—'

She was shaking her head. 'Did you take laudanum tonight?'

I forced myself to draw a calming breath. 'I've *never* taken the laudanum. Listen to me. Are you absolutely sure this is the body we want Konrad's spirit to inhabit?'

'It's the butterflies, just as I suspected!' she said, voice raised against the wind. 'You've abused their power, and now you're seeing things, Victor. How many do you have on you right now?'

'None,' I said. 'I left them behind.'

'So you went *again* tonight. I've told you, that place is best avoided!'

A sudden wave of nausea crested over me as I remembered my last visit. My mind felt filled to bursting. 'I think you might be right. The thing in the pit is growing. Not growing, exactly . . .' The proper word came to me with a chill of cold wind. 'We're *waking* it.'

'What?'

I told her how I'd seen my butterflies disgorge their colour into the massive form, invigorating it. 'They're like worker bees, or termites, feeding the queen. And the food is *us.*'

'Dear God,' she murmured. She took my hands and looked at me urgently. 'Victor, you've strayed too long in that place, and I scarcely know whether to trust you. One thing I do know. We need to get Konrad out of there as soon as possible. And this body we've grown is his only way out. *That* is our goal. And after tomorrow night you must bid that place farewell for ever. Do you understand?'

She took a breath, and her eyes softened. 'I know how hard you've worked to bring Konrad back. I'm sorry I've been so severe with you. You were the one who brought us this wonderful plan, and I know you'll have the strength to follow through with it. But first you need to rest properly. You've let these spirits suckle on you, and they've clouded your judgment. You can't expect to see things clearly and make sound decisions when you're perpetually exhausted.'

'I . . . I don't recognize myself sometimes,' I murmured, feeling overwhelmed.

She led me like a child across the fields the rest of the way to the chateau. Inside, I was surprised when she accompanied me all the way to my bedchamber.

'Into bed now,' she instructed.

I did as I was told.

'You'll take some laudanum to help you sleep,' she said.

I looked at the unopened bottle the doctor had left me. My missing fingers throbbed, and I felt fatigued beyond endurance. I sighed, wanting to surrender, wanting sleep. 'One measure, no more,' I said.

'There now,' she said as she held up the dropper and dripped the opiate onto my tongue. She leaned over me and gave me a kiss that almost grazed my mouth, and seemed to promise more. Then she stood and wished me good night.

After she left, I could still feel the imprint of her lips on my cheek, feel the heat of her face against mine.

But even as my body grew heavier, and my eyes drooped, I could not forget the creature's monstrous face in the nursery.

And then I slept, and dreamed.

I am on a sledge pulled by a pack of dogs, hurtling over a plain of ice, exhilarated. The sky is molten lead, lit from the west by a sinking sun. I am travelling north. At the summit of a low hill, the dogs falter, exhausted.

Before me a massive plate of ice, as big as a field, juts up and grinds over the frozen ground, and I realize that this is not ground at all but the sea, hardened by the same cold that turns the vapour of my breath to ice crystals the moment it leaves my mouth.

What am I doing in such a forlorn place? Surely I must be nearly at the pole. Are Konrad and I finally having our adventure, just the two of us? But as I cast my eyes to all horizons, I see that I am alone.

Mercilessly I drive the dogs onward, intent only on moving north, on finding Konrad. Each pulse of my fevered heart is filled with yearning.

Silhouetted in the distance like a frozen city, great jagged ramparts of ice lean and shriek and crack. My gloved hands are clawed around the reins of the sledge.

My exhilaration is congealing to despair as darkness fast approaches. But then I catch sight of a smudge of movement on the white wastes. Squinting, I make out the telltale shape of a sledge in motion, and standing upon it is a fur-clad figure so familiar that I give a cry of ecstasy. Tears flood my eyes and threaten to freeze them shut before I can clumsily wipe them away with my leather mitt.

I urge the dogs to give me the last of their flagging strength, to speed me to my heart's desire.

I feel as if a promise has been made.

It is Konrad. My brother lives again.

CHAPTER SIXTEEN

SOMETHING MONSTROUS

I slept hard and woke to a morning so bright and still that the tempestuous events of the previous night seemed pure impossibility. A maid must already have been to my room, for my curtains were drawn and on my bureau rested a basin of fresh water and a tray of tea and rolls. I stared out at the blue sky and mountains, and remembered my dream of Konrad and me on the ice. For the first time in a long while I felt calm and properly anchored.

When I looked at my clock, I was surprised to see that it was close to noon. I dressed, and when I stepped out into the hallway, Maria was passing.

'It seems I've overslept,' I said.

'And I'm glad of it,' she replied, smiling with satisfaction. 'You still look peaky, though. You need feeding up.'

'Have you seen Elizabeth and Henry?' I asked.

'They checked in on you, but you were dead to the world. I told them to let you sleep.'

'Where are they?'

'They headed off on their picnic about an hour ago. They said you'd find them in their usual place. But let me fix you something in the kitchen to tide you over.'

'Thank you, Maria,' I said, and we walked together towards the main staircase.

The house was bustling with servants carrying travelling cases and dust sheets, simultaneously starting to put our chateau to bed for the winter while preparing for our hasty departure to Italy in two days.

As we passed the library, Professor Neumeyer emerged, looking distinctly dusty and more than a little excited.

'Ah, good,' he said. 'Is your father at home?'

'He's gone to Geneva to attend to some business, sir,' said Maria stiffly, scarcely concealing her distaste for this man. To her way of thinking, he'd opened a tomb within our family home and unleashed more misery into it. 'And Madame Frankenstein is not to be disturbed.'

'Of course, of course,' he said, looking expectantly at me now.

'What have you discovered?' I asked, feeling uneasy.

'Some remains in the burial pit,' he said. 'They were very deep, and it took us some time, but there's something very interesting indeed.'

My stomach clenched as I remembered the wailing and thrashing of the fleshy womb in the spirit world, but I heard myself asking, 'May I see it, please?'

'Of course, yes.'

The professor led me through the caverns I'd become so familiar with, in this world and the one beyond our own. The walls were lit by the amber glow of many lanterns. We passed several dusty workers, stripped to their undershirts, strong limbs gleaming from their recent exertions.

For the first time my step faltered as we started down the steep passage to the burial chamber. Inside, great mounds of moist, richly stinking earth were piled high, an odour that recalled both rot and a freshly ploughed field.

'The body,' the professor told me, 'was not in one piece.'

A chill prickled my flesh.

'Has it just decayed over time?' I asked.

'No. It was intentionally massacred. Whoever he was, his people must have thought there was a chance he might somehow return. Clearly he was greatly feared. Come. See.'

The professor led me to the pit, and I could see it had been excavated some seven feet. A ladder led down to the bottom, where many pieces of all different shapes had been carefully laid out. The professor nodded for me to descend.

'Just mind where you step,' he said, following after me. His voice seemed to come from a long way away. 'Originally the body seems to have been buried upright on some kind of elaborate bier – a platform on which the dead were often transported. The ones I've typically seen were made of wood. But this one appears to have been constructed entirely of bones.'

Step by step down the ladder, panic and claustrophobia squeezed tighter upon me. I reached the muddy earth and moved aside to make room for the professor.

'You can see those long lengths of bone tipped up against the wall, perhaps thigh bones or upper arm bones. Those appear to have been part of the bier.'

'They're all hacked apart,' I said, noting their splintered ends.

'Yes. My guess would be that the grave was dug up shortly after the burial. The bier was smashed and the body itself torn apart. We've only recovered pieces so far.'

The professor reached down and picked up a large smooth curve of bone. He passed it to me.

'What's this?' I asked.

'That,' he said, 'is part of a skull.'

I swallowed, remembering the shadowy shape I'd seen within the fleshy membrane, how it had jerked as though turning to look directly upon me. 'This . . . this is huge.'

The professor nodded. 'Perhaps twice the size of a normal man's. And here' – he picked up a thick wedge of connected bones – 'the talus, tarsus, and navicular bones are apparent enough, but the metatarsals seem to be fused together into a single mass.'

'I'm sorry. What part of the body is this?' I asked, my empty stomach giving an unpleasant twist.

'That is a foot,' he said. 'A clubbed one, curiously.'

I swallowed. 'It's so large that it seems more of a hoof.'

'Most unusual, I agree.'

'Professor, what was this creature?'

For a moment he looked as shaken as I felt. 'Young sir, I've never seen anything like this. It's possible, of course, that this was merely a person of giant proportions – though, I've certainly never heard an account of one so big. And there are always rumours in my field of study, things that defy scientific explanation. Things so bizarre they could only be monsters.'

He bent low and picked up something else.

'And here, the last piece we've recovered so far.'

He passed me an L-shaped span of bone that I knew at once was part of a very large jaw. On the lower half some teeth were still attached.

They were not the teeth of a human. But I'd seen the like before. They were all strangely serrated into four points, still venomously sharp.

They were just like the one I'd seen on the creature Elizabeth had already named Konrad.

* * *

I ran across the pastures, vaulting fences. As I neared the cottage, my sweat was icy against my skin. I flung open the door to find the place deserted. They must've taken him to the glade again. Before I left, I grabbed a shovel.

Fatigue slowed my steps as I hurried through the forest. How had I become so feeble when I'd once felt so strong? When I reached the little hill, I was out of breath and laboured up to the top, kneading the cramp in my side.

Through the trees I could see the glade spread below me. On a picnic blanket sat Elizabeth and . . . Konrad. For several breaths I could only stare in confusion, for it was exactly like looking at my brother. Indeed, the creature even seemed to be wearing Konrad's shoes and trousers, shirt and jacket. His abundant hair, quite long now, was stylishly tied back. Elizabeth poured a cup of tea and held it out to him; he took it and drank.

Where was Henry? My eyes swept the glade, and there at the far end I made him out near some bushes, picking blackberries.

The scene was so serene, I felt some of my panic ebb.

It was *Konrad*, and all I had to do was walk down to see him. My brother. Elizabeth was pointing things out to him, as she would a child, no doubt naming them. A tree. A cloud. A patch of flowers that grew near their blanket.

287

Konrad stood and looked at them more closely, then grabbed them and ripped them up. He tasted them and spat them out. I heard a trill of Elizabeth's laughter, and she came and gathered up one of the flowers, and smelled it, then held it out to Konrad, tickling his nose. He leaned into the flower, then took it from her hand and held it under her nose.

And then he kissed her on the mouth.

I watched, frozen. For what seemed like a very long moment, she let him kiss her – or perhaps she was not merely allowing but participating. Then she put her hands on his shoulders and gently pushed him back, saying something. He gazed at her for a moment. Then he seized her arms and kissed her again, roughly on the neck.

I shouted, but my voice was hoarse, and I didn't think either of them heard me. I lurched headlong down the hill. Elizabeth pushed against him, but he overpowered her, forcing her to the earth. He lay on top of her, pinning her arms flat even as he continued to ravish her, his mouth on her throat and lips.

Elizabeth cried out, and I saw one of Konrad's hands dragging her dress up, revealing her stockinged legs.

Henry was running across the glade now, but I reached them first.

'Get off her!' I bellowed, my shovel raised.

Konrad and Elizabeth both looked at me in surprise.

'Victor, no!' I heard Elizabeth shout.

Konrad began to stand, and I struck him hard on the shoulder with the flat of the shovel, knocking him over. He looked at me, and those empty eyes were no longer empty. They were filled with anger, and his jaw jutted – his brow furrowed and compressed.

But then, just as suddenly, he looked like a slightly younger Konrad, clutching at his shoulder. There was blood on his fingers.

'Victor, you've hurt him!' Elizabeth cried.

'He attacked you!' I felt Henry's hand on my shoulder and turned to him. 'You saw it, Henry!'

My oldest friend was pale, eyes flicking nervously from Konrad to Elizabeth. 'I saw it too. He was forcing you against your wishes.'

'He doesn't know!' Elizabeth protested.

'What doesn't it know?' I bellowed back, not taking my eyes from the creature. 'It knew enough to try to rape you!'

'No. He has a man's appetites but no conscience yet,' she said.

The creature stood up, and for a moment its face darkened and I thought it might lunge at me, so I struck it again with the shovel on its leg. With a wail it turned and pelted across the glade and into the trees, making a sound like a thrashed dog.

'Look what you've done!' Elizabeth screamed, kicking off her shoes and chasing after him. 'Konrad, come back!'

I ran after her, still clutching my shovel, Henry at my heels.

'Listen to me!' I grabbed her wrist and tried to pull her to a standstill, but she wrenched herself free and kept going. Through the trees I saw Konrad. He was fast, a bundle of will and energy, hurtling through the undergrowth, snapping branches. Even barefoot Elizabeth had no hope of keeping up with him – none of us did – and in less than a minute we'd lost sight of him.

'He'll get lost!' she panted, staggering on, refusing to stop. 'He might come to harm!'

'Slow down! Listen to me! The professor found something monstrous in the burial pit.'

'What of it?' she gasped, refusing to look at me.

'It's some massive thing, not human. But there was a jawbone, and on it teeth, teeth that looked exactly like the sharp one on Konrad!'

She laughed in my face. 'Is this another your hallucinations, Victor?'

'What are you saying, Victor?' Henry demanded at my side.

I grabbed at Elizabeth and this time stopped her. 'Don't you see? It's not just Konrad's body we grew. It's someone else's, too!'

Henry frowned. 'How can this be? We used Konrad's own hair—'

'Konrad's hair *blended* with the butterfly spirit! And those spirits *come* from the creature in the pit. And what that creature wants is a new body! Konrad's body!'

'You can't know this,' said Henry.

A hostile silence emanated from Elizabeth.

'If you don't believe me, come back to the chateau and see for yourselves! You'll see the size of the thing. The professor said its own people were frightened of it. Maybe they were meant to resurrect it, but instead they dug it up and massacred its body. It was a monster, maybe some kind of demon!'

'There's no time for this!' Elizabeth cried. 'We have to find Konrad now!'

'Stop calling it that! I'm Konrad's twin, and I can promise you, what we created is *not my twin!*'

'He needs to be found,' said Henry with surprising calm. 'Imagine if he wanders into a town, looking like you . . .'

'And he'll outgrow his clothes soon,' Elizabeth said. 'He'll take them off.'

I dragged a hand across my brow. They were right. The idea of having a naked facsimile of myself running rampant through the countryside, eating dogs and cats – and who knew what else the thing was capable of. It was too horrific to comprehend.

'All right,' I said grudgingly. 'But surely it'll just come back to the cottage. Or the chateau. Those are the places it knows.'

'And he knows you'll be there too, waiting for him with your shovel,' Elizabeth said.

'It's dangerous!' I said. 'How can you not see this? What would you have done if I hadn't appeared?'

She laughed disdainfully. 'Do you always need to be the hero? I would've stopped him, calmed him, and he wouldn't have run off.'

'You're mistaken,' I said.

'It's you who's mistaken,' she countered. 'And inconsistent. At first you trumpeted your praises of these spirit butterflies! *They give intelligence, power, life!* You kept them on you. You probably have them on you still! But now you expect us to believe they're evil.'

'That body,' I insisted again, 'is made for something else.'

'So, what do you propose we do?' she demanded. 'Destroy it?'

I said nothing, though the idea spread through my head like a bloodstain.

'I don't know,' I said. 'I don't know yet. Right now we just need to find it and get it out of sight.'

'Put your shovel down if you mean to come with us.'

Our eyes locked. I held tight to the shovel. Murderous thoughts filled my head – hacking at the creature that so resembled Konrad, bludgeoning it to death – and my stomach curdled. We needed to get it back to the cottage. It needed to come willingly. Then, once we'd locked it inside, I could decide what must come next. The shovel would only frighten it away. I dropped it.

'Good.' Elizabeth set off at once, leading us deeper into the forest, in the direction we'd last seen the creature. It seemed a poor plan, but I could think of no other, so I followed along with Henry. Strangely, Elizabeth seemed to know exactly where she was going, her face intent, eyes focused on some inevitable destination.

'Look,' she said, pointing to a pair of discarded shoes in the grass. They were indeed Konrad's.

'How do you know the way?' I asked, and remembered how she'd known, even in her sleep, that the creature had been waiting outside the door of the chateau.

'I'm taking the easiest path through the forest,' she said. 'Wouldn't anyone do the same?'

I didn't believe her. After half an hour we found a jacket caught on a branch, and not much farther on, a shirt, its buttons ripped. I hoped the creature was merely hot, ridding itself of restraints, and not bursting through its clothing because of a monstrous growth spurt. I regretted leaving the shovel behind.

Our route was uphill, and after an hour we came upon the creature on the shore of a small kettle lake, fed by a cataract of water running from the mountains. It was completely naked now, my size exactly, if not a bit bigger. On one of its shoulders was an ugly cut, dark with congealed blood, where I'd struck with the shovel. The Konrad creature was crouched by the water's edge, its back to us, staring. At first I thought it was slaking its thirst, but it was gazing fiercely into the glassy water, and I realized it must be looking at its own reflection. Before this moment had it ever beheld itself?

'Konrad,' Elizabeth said gently, walking up to him.

It startled and turned to her, and the look of utter relief and joy on its face was so sincere and innocent that I felt my brutal resolve falter. It stood and shuffled towards Elizabeth with its head lowered, as if in shame. At once Henry took his jacket and tied it swiftly around the creature's midriff to hide its nakedness.

Elizabeth placed a hand on the creature's uninjured shoulder. 'We're going home now.'

It looked at her, surely understanding nothing but her face and the tone of her voice. Then its gaze settled on me. I'd expected wariness, but its eyes widened in amazement. Once more the creature turned to glance at itself in the still water. Wonderingly it touched its own face. Then the creature turned and pointed at me.

'He knows you're twins,' Elizabeth said quietly.

And suddenly I knew it too. Impelled by a force I couldn't control, I walked closer. So like Konrad. So like my twin. Very gently it touched my face. I exhaled. Its fingertips lingered on my cheek and then stroked my hair, then its own.

Elizabeth smiled. 'It's like a reunion.'

Maybe it would work, I thought. Maybe, once Konrad's spirit was inside this body, it would be Konrad, regardless of how the body itself had been formed. The body was just a vessel, after all. Once inhabited by my brother, wouldn't it truly become my brother?

The creature reached out once more and took my good hand, shaking it again and again, like some comic greeting, so that I almost laughed. I remembered Ernest doing something similar when he was little.

Then it pressed the wound on its shoulder, wincing.

'I'm sorry,' I said.

With a disconcertingly blank expression it lifted its bloodied fingers and placed them on my shoulder, gripping tight. I put my left hand on the creature's and tried to move it, but its fingers were locked. I was suddenly aware of a great dormant power in its limbs. I looked at the impassive face.

'Let go,' I said quietly, feeling the first flutter of panic.

With its other hand the creature gripped my maimed one and squeezed, sending a spasm of pain through it

'That's enough!' I shouted, and shoved my full weight against the creature. Without releasing its grip on my hand, the Konrad creature staggered back and fell into the lake, dragging me in too.

The water was surprisingly deep, even right against the bank, and locked together as we were, we both went under. I came up spluttering and splashed towards the bank, mere inches away, but the creature was behind me and grabbed hold, pulling me back and down.

Choking, I thrashed up and turned around to face the creature. I wasn't sure if its face was filled with malice or pure terror.

'He can't swim, Victor!' cried Elizabeth. 'Help him!'

I caught a glimpse of her preparing to jump, and just had time to shout, 'Stay away!' before the creature was upon me, flailing and seizing hold of me in a cold iron grip. I went under again. A murderer could not have been more single-minded.

I came up briefly, enough to glimpse that all our thrashing had actually moved us much farther from the bank. From the corner of my frenzied eye, I saw that Henry had found a long branch and was stretching it out to us. Elizabeth was shrieking, 'Help him grab the branch, Victor!'

But its face was livid with panic, and it clawed its way on top of me once more. Down we went again, for too long. A great cold contracted round my heart, tunnelling my vision. I kicked and hit sluggishly, and managed to knee the creature in its privates so that its grip loosened. Fighting my way up, I broke the surface, gagging for air.

The creature came up, head barely cresting, a terrible bawling coming from its throat.

'He's drowning!' I heard Elizabeth scream, and saw she was in the water, swimming for us.

'Stay aw—'

And the creature pulled me close again, its panicked face spluttering against me. It wrapped its legs around me, trying to haul itself up onto my shoulders. I punched it in the face, and then again harder, my numb fist like a hammer. The creature recoiled, and I would never forget its expression – a kind of bleak incomprehension, and then panic once more – before it sank below the surface.

'Konrad!' Elizabeth screamed.

I hurled myself at her, intercepting her, gripping her with my arms and legs and trying to drag her back to the bank.

She cried and clawed and bit.

'Give me the branch!' I hollered at Henry, and he threw it to me. The water was murky, and I could not see the creature beneath the surface. My great fear was that it was under me and would drag me down for good.

'Dive for him, you coward!' Elizabeth screamed at me.

'You can't drag a drowning man from the depths!' I shouted back at her.

The creature did not reappear. Not in ten seconds, twenty, or thirty. When a full minute had passed, I said, 'It's gone.'

'You killed him!' Elizabeth gasped.

'It would've killed us both!'

'He . . . he wanted you to help him . . .'

'Victor's right, Elizabeth,' said Henry quietly. 'There was nothing he could've done.'

'And where were you, Henry?' she cried.

'I found a branch as quickly as I—'

'Cowards, the both of you!'

We hauled ourselves out, cold and exhausted, and sat hunched on the grassy bank, shivering for some time, staring at the water. The silence was like a dreadful prison, entrapping me in my own bloodstained thoughts. Might I have saved it? But it needed to be killed, surely it did.

Then we stood and started the long walk towards home.

CHAPTER SEVENTEEN

A GROWING FURY

The walk home was interminable, silent apart from the sporadic sounds of Elizabeth's sobbing. She wouldn't meet my eye, wouldn't even let Henry place a consoling hand on her shoulder. We stopped only briefly at the glade to gather our things and dry off with the picnic blankets, working like automatons.

It was like losing Konrad all over again. I had killed him twice.

Only last night I'd dreamed we were to be reunited. The dream had had such substance, such certainty.

When we entered the chateau, Elizabeth immediately started up the stairs towards the library.

'I want to see them,' she said. 'These monster bones.'

Henry and I followed. We found no sign of workers in the library, and as we made our way into the caverns, we found them empty too, though a few lanterns still flickered.

'Professor Neumeyer?' I called out, but heard no reply.

We ventured down the steep passageway to the burial chamber and walked to the edge of the pit. The ladder was still in place, but at the bottom all the skeletal fragments I'd seen earlier were gone.

I turned desperately to a tarpaulin where a few small bits of bone were laid out. I hurried over and knelt down, but these pieces were all so nondescript they might have been from any creature.

'Is this all there is?' Elizabeth exclaimed, snatching up a shard of bone. 'This is your monster?'

'They must've taken away the other pieces,' I murmured, feeling suddenly light-headed.

'If they were here at all.'

'They were here,' I said. 'A bit of the giant skull, a clubbed foot. And the jawbone that bore the exact same teeth as Konrad's!'

'A tooth!' She was shaking with anger now. 'Is that all the proof you can muster? Admit it, Victor. From the moment you saw him growing as a baby, you didn't want him back!'

My voice was hoarse with grief. 'That's a lie! You think you're the only one who suffered today? I saw the hope of getting back my brother, my twin, sink! I want him back, Elizabeth, even more than you!'

She shook her head. 'You were more interested in your stolen spirits and the power they gave you!'

'How can you say that, after all I've done—'

'With you, Victor, it's never clear why you do things!'

I held up my maimed hand and shook it in her face. 'I – gave – my – fingers!'

Dismissively she batted away my hand, and before I could check my rage, I smacked her face.

She flew at me, her fists battering my chest. I pushed her away so hard that she fell down.

'Victor!' Henry said sharply, his hand tightening around my arm.

'Take that hand off me,' I growled.

We held each other's eyes for a moment before he released his grip.

There was a shuffling sound behind us, and I turned to see Gerard, one of the professor's colleagues, emerge from the steep passageway.

'What're you doing down here?' he asked.

'The pit remains, where have they gone?' I demanded.

'The professor's taken them into Geneva not an hour ago,' he said.

'Why?'

'He was concerned they should be preserved properly.'

'The body,' said Elizabeth, 'was it truly of giant proportions?'

'Indeed it was, miss.'

'You saw its teeth?'

'They were unusually sharp.' He nodded at the tarpaulin. 'I'm just here to gather up the last bits of bone.'

'Thank you,' said Elizabeth, walking out of the chamber. Henry and I followed.

As we made our way back through the vaulted galleries, I said, 'You see, I didn't imagine any of this.'

Elizabeth ignored me.

'Whatever that thing was, or is, it wants a body born, and not for Konrad – for itself. You can't blame me for what happened at the lake.'

'Don't worry about me,' she said. 'Worry about your brother when you tell him tonight.'

When he sees the three of us, Konrad beams. He's in the library with Analiese, who is carefully reading aloud to him when we enter. Arranged on the tables is an arsenal of weapons from the armoury, as if he's expecting to be attacked at any moment.

'Are we ready?' he asks, leaping up. 'This is the night, is it not?'

'Konrad—' I begin.

His face falls. 'What's happened?'

My voice is a defeated croak. 'Your body . . . There's been an accident.'

Analiese gasps. Konrad sinks down in his chair. 'What kind of accident?'

I swallow, struggling to govern myself. 'It drowned.'

'How?'

Before I can assemble the words, Elizabeth says, 'Victor fought with him and they fell into the water, and he didn't know how to swim.'

Konrad looks at me, his eyes dark with reproach.

'Listen to me,' I say. 'You must believe me. The body was corrupted. It was violent. It tried to rape Elizabeth!'

'No!' she objects. 'That wasn't the case. It kissed me and became enflamed, as any young man might've done. It had no conscience yet to—'

'The body was not yours, Konrad!' I shout over her. 'It was meant for another.'

'What do you mean?' Konrad demands, standing now, pacing like a caged tiger.

'That creature in the pit, your body was meant for it!'

'How can this be?' exclaims Analiese.

I see how, even now, Elizabeth looks at her, with suspicion and barely veiled hostility.

'The spirit that animated your body comes from that creature!' I tell Konrad. 'And all of these,' I add, looking nervously at the black butterflies that circle overhead.

'Don't let them land! They've been feeding on us whenever we come here, especially me, taking our life energy back to the creature and gradually waking it. When I last saw it, it had changed yet again. It was like some vast embryo.'

'Why didn't you tell me this last night?' Konrad demands.

'My time was up. I . . . I had to leave,' I tell him, unable to meet his gaze.

Konrad's voice is irate. 'You take time to do your reading and collect your specimens – but not enough to warn me about this thing!'

'I still wasn't sure what it was,' I tell him. 'Or how dangerous it might be. It wasn't until this morning, when the professor dug up the remains in the real world. It's some kind of monstrosity, maybe not even human. Some of its features were exactly the same as the body we've been growing for you!'

'One!' protests Elizabeth. 'A single sharp tooth! That's Victor's lonely bit of evidence.'

'No. There were other moments when you – the *body* – became strange and frightening. It bit. It growled. Its face changed into something brutal.'

'Victor has become addicted to the spirit butterflies,' says Elizabeth, 'and they've clouded his judgment. He sees all manner of things.'

Konrad looks at me long and hard, then turns in Henry's direction.

'Henry, you've always had a level head. Tell me what you know.'

'The body we grew for you did have a strange tooth, it's true.' He sighs and looks ruefully at Elizabeth. 'And today I did see those features Victor mentioned. They were like a shadow crossing its face.'

I feel a rush of gratitude for Henry. 'I swear to you, Konrad, there is some infernal design at work. The professor thinks this creature may have been considered some kind of god, and maybe he's right. How else to explain the fact that it created these butterflies from its own dead body?'

Analiese is shaking her head, frightened. 'But the butterflies have always been here. And I've never sensed any evil purpose in them.'

'Until they have living souls to feed upon,' I reply. 'Look how the little parasites hover, wanting to steal more from us.'

Overhead they flutter closer, darting towards Henry, Elizabeth, and me, wanting to touch us. I shoo them away viciously.

'They're like leeches!' I shout. 'They'll drain us and use our power to fully wake that creature in the pit!'

'But you put such faith in these creatures!' Konrad says. 'You said they gave you immense powers.'

'They did,' I say, swatting one that alighted on Henry's back without his realizing. 'But even as they gave, they took away. Elizabeth! Don't let it land on you!'

I am suddenly aware that everyone is looking at me as though I'm a lunatic – and no doubt I look it, my eyes darting about, lunging to and fro to swat butterflies.

'Victor,' says Elizabeth sadly, 'you're deluded. There was nothing the matter with the body we grew. And you let it die!'

'It tried to drown me!'

'He did his best to save it,' says Henry.

'Make me another!'

The shout comes from Konrad, and when I turn, I know that I have never seen his face so angry. He stalks towards me, fists clenched.

'Make me another body!' he shouts.

'It can't be done! It would be another monstrosity!'

'You promised me, Victor!'

His words impale me, and I have no reply.

'It's just like last time,' he rails. 'You make me these promises. The Elixir of Life! How it will heal me! How it will keep me from any illness. Then you tell me you can

307

raise me from the dead! Your promises are meaningless, Victor! Meaningless!'

'Konrad, I've tried my—'

'No. You *tried* to make yourself grand and powerful, as usual, and you have ruined everything!'

I don't realize how close he's come towards me – until he strikes me. His fist actually touches my body. And though it feels like the graze of a feather, I gasp in shock. How is it he's able to come so close?

'I want my life back!' Konrad shouts as he batters at me, his blows like little breezes. I wish they hurt more, to match my misery.

'I'd do anything for you,' I say.

'Liar! I half think you drowned me on purpose, so you could woo Elizabeth and take her for yourself.'

'That's not so!' I protest weakly. But I wonder if all his angry words have the accuracy of arrows.

'You mean to whine at her and worry her like a dog until she takes you!' Konrad says with a cruelty I've never known from him.

Analiese puts a restraining hand on him, draws him back. 'Konrad, his remorse is obvious. Please stop.'

'Don't touch him!' Elizabeth yells at her. 'We don't even know who or what you are!'

A sense of madness throbs through the room, and the

walls are beginning to pulse with our frenzied emotions.

Konrad shrugs free of Analiese and strikes at me again. 'I – want – more – *life*! You've paraded it in front of me, and now I want it! Get me another body!'

Henry steps in front of me, and Konrad recoils, driven back by my friend's light and heat. Why has mine not done the same?

My brother sinks suddenly into a chair, covering his face. 'Victor,' he says, 'I'm—'

'Do you all see?' I shout. 'My light has faded. These spirits have stolen it from me and given it to that thing in the pit. Can't you all see that? How else could Konrad have touched me?'

There's an uncomfortable silence, and for a moment I hope I've finally convinced them.

But Elizabeth just shakes her head stubbornly. 'If you're weakened,' she says, 'it's because you've abused the spirits and dallied too long in this world.'

'But your light and heat are dimmer too,' says Konrad, looking at her carefully. 'Not so much as Victor's . . .'

Henry and I both regard her, surprised, for we've never been able to see one another's auras.

'Have you been coming in, without me?' I ask her.

She nods quickly, and I see Konrad's guilty look.

Konrad stands up and starts seizing weapons from the table.

'What're you doing?' Henry asks.

'What I should've done much earlier,' he says savagely. 'I'm going to destroy that thing!'

'Konrad, don't!' cries Elizabeth. 'It's too dangerous!'

'He's right,' I say, snatching up a crossbow and a sword. 'It must be done.'

'Then I'll fight with you,' says Henry.

But at that moment the spirit clock in my pocket begins to vibrate and shake with such frightening intensity that I fear the thing will burst apart. 'It can't be,' I mutter, pulling it out. 'How can our time be up?'

'Can you slow it?' Konrad asks desperately.

'No . . . it's too late. I can't turn back time.'

He looks at me, desolate, and then his face hardens. 'I'll do it alone.'

'No,' I tell him. 'You might need help. The help of the living.'

'I'm sick of listening to it!' he shouts. 'Waiting for it to come!'

'It won't come,' I tell him. 'It needs more life to wake. Without us here it can't wake fully.'

He shakes his head, refusing to meet my gaze. 'How can you know that?'

'I won't leave you here,' I say. 'I'll come back. I'll solve this somehow.'

He is silent.

'I'll find a way,' I promise him. 'But don't attack this thing on your own.'

He nods. I don't want to leave him, not like this, with all hope drained from his face. I want to stay, to make amends, but the urgency to return to my real body makes a coward of me, and I run along with Henry and Elizabeth, her face streaked with tears, back towards my bedroom – and life – while Konrad remains behind once more, in the land of the dead.

CHAPTER EIGHTEEN

POSSESSED

When we came back to ourselves, we looked everywhere but at one another. From the corner of my eye I sensed Elizabeth's anger just by the set of her mouth.

'Konrad's in no danger right now,' I said, as much to comfort myself as the others. 'The pit demon can't be born without our energy.' I drew a weary breath. 'I'll think of something.'

'Perhaps your spirit friends can help you,' Elizabeth said coldly.

'There are none on me.' Leaving the spirit world, I was most careful to make sure of that.

Elizabeth looked at me. 'You're sure?'

'Will you check me?' I asked Henry.

Elizabeth turned to the wall, and I stripped and let Henry examine my body.

'He's clear.'

'Even so,' said Elizabeth, 'he has some in a flask in his drawer.'

'Just one,' I said. 'And here, if you don't trust me.' I took the key from its new hiding place and handed it to her. 'You hold on to this.'

'Thank you, Victor,' she said, and took it.

After checking to be sure the hallway was clear of servants, she left for her own bedchamber. Henry and I were alone.

'Thank you,' I said, 'for saying you saw how its face changed.'

Henry exhaled nervously, and I caught a welcome glimpse of my old friend. 'I tell you honestly, I don't know what to think.'

'Nor I,' I murmured.

'You haven't made it easy for us, Victor,' he said. 'Your behaviour—'

I wanted to save him the chore of chastising me, and save myself the pain of hearing it. 'I know. My behaviour's been odd.'

'I think sometimes you're half mad.'

'*Only* half?'

He chuckled weakly, and it seemed impossible to imagine a time when one could live with a full and careless heart.

'Let's sleep,' I said. 'Things always seem clearer and more possible in the morning's light.'

He stood and put a hand on my shoulder. I reached up and placed my good hand gratefully on his.

'Good night, Henry.'
'Good night, Victor.'

I slept, but the pain in my hand inhabited my dreams, and when it finally woke me, I sat up, sweating, and lit a candle. I looked at the laudanum on my bedside table and wanted oblivion, if only for a few short hours. I opened the bottle and was about to drop some onto my tongue when I noticed that the locked drawer of my desk was open.

I leaped off the bed and rushed over.

The spirit clock and green flask of elixir were still there.

But the vial that held my one remaining spirit butterfly was gone.

I dressed quickly, ran to Henry's bedchamber and roughly shook him awake. He opened his eyes and sat up, chest swelling with surprise.

'Dress quickly,' I said.

He looked at my strained candle-lit face. 'What's happened? What time is it?'

'We're friends, are we not?' I asked.

With only a slight hesitation he nodded.

'I know lately we've butted heads, but you've been my dearest friend from childhood, and I need you to trust me now.'

'Victor, what's going on?' he demanded.

'Elizabeth's stolen the flask with the butterfly spirit.'

'How do you know she hasn't just taken it away to stop you from using it?'

'She took the key to the cottage and Konrad's brush from my bureau. There are probably more than a few hairs left in it.'

My friend licked his lips. 'Surely she wouldn't attempt such a thing.'

'She still doesn't believe the first body was corrupted. We have to stop her.'

'I can't believe it,' said Henry.

'If I'm right, we'll find her bedchamber empty and she'll already be at the cottage . . . at work.'

He swung himself out of bed, hurriedly pulled on trousers and shirt. We padded down the hallway to Elizabeth's room. I opened the door, and we slipped inside. I parted the curtains at the foot of her bed and in the shadows saw her there, asleep.

I glanced sheepishly at Henry, but he grabbed my arm tightly.

'What?' I said.

He rushed to the side of her bed and shook her so violently that she came apart in an explosion of pillows and rolled linens.

Together we bolted downstairs, slipped on boots and cloaks, and launched ourselves headlong into the night.

Pain seared my missing fingers, and my limbs shook with fatigue. I felt like an invalid not properly recovered from a fierce ague. My body craved the rush of a spirit butterfly against my flesh, even though I knew it was precisely this that had enfeebled me. I slogged on through the pastures, Henry at my side.

The lock of the cottage was unclasped. I shuttered my lantern and cracked open the door to peer inside. A single lamp flickered on the crude table, mounded with damp mud. We were in time! She hadn't created it yet. Behind the table Elizabeth sat on a stool, her back to us. She was very still, her head tilted down. She wore only her nightdress.

I whispered to Henry, 'I think she's sleepwalking. We must be calm but firm with her.'

'And do what?'

'You get hold of the flask that contains the butterfly spirit, and I'll guide her back home.'

We opened the door and walked inside. Elizabeth did not even turn her head.

'What are you doing, Elizabeth?' I asked pleasantly, stepping slowly closer.

As I passed the table, I noticed Konrad's hairbrush and a toppled flask, unsealed.

Empty.

'Look at him, Victor,' she said dreamily. 'Just look at him.'

Still she kept her back to us, but now I could tell she cradled something in her arms.

'I made him anew,' she murmured.

'Ah,' I said, and took another cautious step closer.

She turned to face us then. In her arms she held a mud baby, but this one was much, much larger than the one we'd originally created. I didn't know if she'd simply fashioned a bigger body this time, or if the particular butterfly spirit she'd used was more vital than the first. The baby's body was still crude, its muddy limbs misshapen and scored with hasty finger strokes, but it was obviously, terrifyingly alive. Its crude legs and arms twitched, and its head shifted against Elizabeth's nightdress.

Her gaze seemed directed at someone behind Henry and me, and I fought the urge to turn. It had always been her way, when sleepwalking, to look beyond what was right before her eyes.

'It was very clever of you,' I said, fighting to keep my voice steady. 'You must've found some more hairs on Konrad's brush.'

She smiled secretively. 'A few,' she said. 'But I also had another bit.'

'What bit was that?' I asked, my step faltering.

'A bit of his bone. From the pit. I used that, too.'

I glanced anxiously at Henry, and saw my own horror reflected in his pale face. I remembered Elizabeth in the burial chamber, how she'd bent to pick up a tiny shard of bone. I'd never noticed her put it down.

'He's waited such a long time,' Elizabeth said now.

'Has he?' I asked politely, taking another step, keeping an eye on the stirring creature in her arms. 'How long has he waited?'

Barely audibly, she said, 'Hundreds of thousands of years. I'm to be his mate.'

My flesh crawled, and at that moment I saw a furtive insect-like shadow dart from the neckline of her nightdress and take refuge behind her ear. Henry's small gasp told me he'd seen it too.

I realized in that moment that Elizabeth wasn't simply sleepwalking.

She was possessed.

'Shall we put the baby to bed now, Elizabeth?' I said, my voice shaking. I had no idea what to do. No plan effortlessly constructed itself in my head. I was just myself, unaided by supernatural forces, and all I knew was that this creature could not be allowed to exist.

'Not yet,' Elizabeth replied serenely. 'I want to hold him.'

'I can tuck him up with his blanket,' said Henry, walking towards her with his arms outstretched. This was wise. She'd always trusted Henry with the child.

Elizabeth smiled. 'You'll have to destroy me first.'

And at that moment the creature turned its muddy head to look at Henry and gave a rattling shriek. Its mouth bristled with serrated teeth.

'Good God,' Henry breathed.

'Elizabeth,' I said, 'you must let us take care of the baby properly.'

'So you can kill him?' she asked calmly.

'The baby must be tired,' said Henry soothingly. 'His eyes are drooping, see? He needs his sleep if he's to grow.'

Elizabeth's own eyelids drooped, and she nodded. 'All right.'

Henry stepped closer, and the creature sprang from Elizabeth's body towards Henry, its jaws wide. It didn't bite him, merely knocked him backwards and sprang off him towards me, hissing like a feral cat. I struck out with my arm. I felt its teeth catch my cloak, trying to bite deeper, before I threw it off. It sailed across the cottage and landed somewhere in the darkness.

Panting in terror, Henry and I tried to track its quick scuttling movements across the floor. So many hiding places.

'Konrad!' Elizabeth cried. 'Where are you?'

Against all instinct I had the sense to rush back and close the cottage door firmly. We couldn't let this creature escape into the world. I grabbed a thick burlap sack, seized a lantern, and leaped up onto the table, hoping for a better view. But there was so much debris upon the floor, so many tools and shadows, that it was quite hopeless. To my left a scrabbling, then to my right. The little monster moved with supernatural speed. I saw Henry pick up a rake. Elizabeth was looking about, distraught, urging the creature to return to her arms.

Then the scuttling ceased. Elizabeth stopped calling out. A terrible silence lowered over the room like a night mist.

Upon the table I turned slowly in a circle, never letting my eyes settle on any one place, watching for a blur of movement in my peripheral vision. I was fervently hoping it had fallen asleep, and then our dreadful job would be much easier.

A ghastly pain pierced my toes, and I looked down to see the creature's jaws biting through my boot as it climbed up from underneath the table. I tried to kick it off, but its grip held, and the thing's compact weight was enough to throw me off balance. With a cry I toppled and hit the table hard. The monstrous thing was jarred loose and leaped on all fours for my face. I threw my sack at it, and the creature dropped, entangled, to my stomach, thrashing. But it quickly freed itself and jumped for me again. I rolled off the table altogether, and as I hit the floor, I heard the sound of breaking glass and a terrible screaming.

I scrambled up and stared. The creature had landed on the lantern, cracking the glass. Soaked in oil, it flailed about, burning.

Elizabeth grabbed the sack and threw it over the creature, trying to smother the fire. But the abundant oil saturated the burlap, and it too burst into flame. Within moments the mud creature became still and hard, like something blasted in a kiln. But from the centre of its chest, I caught sight of a spiralling tendril of darkness trying to break free from the clay. The flames licked at it hungrily, devouring it as quickly as they would a strand of hair, and by the time the mud body had cracked into several pieces, the spirit had been reduced to ash.

With the rake Henry flung some soil onto the table to extinguish the last of the oily flames.

'You murderers!' Elizabeth wailed at me.

There was, suddenly, a hammer in her hand, and she

swung. A peal of pain and light exploded through my head, and I crumpled to the floor clutching my temple. When I could see again, Henry was wrestling the hammer from her grip, but then she came at me again like a lynx. She was preternaturally strong, empowered by the spirit upon her. It was all I could do to fend off her blows.

'Help me pin her down, Henry!' I shouted. 'We need to get that spirit off her!'

Henry helped me force her to the floor, fighting hard the whole time.

'We're too rough!' he cried in distress.

'Hold her, Henry!' I shouted, for I knew I didn't have the strength to do this alone.

I clambered onto her kicking legs while Henry tried to keep her flailing arms away from me.

'How dare you!' she cried. 'You brutes, both of you! Get off me!'

'The flask!' I yelled to Henry.

He reached back to the table and tossed it. I knew I had but one chance, for these things were quick and wily.

'He needs a new body!' she wailed.

I pulled her hair back from her ear and saw it, a darker bit of shadow. Swiftly I plunged the flask's opening hard against her flesh.

The spirit was trying to squeeze beneath the rim,

and with Elizabeth thrashing so hard, I feared I'd lose it.

'Light!' I cried. 'Turn her towards the lamp!'

We wrenched her over onto her side, and the sudden flare was enough to startle the spirit deeper into the flask. At that moment I slid the seal securely over the rim and trapped it.

The instant the spirit left her body, Elizabeth stopped fighting and instead seemed to wake, as though from sleepwalking. Eyes wide with childlike confusion, she gazed all around, at me and then Henry, and then she pressed her face into Henry's arm and wept. I envied him more than I could say as he held her and stroked her hair.

'There, there, now,' he said.

I knew she didn't love Henry, but at that moment I wondered if she could ever love me.

'Tell me what happened,' she gasped after a few seconds.

Between us we told her what we knew. She sat, incredulous, staring at the dark spirit whirling frenzied against the glass.

'I was almost certain I saw one on you yesterday,' I said, 'but now I wonder if you had one from the very beginning.'

'I can't believe it,' she murmured.

'Maybe that's why you were so devoted to the creature and kept making excuses for it,' I said, 'even when it bit me and tried to ravish you. It must've urged you to take that piece of bone from the burial chamber.'

'And when I was sleepwalking,' she said with a shudder, 'to come here and make a new body for whatever's in that pit. And afterwards . . .'

She sat up and felt the pocket of her nightgown. She brought out the key to the cottage and, with a frown, a small brown vial.

'What is that?' Henry asked.

'The spirit elixir,' I said. 'Her own private store. You meant to make the baby tonight and take it into the spirit world for the pit god to inhabit – right away.'

She looked astounded, and then gave a small nod, as if remembering.

We were all silent for a moment, imagining Elizabeth rearing the pit god as it grew with freakish speed into its full giant form.

'You said you were meant to be its mate,' Henry said, looking ill.

'Dear God,' she murmured. 'What have we done?'

The immensity of it was almost too much to grasp.

'That thing, that pit god—'

'Please don't call it a god,' said Elizabeth fiercely. 'It can only be a demon.'

'It stole from us to make itself strong,' I said. 'Every

time a butterfly spirit touched us, it stole our energy and used it to wake the demon. And whenever I brought a butterfly out from the spirit world and then returned, it was bloated with my life – I saw it – and carried that to the demon too.'

'Why weren't you possessed like me, then?' Elizabeth asked.

I rubbed at my bruised head. 'I *was*, just differently. Your spirit promised you Konrad. Mine promised me knowledge and power and release from pain. And it needed me to keep coming back for more so I could wake the demon from its slumber.'

I looked at Henry cautiously. 'And no doubt you have one on you as well, my friend.'

His eyebrows shot up. 'Me?'

'How else do you explain this new valour and confidence?'

He looked away shamefaced for a moment, but when he looked back, there was defiance in his eyes. Wearily I wondered if I would have another fight ahead of me.

'Check me, then,' he said.

We placed the remaining lanterns nearby, and Elizabeth turned away as he disrobed. I checked every inch of his body, with growing consternation.

'Incredible,' I said. 'There is nothing on you. Nothing.'

'Ah,' he said wryly.

'I don't understand how . . .'

'Perhaps, Victor,' he said, pulling his shirt back on, 'some people can just change all on their own.'

I sank down onto the dirt floor, exhausted, sickened by the noxious vapours still emanating from the charred remains of the mud creature.

'We have to go back and warn Konrad and Analiese,' I said. 'We have to finally destroy that thing in the pit.'

'Can we truly destroy it, though?' Henry said.

'We have to try!' I said, standing. 'And now!'

'Just wait, Victor,' Henry said, lifting his hand. 'You yourself said it wasn't fully born, that it needed our lives to waken it.'

I nodded. 'Yes.'

'Well, then, if it gets no more life energy from us, it can't be born. And maybe, if it's starved, it'll go back to what it was, an ancient block of stone.'

'You're suggesting we never go back inside again?' Elizabeth said, her pain obvious in her voice.

'Can we risk it?' Henry asked us. 'There are too many butterflies now, and they're devious. If even one feeds on us, that might be all it takes to unleash the pit demon.'

His logic was true; it was also unbearable.

'But I promised I'd go back,' I said. 'I said I'd think of something . . .'

'Henry's right. There's nothing you can do,' Elizabeth said quietly. 'If only we hadn't interfered from the start. At least this way Konrad will be gathered and will find his new home. Which is as it should be.'

'I won't accept it,' I said. 'There must—'

'Accept it, Victor,' Henry told me.

'No.'

In my dream I'd seen him. He'd been ahead of me on the ice, but I was going to catch up.

And suddenly I had my answer. It was such an obvious one.

I flung open the cottage door and ran, ignoring the urgent calls of Henry and Elizabeth. Where my strength and speed came from, I didn't know, but I sprinted through the night. They could not keep up as I bolted back to Chateau Frankenstein, to bring my brother back to life.

CHAPTER NINETEEN

THE BODY THIEF

For a second I lie very still on my bed, looking all around my room. There's no sign of black butterflies lying in wait like vampire bats. Outside my windows the eerie white mist gathers angrily and thumps against the glass. I'm suddenly aware that this is the second time I've entered the spirit world in a single day – something the instructions warned us was dangerous. But it's too late for worries now. Hastily I steal from my bedchamber and make my way down the hall, checking in Konrad's room. Empty.

I won't call out. I want no unwanted attention. As I put my hand upon the library door, a shrill howl of frustration rises up from the depths of the house, sending my heart into a gallop. But at least I know that thing is still trapped in its pit.

When I open the door, I fully expect to find Konrad here, armed, a crossbow aimed at the secret doorway. The weapons are still laid out ready on the table, but the library is abandoned except for a small cluster of butterflies. I close the door quickly behind me, hoping they didn't sense my presence. I slip down the great staircase and make my way towards the armoury. The house is so quiet and still.

What if Konrad has already been gathered? The thought should make me happy, but a spasm of sadness racks me. I will never see him again, and our parting was such a bitter one.

The armoury, too, is empty. I walk past our ancient chapel and stop to peer inside. My heart unclenches, for I see him sitting alone in a pew near the altar, hands clasped in prayer. Warily I look all around, and see no black butterflies. I enter.

'Konrad,' I whisper.

He turns in astonishment.

'Victor!'

'Shhh!'

He stands, walks towards me, scarcely squinting, his kind face furrowed with regret. 'I'm sorry. My behaviour last time, it was ugly.'

'Never mind. I understand completely.' I take a breath. 'The creature in the pit seems to be staying put.'

'It howls, but I can't bring myself to go down to look.'

I quickly tell him what happened after we left him, including what just passed in the cottage.

'The body you grew truly was malignant, then,' he says. He smiles bravely. 'There's no hope of my returning. Victor, you must go. Tell Elizabeth I love her, and tell Henry he was my dearest friend, and go.'

'I won't say goodbye to you this way.'

'There's no way out for me, Victor! Resign yourself. I have.'

'You needn't.'

He shakes his head and almost laughs. 'Victor, when will you stop playing God?'

Beyond the narrow stained-glass windows, the spectral wind wails, shaking the casements.

'Konrad, I've got a way for you to return. The simplest of ways.'

He says nothing, his brow creased.

From my hand I take my ring talisman. From my pocket I take the spirit clock. Both of them I place on the pew and step back.

Konrad stares at them.

'Do you understand?' I ask.

He swallows. 'Don't do this, Victor.'

'Take them. Take my body.'

He is silent.

'Come,' I say with a chuckle meant to be jocular, but it comes out sounding parched. 'It's not such a bad deal for you. Only three fingers on the right hand, and a difficult personality, but you can take care of

330

that in short order. Your soul was always the better.'

'You can't mean this,' he whispers.

'Why do I deserve life when you've lost yours? Elizabeth is yours, and she'll never love anyone as she loves you. I've promised you so many things. And I've not made good on any of them. This time I deliver. Take them and go. *Now!*'

He cannot rip his gaze from my ring and clock, the two things that will take him back to the real world, in my body. I can see the hunger in his eyes.

'Don't tempt me this way,' he murmurs.

'For God's sake, Konrad,' I growl, 'don't be a bloody fool. Do it before I change my mind!'

He takes a step closer to the ring and clock. 'It's like murder, don't you see?' he says. 'It is me stealing your life.'

'No. I'm *giving* it to you!'

He tears his gaze away and looks at me. 'Your light's dimmer than ever, Victor, and scarcely any heat comes off you. You've weakened yourself more just coming here. Now say goodbye to me, Victor. And do not come back!'

I shake my head.

He storms out of the chapel. I stand there, and wait. He'll return. How can he resist such an offer? I couldn't. But he doesn't come back. The stubborn idiot! Doesn't he know what it cost me to make such an offer? Does he think

I can be noble for much longer? Cursing under my breath, I pocket the ring and spirit clock and go to find him.

In the hallway I see Analiese at the foot of the great staircase.

'Analiese,' I call out, surprising her, 'have you seen Konrad?'

'Going upstairs in great distress. I was about to follow to see what the matter was.'

'It was my doing,' I tell her. Her face is so sympathetic, I find myself telling her about our conversation, the offer I made.

For a moment she says nothing, and when she does, her voice is thick with emotion. 'From the very first your love for your brother was obvious, but I don't think I've ever known such selflessness.'

She has never been so close to me, and she is so beautiful. If I reached out, I could touch her.

'Are you really so willing to part with your life?' she asks me.

I look away. 'I can't fail him again. If this is to be the only way, so be it.' I think of Elizabeth in anguish, knowing she'll never properly love me, knowing my very nature makes me unlovable. I think of my many faults, the unceasing pain in my hand. Right now to be free of these things would be almost a relief.

'Did you know,' Analiese says calmly, 'that your light has gone out altogether?'

Stupidly I hold out my arms, as if I'll see a difference. How could this happen? Panicked, I cast around, but I see no sign of colourful butterflies. Then I look down. On the floor three of them scuttle silently under my trousers and up my legs. Whirling, I look over my shoulder and see six of them on my back, blazing with light, feeding on me.

'Did you see them coming?' I cry out, knocking them off in a crazed fury. I try to catch some of them as they abscond with the last of my light, but they are hummingbird-quick.

Devastated, I turn back to Analiese, and she punches me hard in the face. This is no breezy touch, like the last time Konrad struck me. This is real contact, without any protective veil. Her fist snaps my head back with a sickening crack, and my legs buckle. I hit the floor. Dazed, I watch as this small young woman strides towards me with a terrifying detachment and kicks me in the stomach. A wave of nausea breaks through me, stealing my breath.

'Your idea isn't new, you know,' she says as she plunges her hands into my pockets and plucks out the spirit clock and ring. 'A clever fellow thought of it some three hundred years ago when he stole *my* body.'

As I cough and retch, she steps back, mutters some words I don't comprehend, and grasps the neckline of her black dress. A single downward rip, and the dress explodes towards me like a jigsaw puzzle, each piece a black butterfly, its wings perforated with suture marks and trailing the threads that once bound it into this super-natural fabric. When the cloud of butterflies disperses, I see that Analiese is gone and before me stands Wilhelm Frankenstein, as though he's just stepped from his portrait.

'I lingered too long here, just like you,' he says, 'seduced by the power of the place. I didn't realize that my living presence woke the monster from its slumber. There were other human spirits here then, and I became too friendly with one of them. He waited till I lost my light, then stole my talisman and rode off in my body.'

I start to push myself to my feet, but with a savage, well-aimed kick he knocks my legs out from under me.

'But now,' he says, 'your life is mine.'

He is already running. I scramble up and give chase, down the hallway towards the grand staircase.

'Stop!' I bellow like a child. 'You can't leave me here!'

At the top of the stairs he turns instinctively towards my bedchamber, drawn by my ring. I know this is a race I must not lose, and I put on a burst of speed. Halfway down the hallway I hurl myself at his legs and bring him to the floor. I still have some strength left. I punch at him, trying to claw the ring from his finger.

From beneath the chateau rises the loudest, most terrifying shriek I've yet heard – because this one is unmistakably filled with triumph.

For a split second Wilhelm's eyes meet mine, and I see his utter horror. Then he drives an elbow into my face and sends me skidding against the wall.

He's up again, running, hurtling through the doorway of my bedchamber.

'No!' I roar. I burst in, murderous with fury, and see him reclining on my bed, clutching the spirit clock and ring. I launch myself at him, ready to bite his hand off if need be—

But he's gone. I land atop an empty bed.

Panic pounds at all the doors of my mind, hungry for entry. I touch my chest, grip my arms. The missing fingers of my right hand are still there, but they are fiery with pain. I can't be dead. Nothing dead could feel such pain. My body lives on, elsewhere, but inhabited by another. I jump off my bed and pace the room, as though some other exit will magically present itself.

This isn't happening. It's not true. Please let it not be true.

Black butterflies swirl about my room but leave me unmolested. I'm no use to them any more.

'No, no!' I bellow, and sink to the floor.

And the moment my eyes shut, I am seeing—

—through the eyes of another. I am in my room, sitting up on the edge of my bed as Henry and Elizabeth burst in, their faces alive with dread.

'Did you go back inside?' Henry demands.

'I needed to make sure all was well,' I hear my voice – my very own voice – say. And I realize I'm seeing through the eyes of my thief, Wilhelm Frankenstein. The sensation is indescribable, to be within and without oneself simultaneously, to hear myself, to feel myself move, without having any control whatsoever.

'The pit monster is lapsing back into its dormant state,' I lie to Henry and Elizabeth.

'You went to see it?' Henry asks, incredulous.

'I had to, to make certain. And it already looks more firmly entombed in cocoon and stone.'

Elizabeth lets out a long-held breath. 'That's good news, truly good news.'

'Konrad will be gathered,' my voice says. 'I have no doubt, his heart is so pure.'

'It's a pure heart,' Elizabeth says, her eyes moist. 'I've got so much to atone for. What we did was a terrible interference with God's law. And yet . . .' She bites her lip. 'I want to say goodbye to him.'

Henry scratches his chin uncertainly. 'Isn't that too

336

risky? Victor, there must still be so many butterflies about . . .'

'They're numerous, though they seem to be getting sluggish too, without nourishment.'

'Don't go,' Henry tells Elizabeth.

'I must,' she insists.

'Yes, of course, of course,' I hear my imposter's voice say.

But Henry holds firm. 'No, Victor. What if they feed on her and wake the pit god fully?'

'I'll be quick,' she promises.

I watch as my hand, which is no longer my hand, reaches for the flask of spirit world elixir. I feel my fingers grasp it, and then intentionally release. The flask falls to the floor and shatters. There is little fluid left, and even as my body drops to its knees and makes a show of trying to wipe the liquid furiously back into the flask, the elixir is quickly absorbed into the wood and its cracks. Not a single drop remains.

Watching this scene from the spirit world, I'm aware of making a low whine, like a kicked dog.

'I . . . I'm so sorry,' the false me says, looking up at Elizabeth's stricken face.

'It's for the best,' Henry says, putting a hand on her shoulder. She shrugs it off.

'Did you do that on purpose, Victor?' she demands.

'Of course not,' I reply, amazed at the sincerity in my voice. 'I'm so sorry, Elizabeth. I'm still weakened—'

—someone is shouting my name, and I realize it's not in the real world but here in this spirit one. I open my eyes to see Konrad standing over me, brow furrowed.

'What's wrong? I heard shouting!' he asks.

I look up at my brother, so overjoyed to see him that for a moment I'm speechless.

'Victor, what's the matter?' he demands, and then frowns. 'Your light. It's gone altogether!'

'He stole my body,' I rasp.

'Who?'

'Wilhelm Frankenstein. He stole it. I'm trapped! Trapped here!'

Speaking the brutal truth aloud, panic grips me again in its vise and tightens fast. I pound my fists against my temples. I'm a bird in a house, my eyes flitting everywhere, unable to focus.

'There's no more elixir!' I rant. 'He broke the bottle. There's no more! There's no hope of rescue! None!'

'Victor!' my twin says. 'Calm down.'

He reaches out his hand, pulls me to my feet – and at his touch, this first touch between us in months, a wonderful stillness fills me. I look at him, then embrace him, squeezing with all my might. There is such comfort in this simple physical contact that I never want to let go. But finally I pull back and behold him. We are, at last, properly reunited.

'Tell me everything,' he says. 'Talk sense.'

With all the calm I can muster, I explain.

'It was him all along,' Konrad murmurs. 'Elizabeth was right. Analiese *was* keeping a secret.'

'I'm such a fool,' I say. 'When that mist spirit broke in and grabbed her, I saw something change in her, but I thought it was just another mystery of the spirit world.'

'He's been waiting for three hundred years,' Konrad says. 'The message from your spirit board – it was from *him*, trying to lure you inside!'

'Why was he never gathered?' I ask uneasily. 'How can he still be here after so many years?'

'Maybe because he was separated from his own body.'

I shudder. 'He's *inside* my body now.'

'And you can truly see through his eyes?'

'Only when mine are closed.'

What torment to watch someone else live my life. And when my body dies, what will happen to me then? Will I wait here for ever and ever, abandoned, like Wilhelm Frankenstein?

Another wail emanates from beneath us, and this time it

is no primal cry; it has a shape and rhythm that suggests language. A slight tremor passes through the very bones of the house. The black butterflies that have been swirling about the ceiling now gather into a thundercloud and scud swiftly into the hallway.

I lick my lips and look nervously at Konrad, and together we follow them. I see them disappearing into the library, joined by several other converging torrents. When we cautiously enter, we see the last of them slipping through the gaps in the secret doorway.

'Before your light disappeared,' Konrad asks, 'did butterflies feed on you?'

'A great many.'

He needs say no more. We both know what has happened. The last of my syphoned life force has already been fed to the pit god – and it is fully awake, and moving. Again from beneath the house comes the sound of earth shifting, something hard striking stone.

We run to the secret door, open it, and peer down. Echoing up to us through the vaulted galleries comes the unmistakable sound of a heavy footfall. It shakes the house.

'Dear God,' says Konrad, closing the door.

'Wait, wait!' I say. 'We need a place to hide!'

I reopen the door and run down the stairs towards the Dark Library.

'Victor!' he cries out. 'What're you doing!'

'I need a key!'

Inside the library I scan the sagging shelves, looking, looking, until I find it. The red metal book that I plucked from the fire. I snatch it and vault back up the stairs. Behind me I can hear the sound of footfalls, like the clopping of a horse's hooves. Breathless, I rejoin Konrad and slam the door behind me, checking to make sure the secret latch is secured.

'What did you get?' my brother demands in bewilderment.

I open the metal book and take out the star-shaped key.

'The chapel ceiling?' he says, remembering the tale we told him.

'That thing might not know about it.'

Together we grab a table and push it against the door, and then heave a small bureau on top of it.

'Will this do any good?' Konrad asks.

My laugh croaks from my fear-parched mouth. 'I doubt it.'

I look at all the weapons Konrad has assembled, and at once we both arm ourselves with everything we can – crossbows, quivers of bolts, swords, daggers. The mere weight of all this military metal gives me some comfort, but my hands and knees are shaking.

'We can fight this thing,' I say. 'My light might be gone, but my body's still alive in the real world. Surely that gives me some power here.'

Konrad nods vigorously. 'Absolutely. This thing was destroyed once before, and we can destroy it again.'

A footfall like an anvil blow shakes the floor. Books jump from the shelves.

'It's coming,' I gasp.

We flee the library, careening down the chateau's grand staircase and along the hallway to the chapel. Upstairs, heavy footfalls shake the ceiling. Outside, the wind howls furiously and pounds at the windows so hard that I'm sure they will explode.

'Demons within and without,' Konrad says as he helps me hurriedly lower the chandelier.

'Has it occurred to you,' I say as we clamber onto the wooden arms and proceed to haul ourselves up, 'that our house is a bit gloomy?'

We reach the ceiling and tie off. I insert the star-shaped key, and then pull open the hatch. We scramble inside and pull the door shut behind us.

'This was good thinking,' whispers Konrad, lighting a candle. 'If it's truly a demon, it won't dare come into a chapel.'

'You really think so?' I ask.

'Well, it's a nice thought.'

'I was actually just thinking it was a mistake. If we're discovered, we have no means of escape.'

'We'll fight all the harder, then,' Konrad says, winding back the string of his crossbow.

I do the same, and for a moment we work in silence, spreading out all our weapons as the thunderous footfalls move about the house overhead.

'She was Wilhelm Frankenstein all along,' murmurs Konrad to himself. 'I can't believe I thought her so . . . attractive.'

'Well, she *looked*, um, very beautiful.'

'I'm more disturbed than I can say.' He shudders, then asks, 'What's happening in the real world?'

I take a breath, close my eyes, and—

—'It doesn't matter,' Elizabeth says to my imposter. 'I can still enter to say goodbye to Konrad. There's this, remember.'

From her pocket she takes the small brown bottle of the elixir she syphoned from the main flask. In the spirit world my heart beats hard. In my panic I forgot about Elizabeth's private store. And Wilhelm Frankenstein knew nothing of this. He's silent, but I feel his tension in my real-world body.

343

Elizabeth picks up the spirit clock and turns to leave my bedchamber.

My body catches her by the arm. 'Wait. Maybe Henry's right. Maybe the smashed flask is a portent from God that we're not meant to go back.'

'I'll go in only very briefly, to make my goodbyes,' says Elizabeth.

Through Wilhelm's eyes I helplessly watch Elizabeth, trying to gauge her reaction. I see her glance quickly to Henry, then back to me. Does she suspect?

'No, I was too rash. It's too risky,' Wilhelm Frankenstein says with my voice. 'The light about you, it will be too tempting to the butterflies. When I went, I was as pale as a wraith. But your life will blaze a beacon trail. Konrad knows you love him. And he loves you. He told me so before I left. His last words. He wants you to be safe, Elizabeth. He told me not to let you come back.'

This seems to quell her determination. 'He really said that?'

My body nods. 'It is too painful for him. And dangerous for you.'

She hesitates.

I feel my real-world hand rise and stroke my earlobe absently. 'Give me the elixir, Elizabeth.'

She gives me an odd look, then says calmly, 'So you can destroy it, or use it yourself?'

'I mean to destroy it right now.' I see my hand reach out.

'Prove it,' says Elizabeth. She uncorks the brown bottle and hands it to him. 'Pour it out right now.'

Watching, I gulp in anxiety. What's she doing? He'll destroy it! And with it my last frail hope of rescue!

'Happily,' says my imposter, and I feel my eager hand clench the bottle and begin to tip it.

In an instant Elizabeth's quick hands have snatched back the bottle and she retreats, her face fearful.

'You're not Victor,' she says.

'Don't be ridiculous,' my traitorous body says.

'No. The real Victor would never be so eager to get rid of it. And he never sees signs from God either. And there's only one person I know who strokes their ear like that!'

She takes a step towards me and smacks me in the face. 'I knew there was something vile about you, Analiese!'

I feel my real-world chest rising and falling more quickly. My body lifts its hand to strike her back. 'You're talking nonsense. Now, do as I say and give me that bottle!'

'Henry, punch him!' Elizabeth cries. 'Hard! *Knock him out!*'

I pivot to face Henry, just in time to see his boxer's fists

345

clench and his right come sweeping up towards my chin, and then—

—blackness. I open my eyes with a gasp.

'What've you seen?' Konrad demands.

'Henry has knocked me unconscious!' I say jubilantly.

'What?'

'Elizabeth *knows*! She knows it's not me! She thinks it's Analiese! And she has more elixir!'

Even as my heart swells with hope, I feel an opposite contraction of grief, for even if they enter the spirit world, they can only rescue me, not Konrad. And I can't abandon my twin to the fiend now stalking the house.

'How did she know it wasn't you?'

'I talked as though I believed in God!'

Konrad laughs and then goes silent, staring down at something near our feet. I look. Something is wriggling through the seam in the trapdoor. First a pair of antennae pokes through, then the black head of a spirit butterfly. I seize my sabre and impale it, pulling it inside and slicing it in two. It flinches briefly and then is still.

'It can be killed,' I breathe.

If this thing, birthed from the pit demon, can be destroyed, then perhaps its master can be too. Hope flares within me.

A second butterfly suddenly thrusts its way into our hiding place, as angry as a hornet, and Konrad slices it in half in midair. A third one bursts in. It evades my slashes and plasters its wings against my face, blinding me. I claw at it with my hands, peel it off, and then hurl it to the floor, where Konrad crushes it.

We turn to each other, breathing hard, and smile. For a small beautiful moment I can almost pretend this is a grand adventure.

But something moves, and I look down to see a butterfly scuttling towards the trapdoor. I stab at it, but it slithers through the seam and is gone.

'It knows we're here,' Konrad says quietly.

'It'll tell the others,' I say, 'and then its master.'

We look at each other, then busy ourselves checking our weapons, making sure everything's within easy reach.

Then comes a tectonic hoof-like stomp on the marble of the grand staircase. It's coming downstairs.

'I must confess something,' I say. 'I meant to win Elizabeth.'

A second massive stomp, and a third.

'Well,' Konrad says, 'I was dead. It's only human.'

'No,' I say. 'Even after you came back to life, I meant to have her for myself. I was . . . I am . . . a terrible scoundrel.'

'I'd expect nothing less of my evil twin.'

Stomp . . . stomp!

'I'm sorry,' I say. 'Please forgive me.'

'No need,' he says. 'If I *had* come back, she would've been mine anyway.'

I give a dry chuckle. 'Yes, I've realized that.'

The lopsided footfalls grow in intensity as the demon draws closer. I feel each impact in the roots of my teeth. There's a moment of eerie silence when the demon reaches the bottom of the staircase, then a gut-churning scream as the footsteps resume in our direction.

All the vigour I used to feel in this spirit world has long evaporated and been replaced by numbness. The only part of my body that feels truly alive is the two fingers of my right hand, the fingers that don't properly exist. But the fiery pain within them is almost welcome, for it reminds me that my body, somewhere, is still alive.

The great stomping stops outside the chapel; then there's a poisonous silence.

Is it standing here at the threshold, unable to enter because this is a holy place? I've never believed in God but at this moment find myself wishing fervently for a powerful, protective presence.

One heavy thumping step, then another. It's inside.

Konrad reaches out and grips my arm. Our eyes meet. He points at the crossbows, and I nod. We each take one, backs against the wall, aiming at the trapdoor.

More colossal footsteps, each one closer than before. I can tell the pit demon is directly beneath us.

It must know we're here. But surely it isn't tall enough to reach the ceiling. Will it realize the chandelier is an elevator? Even if it does, the chandelier won't bear its massive weight, will it?

There's a great wrenching sound from the chapel, and moments later the trapdoor of our hiding place explodes, shattered to splinters by a long wooden pew used as a battering ram. The pew pulls back, and the wreckage of the trapdoor dangles down on mangled hinges.

Through the madly swinging spokes of the broken chandelier, I catch a quick glimpse of a massive form churning with black butterflies. It's shockingly like the crude cave drawing of the giant – two writhing long legs, a huge torso with seething arms, and a black hive of a skull.

'Let fly!' Konrad shouts.

We fire in unison, and our two crossbow bolts bury themselves in the swarming black mass of its chest, disappearing.

For just a moment some of the butterflies on its head flutter away, and I catch sight of a long, crooked slash of lipless mouth, parted to reveal serrated teeth. As it screams, a terrible slaughterhouse smell emanates from its throat. Then the butterflies once again swarm over its face, as though they cannot bear to be parted from its flesh.

Frantically Konrad and I wind our strings back, load, aim, fire. I give a cry as the pit demon leaps, one long arm outstretched, black fingers tapering to claws. The thing is at least ten feet in height, and the strength of its jump is terrifying, but its talons reach only to the chandelier, which it rips from its moorings as it falls back to the floor. Again the pit demon jumps, and again falls short.

'It can't reach us!' Konrad cries out hopefully.

'Again!' I shout, reloading my bow.

We fire volley after volley into its body, and though the demon wails, it does not seem at all weakened, or deterred from its quarry. It makes one last futile jump to reach us, and then stops.

'Look!' Konrad cries.

Butterflies are leaving the pit demon's body, whirling about it like a tornado, stretching themselves into a line that reaches up and up towards the ceiling and into our hatchway.

Below, the demon clasps hold of this infernal writhing rope and begins to climb towards us.

CHAPTER TWENTY

THE PIT DEMON

Konrad and I stab at the nearest butterflies, severing and impaling, cutting short their writhing rope, but even as they fall away, new ones take their place.

The pit demon climbs, claw over claw, and with fewer butterflies upon the creature, I glimpse flashes of flesh, pockmarked with burst pustules, a knee that looks as though it's jointed backwards. And then there's no more time for looking, for it's nearing the hatch, no matter how fast Konrad and I slash at the butterfly rope.

I drop my sword, and Konrad and I take up our crossbows once more and fire all our remaining bolts into the monster. But the demon seems completely unharmed.

'Should've – killed this thing – before it woke,' Konrad gasps.

The demon hangs from its rope with one clawed hand, shoots up the other, and nearly catches me in its talons. Konrad stabs it with his sabre, and a shriek rises from the creature's hidden maw.

Closer it climbs. I look at Konrad, wanting to say something – to tell him I love him, to apologize again – but my mouth is so dry that it's all I can do to swallow. I tighten my left hand on my sabre, my right on my dagger.

A low howl fills our secret chamber, making my ears vibrate painfully. At first I think the noise comes from the demon, but then I realize it's from outside the house altogether. With a great rattling, I hear, and feel, the windows of the chapel shake.

The pit demon must have heard it too, for I see its seething black skull jerk towards the windows. And even though I can discern no expression on its pullulating face, the tilt of its neck, the hunch of its shoulders, conveys emotion.

'It's frightened,' I say to Konrad, who nods.

Is the spirit outside more powerful? The evil spirit – and only at this instant do I realize that everything Wilhelm Frankenstein, in the guise of Analiese, has told us might be a lie.

The pit demon's head turns back to us. Again I see a flash of its serrated teeth, and above them a featureless expanse of skull that has no eyes but for the eyeholes of a huge black butterfly, wings spread. The monster climbs higher, and this time an entire forearm flails into our tiny chamber, rearing and striking like an alligator. Time and time again Konrad and I throw ourselves clear, stabbing with our blades.

My frenzied mind carves out a splinter of time, and I remember how once, in a play, we pretended to fight a monster side by side just so.

And then the demon's claw catches Konrad across the right arm, tearing his shirt and opening a long gash in his flesh. No blood issues forth, only a dreadful line of darkness. My twin cries out, and I realize that all during his illness I never once heard him make such a heartrending noise.

I turn on the pit demon's arm with such hatred that my vision contracts, and with my sabre I chop at its thickest part, like a hatchet into wood. Amputated butterflies scatter and swirl, and I feel the blade bite deep. There's an outraged howl, and the arm pulls back.

'If you feel pain,' I bellow down at it, 'there's more to come!'

I rush to my brother. 'Are you all right?'

He nods weakly, looking at the strange dark gash on his arm. This thing can cut. It can wound, and in a way that makes my blood run cold.

Part of me has clung foolishly to the hope that this spirit world monster cannot truly harm us. But I'm wrong. If it can cut, surely it can destroy us altogether.

The demon's head suddenly twists on its writhing neck, looking back towards the chapel entrance. The butterflies' wings contract and tighten with anticipation.

'Dear God!' I hear a familiar voice exclaim.

'Henry?' I shout.

'Victor? Konrad?' Elizabeth calls out, her voice constricted with fear.

'Up here!' I yell.

The pit demon drops from its butterfly rope and hits the floor with a thunderclap. It turns to face my friends, shoulders hunched, knees bent backwards in a freakish hunter's posture.

I risk sticking my head out of the hatchway and see Henry and Elizabeth just as Konrad first saw us, as creatures enveloped in light. With their swords raised before them, they might be archangels.

'Henry's ablaze,' I tell Konrad.

He grunts in pain as he moves beside me. 'But Elizabeth's light is greatly faded.'

The demon takes a tentative step towards them, then stops, one freakishly long arm outstretched as though testing the heat from a fire.

'You're powerful!' I shout to Henry. 'Remember that! You're both alive with light and heat!'

'We have your talisman, Victor!' Elizabeth cries. 'Get out of there!'

'How?' I shout back, for the pit demon is still almost

directly below, and its skull jerks up at us once more.

With a roar Henry is running at the pit demon, a streak of light, his flashing sword lifted over his shoulder. Frozen, I watch, my breath stoppered in my throat, as the pit demon takes a step backwards, shrieking, one arm thrust forward to ward off Henry's light and heat. As its talons sweep towards Henry's head, Henry strikes with his sword, severing two of the monster's claws. Howling, the pit demon staggers back, stunned, foul vapours pluming into the air.

Gagging, Henry peers up at us. 'Now!'

The infernal rope disintegrates into individual butterflies as they rush to their master, but I can see that the chandelier rope still hangs from its pulley in the ceiling. 'Go!' I shout at Konrad, who is wincing even as he nods.

We don't hesitate. I let him jump first and grab hold of the rope. Then I quickly follow as the rope starts to swing outward with the momentum. We lower ourselves quickly, and when we let go, we hit the floor hard and stumble. Konrad cries out as he pushes himself up with his wounded arm.

I take hold of him and we run. From the corner of my eye, I see the pit demon clutching its severed fingers to their stumps, and butterflies crawling over them, excreting a black gossamer that seems to be fusing them back together.

With Henry and Elizabeth blazing the trail, we bolt from the chapel.

'Where are our bodies?' I gasp as we rush down the hallway.

'Your bedchamber,' Elizabeth says.

'The spirit clock, you brought it?' I ask.

'I have it,' Henry shouts back to me.

The pit demon's hooves crack behind us. I glance back and see it stooping through the chapel doorway. Its skull turns left and right, searching for us, and then a torrent of butterflies issues from it in all directions.

'It's blind,' I say. 'It needs the butterflies to see.'

That fact will buy us a little time. Elizabeth turns and holds my ring in the air. I know she cannot hand it to me; her heat is a barrier between us now.

'Catch,' she says, and throws it. I clasp it gratefully in my hand, and the moment I push it onto my finger, I feel a surge. My spirit is reconnected with my body. We race for the staircase.

'I quite enjoyed knocking you out,' Henry says, completely unwinded as we take the stairs two at a time. 'But when we put a drop of elixir into your mouth, and arrived in the spirit world, it was quite a shock to see you were Wilhelm Frankenstein.'

'I thought it was Analiese,' says Elizabeth.

'There was never an Analiese,' I reply. 'You were right. Where's Wilhelm?'

'We tied him up and dragged him into the library,' Henry says. 'He was still out cold.'

When we're halfway up the stairs, a swarm of black butterflies strafes us, then circles back to tell the demon.

'It'll come for us soon,' I pant.

Almost at once the sound of clopping hoofs, getting louder, shakes the foundations of the chateau.

'We can't leave Konrad behind with that thing!' I cry.

'I'm not sure we can destroy it,' says Henry. 'But I'm willing to fight it to the end.'

'No. It heals itself,' says Konrad, wincing with pain. 'We can't kill it.'

I look at his arm and see that the eerie black line has spread in a series of spider veins.

'Then, we need to open the house!' I say impulsively. 'A door! A window!'

'What about the evil spirit outside?' Henry asks, startled.

'It might help us. Whatever it is, it's no friend of the pit demon's,' I say.

'Or Wilhelm Frankenstein's,' Elizabeth adds. 'I think that mist might be the gatherers, trying to get inside all along.'

357

'Are you sure?' Henry asks.

'I'm sure of nothing,' she says. 'But going out may be Konrad's only chance of escape.'

'And I'm not leaving,' I say, 'until I'm sure he's safe from that thing.'

We reach the top of the stairs, and Henry suddenly falters, putting a hand to his chest.

'What's wrong?' I ask.

'The spirit clock,' he says in shock, pulling it from his breast pocket. 'So soon?'

I can see it vibrating as the fetal sparrow limb beats urgently at the glass, and then I whirl to see the reeking, churning shape of the pit demon at the base of the staircase. Its claws are completely intact. It takes the steps three at a time on its hoofed feet.

Down the hallway towards my bedchamber we charge.

'We'll throw open the balcony window in my room,' I say. 'Let in whatever wants to come in!'

We burst through the doorway. I know instantly where my body lies in the real world, and I want more than anything to lie down, to return. But not before we open the window. I stride towards it and hear Elizabeth give a shriek of surprise, and—

From behind the door Wilhelm Frankenstein lunges, knocking me over. My sabre and dagger fly from my hands.

358

We crash to the floor, him on top of me. I punch and kick to drive him off, but he is single-minded, crazed by his three hundred years of captivity, and he swiftly seizes my hand and wrenches the ring from my finger.

'Give it to me!' shouts Henry, striding towards Wilhelm. My friend's face is fiercely ablaze, and his arms are spread to radiate his light and heat.

Wilhelm staggers back, and just as Henry is about to lay his searing hand upon him and grasp my ring, Wilhelm throws it. It sails high over all our heads and out of the bedchamber door. I hear its clink as it hits the stone, and the thin metallic sound of it rolling farther down the hallway.

I don't think. I run madly after it, see its sparkle as it comes to a halt, and then see the pit demon's insect-infested hoof stamp down before it. I slowly look up. The demon towers above me. With one clawed hand it reaches down and picks up my ring.

I feel Henry's hand on my shoulder, pulling me back.

'Henry—' I begin to say.

But he is already advancing on the giant, crying, 'Get back, get back!' He never reaches it, for a torrent of butterflies comes at Henry, and even as he struggles against it, slashing with his sword, I see the butterflies flaring with colour as they drain him. With every valiant step Henry weakens.

Elizabeth rushes forward, and before the pit demon can fall back, she swings her sword with both hands at its leg. Her blow has such force that she can't wrench the sword free from the demon's churning flesh. It roars from the vast serrated gash of its mouth, and more noxious fumes boil from its wound.

Suddenly Konrad is at my side, pressing my sword back into my hand, and we strike at the thing's torso, as high as we can reach, again and again. I can see my ring glinting in its clawed fist, and I try to sever its hand, but it keeps it out of my reach.

I give a cry of triumph as the pit demon's wounded leg buckles and cracks at the point of its wound, the two halves of its leg held together with only ghastly sinew and the efforts of writhing butterfly wings.

Once again hope swells within me. Maybe we truly can destroy this foul thing. I look over to see Elizabeth and Henry both trying to fight off the black butterflies that now cover them, bleeding them of their lives.

'Your light!' Konrad calls in anguish to Elizabeth over his shoulder.

And then I can no longer see her light, nor Henry's, for the butterflies have done their devilish work and return to their master with bloated colourful bodies. They fly to its wounded leg, and as their own bodies become black once more, new energy seeps into the pit demon. It stands tall, its leg freakishly re-fused.

With one claw the pit demon slashes a black gash across Konrad's chest, and before I can rush to his aid, the monster swats at me as though I were no more than a dog. I fly back and hit the ground.

'Konrad!' I cry out.

Elizabeth and Henry are helping drag Konrad's limp form back as the pit demon advances slowly down the hallway. It is a nightmare drawn with black lightning.

We have no more light, no heat left to fight this thing.

And precious little life. As I stagger to my feet to help the others, I feel dizzy with weakness. I hear my pulse in my ears, tapping like the faltering alarm of the spirit clock. In the real world our bodies are dying.

'We need to return,' Henry gasps when I reach him.

'I can't return without my talisman,' I wheeze. 'Get to the bedchamber! Open the windows!'

With a roar I rush at the pit demon, eyes locked on the clawed hand that clutches my ring. I aim for its wrist but never even get to swing my sword, for once more the monster swats me and I sail back, my sword spinning from my hand and clattering along the floor.

At that moment Wilhelm Frankenstein bursts from my room, pushing past Henry, and snatches up my sword.

'Where's your talisman?' he roars, running at me.

'I don't have it!' I shout back.

For a moment I think he is about to impale me, but a torrent of butterflies intercepts him and drives him back against the wall, pinning him, helpless. He turns to look at the pit demon, and on Wilhelm's face now – that fine, smug face that gazed down at me from its portrait – is pure terror. He stares at the pit demon, and to my amazement the pit demon stares back, suddenly motionless.

And I understand instinctively that there is a history between these two that goes back centuries. Wilhelm was the one to first wake it, to suckle its butterflies and use their bounteous powers, to promise the pit demon in some perhaps unspoken way that it would rise again.

Terrible noises emerge from the pit demon's throat, that same brutal language I heard earlier. I turn to look at Wilhelm, and see a black butterfly crawl into each of his ears – not to stopper them, I realize, but to translate.

'I had no intention of abandoning you!' Wilhelm cries. 'I was going to return!'

At this, a violent gale of noise explodes from the pit demon.

Wilhelm persists. 'I was going to bring back a new body for you, one made from your very own flesh. They have found your bones!'

For a moment the pit demon is silent, as though considering, its body a quivering mass of insect limbs and antennae and pointy wing tips. Then it lunges. I throw myself from its path, as do Elizabeth and Henry, dragging Konrad's limp body with them. The monster lands in front of Wilhelm Frankenstein. It takes him in its two clawed hands and lifts him off the floor.

For the first time the butterflies around the pit demon's head disperse completely, and I can see it truly has no other features but a diagonal gash that spans its jutting, low-browed skull. It opens wide, and its teeth sink into Wilhelm's head, biting it clear in half even as he screams. It then proceeds with terrifying speed to cram the flailing body into its enormous serrated mouth, devouring Wilhelm utterly.

All my resolve fails me.

It consumed Wilhelm. Can it consume Konrad – perhaps all of us without our light and heat?

'Hurry!' I bellow to the others. 'Open the windows!'

Instantly the demon's head turns to Elizabeth and Henry as they wearily drag Konrad into my bedchamber. Immediately twin torrents of butterflies leave its body and swirl about Elizabeth and Henry, dragging all three of them back.

The pit demon turns to me briefly, and then ignores me as it thumps towards my bedchamber. It crouches low to fold its massive frame through the doorway. I see my ring in its hand and realize it has only one intent now – to unite itself with my body in the real world.

I manage to stagger up and lurch after it. Great swirls of mist pound their fists against the windows. Henry and Elizabeth are fighting to reach them, but the butterflies create a riptide they cannot defeat.

The pit demon's head locks on to the place on the floor where my body must rest in the real world. As though I'm already dying, I feel a dreadful numbness seep through me – from my feet, through my legs, up my torso.

The pit demon begins to lower itself to the floor, folding itself into a grotesque facsimile of my body's shape in the real world.

With a final surge of strength I rush towards the windows. But with a flick of its arm, the pit demon flings a noose of butterflies around me, tightening and tightening so I can scarcely move. The window is no more than ten feet away, but it might as well be ten miles.

We will all die.

I hear a cry and look over to Konrad, hunched in pain

over the pit demon, his sword raised high. He brings the sword down on the pit god's hand, cutting it clean off. My ring springs onto the floor and rolls.

As the demon shrieks in dismay, the butterflies around me seem to lose their strength, and I pitch forward, hurling myself at the balcony doors. I grasp the handle and throw the windows wide.

Mist roars in, making a maelstrom of the room. As I cower, I watch butterflies being sucked out of the house in vast black swathes, the mist all the while coalescing into something huge and powerful.

What have I done?

The mist surges across the room towards the pit demon with the ferocity of a cobra. As the demon rises to its feet, the mist slams against it, scouring away the last of the butterflies until, finally, the pit monster is stripped bare, revealing something so ghastly that my mind cannot quite comprehend it.

The great column of mist wraps itself around the pit demon and splits into multiple heads, like those of a Hydra. Viciously the pit demon fights back, slashing one head with its claws, clamping its serrated teeth into another head until it goes limp and disintegrates to vapour.

In the whirl of the spectral storm, I'm only dimly aware of Henry and Elizabeth and Konrad watching, stunned, like me, as these two supernatural creatures roar and shriek and battle, and I'm not sure which is the stronger.

The pit demon crushes yet another of the mist's many heads, and in horror I watch as the other heads wither. The single column of mist seems to loosen its grip around the creature, and the demon rears to its full height and gives a shriek of triumph.

At that moment the mist flexes and, with a surge, plunges into the demon's open mouth, pouring more and more of itself inside. The demon flails about, gagging, clawing uselessly at the seemingly endless torrent.

A gaping hole bursts in the demon's belly, and mist streams out. Then its thigh erupts with mist, and next its shoulder. The monster buckles over, collapsing onto the floor as yet another column of mist bursts out through the top of its ghastly head. Its entire body explodes then, mist swirling, as the demon's remains are sucked out through the window.

The storm calms, but the mist thickens once more and seeps through the air towards me. It swirls around and around me, as if sniffing, and I feel its tremendous strength. Does it remember how I butchered one of its tentacles? Does it see some dark seam in me worthy of annihilation? Reluctantly it leaves me, eddying around Henry and Elizabeth very briefly before flowing over Konrad.

It envelops him utterly for a moment, and then gathers itself and retreats in a great rush through the open window.

An impossible silence fills the room.

I rush over to Konrad. His eyes are closed. 'Konrad,' I whisper, shaking him. He stirs and looks at me, then at his own body. The frightening black rents in his arms and chest are healed.

'Your bodies,' he says anxiously, and I suddenly remember the ticking of the spirit clock.

With a shaking hand Henry drags it from his pocket and frowns. A residue of mist wafts up from the clock, and its glass face is frosted over. Henry scrapes away the ice and holds the clock to his ear.

'It's not ticking at all,' he says, 'but—'

'I don't feel any weakness,' says Elizabeth.

I come for a closer look. 'The little claw's flexed, like it's about to tap, but it's not pointing quite straight up.'

'Surely our time has run out,' says Elizabeth.

'Or paused,' I say, for there is the strangest feeling of time suspended, a breath calmly taken but not yet exhaled. The mist seems to have frozen time for us.

Konrad stands, and Elizabeth rushes to him and throws herself into his arms.

'How good it is to hold you,' she says, pressing her face into his neck.

I watch as they hold each other, and touch each other's faces. He kisses her mouth, brushes the tears that spill from her eyes, and what they whisper to each other I cannot hear.

'I'll come back,' she says.

Konrad shakes his head.

'I'll come back,' she repeats.

'You mustn't,' he says. He looks at me. 'You especially, Victor. Let this be an end of it. There's no true way to bring me back.'

I walk to him and hold out my ring. I hear Elizabeth draw in her breath.

'Take it,' I tell my twin.

Very slowly he takes my hand and closes my fingers around the ring.

'This isn't how it's meant to end,' I say. 'I had a dream, of you and me, having an adventure, and—'

'We've had our adventures,' he says. 'Enough for two lives.'

He takes my right hand. 'Does it hurt even in here?' he asks.

I nod.

'Be done with it now. You've no reason to blame yourself for my death.'

I look away.

'Victor? Do you hear me? It was never your duty to save me. Or bring me back from the dead.'

'Perhaps.'

'Henry,' he says. 'I've never seen more valour. I don't think I could've charged that thing the way you did in the chapel.'

Henry smiles, his old smile.

'But how can we leave you here alone?' Elizabeth says miserably.

'Oh, I'm not staying here,' Konrad says. 'I am going for a walk. It was what I first wanted to do when I arrived. Only, Analiese – I mean Wilhelm – stopped me.'

He gives Elizabeth one last, long kiss. Then he hugs Henry warmly. Last, he opens his arms to me. He doesn't feel cold. He's the same as me.

'No more of this,' he whispers into my ear.

I try to laugh.

'Promise me you'll hatch no more mad schemes.'

I hold on to him tightly just a moment longer.

'I knew I'd get no promise from my little brother,' he says.

Then he turns to the open balcony and steps outside into the mist. The moment he does so, the mist closes around him, not ferociously but gently, like a travelling cloak, and he is gone.

* * *

The house was bustling, things being packed, things being cloaked with dust sheets. We were to leave the next morning, first towards Venice and then, after several weeks, farther south, to where the healing sun would wait for us.

In the privacy of my room, I packed a valise for the things I wanted with me on the coach.

I looked at my notebook, the one I'd kept when I'd had the spirit butterflies upon me and was reading like a madman. I scarcely recognized my scribbling now. There were some passages I was simply unable to read, and those I could read didn't make a jot of sense to me. There seemed to be information not just about turning lead to gold, but about many other things too, including the mysteries of the human body. Numbers and notations and equations that might as well have been the hieroglyphs of a lost civilization.

Nothing good had come out of the spirit world with me. Nothing.

It was just gibberish all along, a mockery of knowledge spun like a cocoon about me by those butterflies.

I ripped out the pages from the notebook and held them close to the candle flame.

And yet I couldn't burn them.

What if the knowledge was real but I wasn't clever enough yet to understand it?

Quietly, as though I were keeping a secret from myself, I folded the pages and locked them away in my drawer.

Later.

That evening came on stormy, and Henry, Elizabeth, and I stood under the awning of the great balcony and looked over the rain-pelted lake. Mist obscured the mountains, and I couldn't help wondering if Konrad were somehow in it.

'Can I ask you a question?' I said to Henry. 'Your talisman. You never did tell us what it was.'

'Oh,' he said, a little sheepishly. 'It was just some inspiring words. I don't mind showing you now.'

He reached into his pocket and drew out the bit of paper for me.

I unfolded it and read,

'I will drink life to the lees,

To strive, to seek, to find and not to yield.

You wrote these?'

He nodded.

'They're very fine,' said Elizabeth.

'It suits you well,' I said.

'We'll miss you on your journey,' Elizabeth told him.

'And I'll miss you on yours,' he replied. 'I wish my father and I were going to Italy and not Holland. I've heard the winters can be quite dismal.'

'I wish you were coming with us,' she said.

He blushed. 'Do you?'

'Of course she does,' I said, wondering if he still harboured ambitions to win her heart. And then I added, 'You're practically a brother to her.'

I clapped him on the shoulder, and he looked at me wryly. Then we both smiled, as two friends do before a fencing match.

The rain came harder, pockmarking the lake. The wind picked up, and I felt the great cool drops against my skin. Light flickered behind the clouds.

'You should come in now,' Father said, joining us on the balcony. 'You'll be soaked in a minute.'

'That lightning,' I asked him, 'what form of matter is it?'

'Electricity,' he said. 'A discharge of energy between oppositely charged particles. It's a relatively new science, a potent and promising one.'

A great fork suddenly impaled the lake. From the sky came a deafening crack, like someone taking a chisel to the very heavens. There was another flash, and about fifty yards along our shoreline a massive oak erupted in a stream of blinding fire. When the light vanished, the tree was nothing more than a blasted stump.

'Come inside, Victor,' Elizabeth said from the doorway, and held out her hand to me. But I hesitated.

'Yes,' I said, 'in just a moment.' And I turned back to the storm and thought: *Such astonishing power.*